TRAGICALLY YOURS

A STANDALONE FANTASY ROMANCE

JAMIE APPLEGATE HUNTER

FAE KINGS OF EDEN BOOK III

Tragically Yours
An Unhinged Standalone Fantasy Romance
Fae Kings of Eden Book Three

Cover Design: Books and Moods

DEDICATION

To everyone who hates the word folds—

At least it's not flaps.

WORLD GUIDE

Please note: this is a guide to use as reference if needed. It does not have to be read before the story.

HUMANS

- No magic
- Not immortal
- Do not have fated mates

NON-ROYAL FAE

- Stronger and faster than humans
- They can glamour small areas around themselves.
- Their glamour works on humans and animals.
- It takes their magic thirteen years to fully manifest.
- They do not have fated mates unless mated to a royal fae.
- Not immortal

ROYAL FAE

- Stronger and faster than non-royal fae
- Their glamour works on every living creature, including non-royal fae.
- Their glamour is stronger than non-royal fae (they can glamour entire kingdoms at one time).
- They have fated mates.
- Royals traditionally only have one child.
- It takes twenty-five years for their magic to fully manifest.
- They cannot leave their kingdoms until their magic fully manifests at twenty-five years of age.
- Royal fae heirs take over the throne at twenty-five years of age.
- Royal-born fae receive a *familiar* and *familiar* mark on their fifteenth birthday.
- Not immortal

MATES

- Only royal fae have fated mates (their mate can be a non-royal fae).
- On a royal fae's thirteenth birthday, the name of their fated mate is whispered into their minds by the gods.
- Fated mates can feel each other's stronger emotions.
- A mate bond can be broken if one of the mates marries another person before the two fated mates marry.
- A mate bond does not make them love each other.

- Mate bonds are the strongest form of pure magic from the gods and were created to ensure the strongest royal fae heirs.

FAMILIARS

- An animal bonded to a royal-born fae on their fifteenth birthday.
- The "bonded" (royal fae) can see and hear through their *familiar*.
- The bonded receives a tattoo of their *familiar* on their upper left chest at midnight on their fifteenth birthday, and their *familiar* finds them within a few days.
- *Familiars* and their bonded can communicate telepathically.
- *Familiars* have immortal healing to ensure they live as long as their bonded. When their bonded dies, so do they.

KINGDOMS

- Mountain Kingdom (fae—cold, snowy, mountainous)
- Desert Kingdom (fae—desert land with mountains and plateaus, hot days with cold nights)
- Tropical Kingdom (fae—thick canopy of tropical trees, humid, mild temperatures, borders the ocean)
- Garden Kingdom (fae—lush flowery greenery with comfortably mild temperatures all year)

- Human Kingdom (human—surrounded by the four fae kingdoms. Made up of all four habitats, depending on which fae kingdom the human regions border).

Note: Fae kingdoms possess magic that the Human Kingdom does not. Their vegetation, animals, bodies of water, etc. are different and can be dangerous to humans.

THE BARRIER

- A magical wall that protects the humans from the dangerous fae lands
- Fae can pass through the barrier freely, but humans require a fae escort in order for the magic to allow them through.
- The five kingdoms agreed to erect a wall along the barrier with only one gate to each fae kingdom.
- Any fae or human who passes through the barrier must have a legal permit to do so.

FALLEN FATE

- A Fate from the heavens who has forsaken or given up their duty in the aether.
- Can only see parts of fate.
- In this world: Lilith, who has been in the Garden Kingdom, secretly guiding them since Eden's creation.

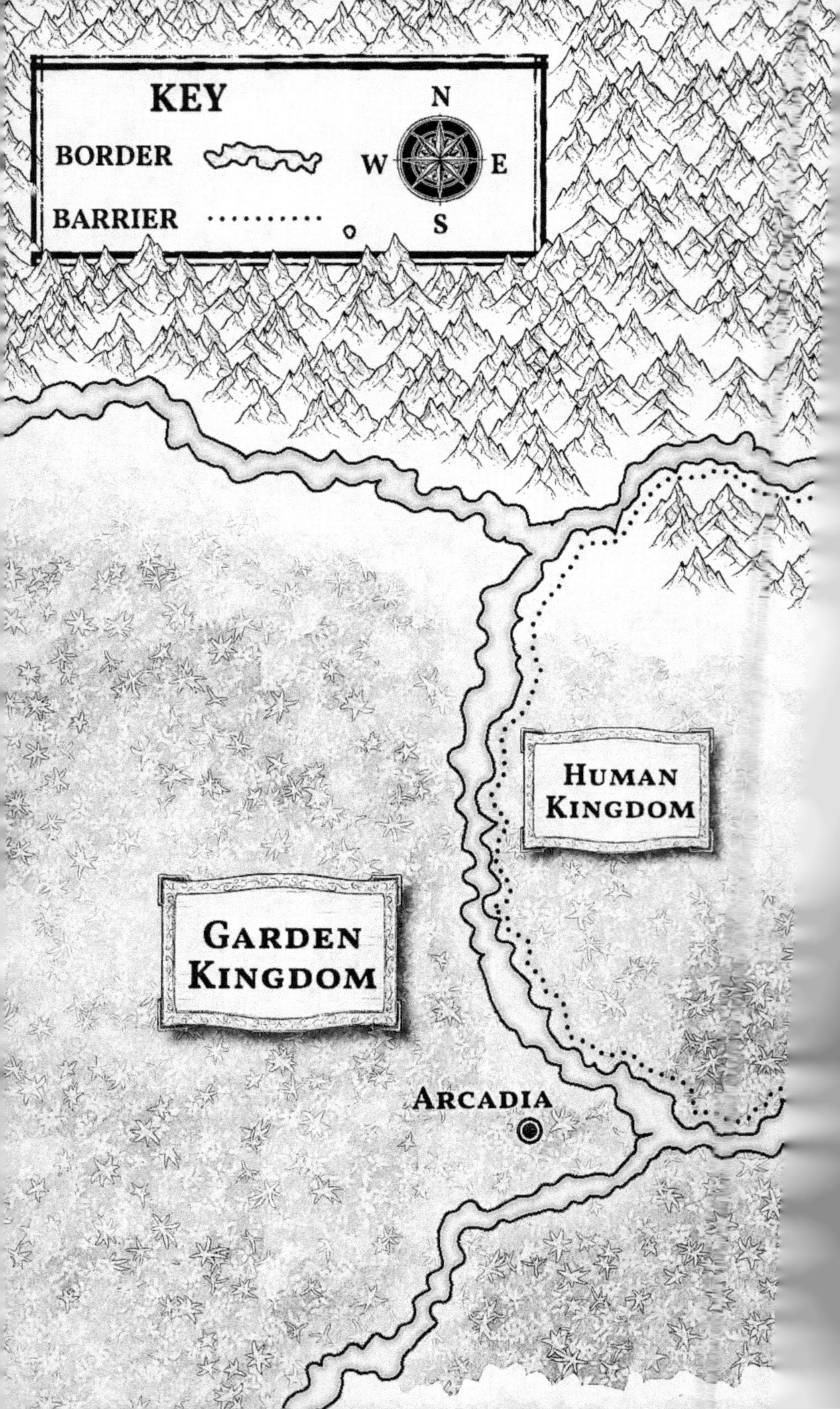

KEY
BORDER
BARRIER
N
W
E
S
HUMAN
KINGDOM
GARDEN
KINGDOM
ARCADIA

EDEN
MOUNTAIN KINGDOM
VALE
FRIYA
DESERT KINGDOM
LUNARI
TROPICAL KINGDOM
SALTU

SPOTIFY PLAYLIST

SCAN THE QR CODE BELOW TO START LISTENING

PLEASE NOTE

Content warnings can be found on the last page or on the author's website at www.authorjah.com/content-warnings

IF YOU'RE LOOKING FOR AN AMAZING FANTASY WITH AN INTRICATE PLOT, THIS MIGHT NOT BE THE BOOK FOR YOU

This is an unhinged fantasy romance.
There's no intricate world building or big fantasy plot.
The plot focuses **solely on the romance** between the two main characters.

The books in this series were written to be quick, fun reads, and are great for a palate cleanser or a book slump. (unless you hate them)

The hero makes a few morally black choices in the name of love, and thinks it's completely normal behavior.
Do not expect him to have a moral compass.

You might have a good time. You might not.
Good luck.

PART ONE
TRAGIC LONGING

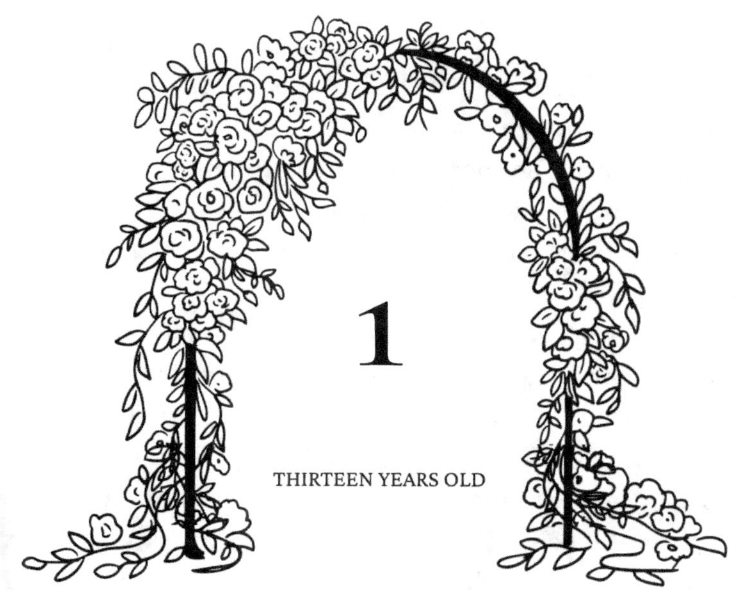

Fawn never caused trouble, but in that moment, she deemed violence worth whatever punishment her teacher might hand down. She curled her hands into fists and considered the best way to break Robert's nose.

"If your teeth were any bigger, they'd cut through your bottom lip," Robert taunted. She pictured blood spurting across his smug grin, the gasps of classmates feeding her like fuel.

Her front teeth were big, but her mother said hers had been large at Fawn's age too. Her tongue pressed against them now, oversized tombstones that seemed to announce her every flaw. Fawn would grow into her teeth, her mother assured her, just as she had. *Hopefully*. She didn't know if punching someone would get her expelled, but today seemed like a great day to find out.

Being half-human and half-fae—plus those too-large front teeth—put a target on her back. Sometimes she swore she could feel that target, hot and prickling between her shoulder blades whenever the other kids laughed.

"Hey, William, do you think *Horse Teeth* here is pretty?" Robert asked one of his friends.

Heat shot up her neck, settling sharp in her ears, but her pride screamed louder than her shame.

William sneered. "Pretty? With hair the color of a barn mouse?"

Fawn struggled to suppress the tears forming behind her eyes. It didn't escape her attention that none of their classmates watching came to her defense. She clenched her hands tighter. "Maybe I'll knock your teeth out," she snapped. Her nails dug crescents into her palms to keep from crying. The thought of his toothless smile brought her a sick kind of joy. She pictured it and shifted her target to his mouth. What would his friends think then?

Robert's face split into a nasty grin. "I'd like to see you try."

A chorus of fear and disbelief rose from the crowd of students, and Fawn looked around. *What are they yelling about?*

"Where are your teeth?" one of Robert's friends asked, stepping back.

"My teeth?" Robert poked at his mouth. "What do you mean?"

Fawn's brows drew together. His teeth looked fine. *Not for long.*

"Oh my gods," another girl exclaimed, staring at Fawn. "Are you using glamour?"

Glamour? Only fae had the magic to glamour, an ability that allowed them to create illusions only effective on humans and animals. Fawn didn't have fae magic, nor could she see through glamour like other fae. Her father explained that since she didn't grow up in the fae lands, her magic never developed.

Fae drew their power from the fae lands, and until they're thirteen, they're advised not to leave the magical lands, lest their magic weaken.

It was why the gods bound the royal heirs to their respective kingdoms. Royals couldn't leave their kingdoms until they turned twenty-five and their magic fully manifested. Being infinitely stronger than non-royal fae, the royals took longer to fully come into their power.

Fawn's father insisted that having no magic kept her safer in the Human Kingdom. A lot of humans feared fae, and her father often glamoured his slightly pointed ears to look rounded in public so strangers thought he was human.

Being half human, Fawn already had rounded ears.

The chatter around her swelled; curious, wary eyes pinned her in place.

"I can't glamour," Fawn said defensively. "I don't have fae magic."

She wanted to scream it, to carve the truth into their skulls—she wasn't special, not chosen, just a mixture of species.

A few students ran inside the school building. "We saw it," Cheryl, another classmate, accused. "You said you would knock his teeth out, and they disappeared!"

I would know if I had glamour, right? She tried wiping her sweaty palms on her skirt, but the feel of the cloth against her clammy skin made her shudder.

Their teacher appeared from the school building and looked from Robert to Fawn. "Did you glamour Robert?"

Fawn shook her head. "No, Miss. I don't have fae magic." Every year, her parents informed her teachers she had no magic. Why were they questioning her now?

The teacher turned to Robert and studied him. "He looks fine." She addressed the others. "Lying to get another student in trouble is wrong."

"I swear, Miss Cadence. He teased Fawn about her teeth," one of the girls said, shooting Fawn a sympathetic look. "She said she would knock his out, then his teeth disappeared and reappeared a few minutes later."

Their teacher studied Fawn carefully. "Have you ever been to the fae lands?"

Fawn's eyes widened. "Only once for a couple of weeks last year." She'd stayed with her grandparents while her parents took an anniversary trip.

Miss Cadence sighed. "Everyone back inside. Outside time is over." Placing a gentle hand on Fawn's back, she guided her to her office and lowered her voice. "I'll have to send for your parents. It's possible your trip to the fae lands infused you with a bit of magic. We'll perform a test to see."

Beads of sweat dotted Fawn's forehead. "How?"

"Make me see something that isn't here," Miss Cadence instructed, pointing to an empty spot on her desk. "If I guess what it is, then we have our answer."

Fawn started to nod, then stopped. "I don't know how to glamour."

"Let's see," Miss Cadence said slowly as she thought. "Focus hard on what you want me to see."

Fawn drew in a deep breath and concentrated on the empty space, willing her teacher to see a vase filled with pink flowers.

Miss Cadence gasped, pulling Fawn's attention from the task. "Flowers," her teacher whispered. "I saw a bouquet of pink flowers."

Fawn's stomach plummeted. Magic wasn't freedom. Magic was exposure. Every eye would see her now.

She should have been excited to possess fae magic. As a girl, it was all she wanted, but after seeing the reaction of her classmates today, it felt like a curse.

Fawn burst into tears.

The Garden Kingdom prince stood in the middle of his sitting room as anger, shock, and fear churned in his chest. He rubbed a fist over his sternum, wishing he could ease the knot forming there.

He'd never met his mate, but her emotions were as familiar to him as his own. Happiness and humor were the most prevalent, something he himself rarely experienced in his own life, and sometimes annoyance or embarrassment filtered down the bond during the day.

But never fear, and that's what worried him.

Why is she scared?

Thinking of his mate in distress blackened his bleak mood. He'd already had an altercation with his father, a normal occurrence, and knowing something happened to his mate almost sent him into a blind rage.

If she were here, he would let nothing touch her.

But she *wasn't* here. According to the records, she didn't exist.

When a royal fae turned thirteen, the gods whispered the name of their fated mate for only them to hear. Mates were born on the same day and finding them should be as simple as checking every fae kingdom's birth records. Yet no record had anyone matching his mate's name and date of birth.

His father traveled to each of the other fae kingdoms—Mountain, Desert, and Tropical—to double-check the records himself with no luck.

It didn't make sense.

Dean fought the urge to rake a hand through his neatly styled light golden-brown hair. Anything less than perfection was unacceptable to his parents, and the last thing he wanted was to be locked in his rooms for a week.

What if we never find her?

The intensity of Fawn's turmoil deepened, and he longed to destroy everything around him to release the growing agitation.

Braddock, Dean's oldest friend, reached out and punched his shoulder. "Why do you look like that?"

Dean grunted and rubbed his arm. At thirteen, Braddock already towered over most men. He eyed his best friend. The boy's bronzed, medium-brown skin and sun-streaked brown hair attested to the time he spent outside training. Dean glanced at his own lightly suntanned beige skin. He trained a lot too, but his mother lost her mind if he didn't wear sun protectant.

Braddock's large hand landed on his shoulder and shook lightly. "Dean?"

Dean gave up and shoved a hand through his hair. "My mate is upset."

"I can go look for her," Braddock offered. "I'm a better tracker than anyone in the kingdom." Dean suppressed a laugh. His friend thought he was the best at everything.

He fell into a nearby chair and stared at the ceiling. "What if we can't find her?" He cringed at the hopelessness in his voice. If his father had been here to hear it, he would have punished Dean for showing weakness.

Braddock stared out the sitting room window, lost in thought. "You'll have to marry someone else," he concluded, wrinkling his nose.

A lump formed in Dean's throat, but he kept his face neutral. He didn't want to marry someone else. He wanted his mate. Since gaining access to her emotions, his life had been bearable. Her joy often held his darkness at bay.

Every time Dean felt her laugh, he wondered how she looked doing it. Did she throw her head back and laugh loudly, or did she sound like a teapot? He almost smiled at the thought.

If only she were here. When he found her, he'd make sure she laughed all the time.

"This has never happened before," Dean admitted, hating that his situation would make history. Another indiscretion in his parents' eyes.

The gods only blessed royal fae with mates; the magical bond kept the royal bloodlines strong. No royal in the history of Eden had married anyone other than their mate.

"You can marry Cali if you don't find her," Braddock suggested with a shrug.

An uncomfortable feeling slithered around Dean's neck like a too-tight collar. Cali was Braddock's cousin. She was a pretty girl with medium brown hair just past her shoulders, light olive skin, and brown eyes.

Dean didn't know her well, and Braddock didn't spend a lot of time with her either—or at least not that Dean knew of. He forced out a laugh. "Don't worry. It won't come to that. I'll find her."

I hope.

The door to Dean's sitting room banged open seconds before his father's booming voice filled the space. "Dean!"

Braddock and Dean both shot to their feet. They'd been friends long enough to know that anything less than a perfect display of respect would not be tolerated by the king, even in private quarters. "Sir?"

His father surged forward, ignoring Braddock, and grabbed Dean by the arm to drag him toward the hallway. Dean's already tall, muscular frame easily kept pace—he was used to his father's theatrics.

"I spoke with General Craven this morning," his father seethed.

By some miracle, Dean kept the contempt from twisting his face. General Craven, the king's closest friend, reported every misstep—or anything his father deemed a disgrace. The general either hated Dean, or the king paid him *very* well.

"Instead of concentrating on your technique, you were standing around with other junior warriors, *laughing*," the king spat. "Training is not the time to stand around being useless."

Dean and the other junior warriors had taken a water break, and gods forbid he allowed himself to enjoy the conversation as they did so. He kept his mouth shut, having learned long ago that defending himself only worsened his punishment.

"You're going to make up for the time you wasted. The general is waiting."

Dean's blood ran cold as the realization of what his father had in store doused him in panic. Last year, his father rotated punishments: sometimes sparring with General Craven, sometimes isolation in locked rooms, and sometimes he'd surprise him with something new and equally as horrifying.

General Craven was a large man, rock solid, and the king's favorite instrument of discipline. Even with royal strength and speed, at thirteen, Dean was no match for the most skilled warrior in the kingdom.

Yet. By the time his powers fully manifested, he would be able to bat the general away like a fly. The general didn't take it easy either. He never injured Dean enough to incapacitate him for longer than a day, but some cuts were deep enough to scar.

"Yes, sir," Dean conceded with resignation. As he followed his father to the horrors awaiting him, he silently prayed that Fawn laughed hard tonight. He was going to need it.

• • •

Dean's head snapped back from the full force of the general's hilt slamming against his face. The general brought down his sword in a wide arc and sliced across Dean's side hard enough to cut through his leather vest and split the skin.

Dean grunted and fell to his knees. If he stayed down, General Craven would berate him, but the *lesson* would stop. Pain radiated across his cheek and side.

"Pathetic," his father commented from the side of the sparring circle.

The only saving grace was no other warriors were around. No, his father liked to conceal his disciplinary lessons, claiming it was so no one saw Dean's weakness. It was more likely he didn't want anyone to interfere with his barbaric methods.

"Get up," his father snapped. "You are a royal. Royals do not lose."

Dean lifted his head. "I can't."

The king walked over and squatted in front of his son to inspect his side. "You're a fucking embarrassment to the Hawthorne line." He straightened and addressed the general. "Patch him up. We'll start again once his wounds heal."

Dean hung his head. Hatred in his heart multiplied, and he wondered what he'd done to deserve this life. He was *tired*.

Later, as he gingerly laid down in his bed, Fawn's laughter bloomed in his chest. Her warmth radiated through him. He closed his eyes and savored the sensation.

If not for her, he didn't know if he could keep going.

A week later, Fawn stared miserably out the carriage window as it bumped along the gravel road of the Mountain Kingdom, trying not to drop the leftover piece of cake balancing on her lap. She didn't want to go to the cold mountains; she wanted to return home to the garden region of the Human Kingdom.

After discovering her magic, her parents decided to return to the fae lands where her father had grown up.

The human children at school feared her, and her father said fear made people dangerous.

She didn't understand how she'd gone nearly a year with magic without realizing it. Her newfound magic was weak at best—almost non-existent by fae standards. She couldn't glamour half as far as her father, nor was her body strong or fast. She had just enough magic to uproot all of their lives.

Fawn's mind wandered to the life that awaited her. Her grandparents had once owned a produce stand but sold it years ago to buy a ranch. They now raised fae Shire horses—massive beasts standing at *least* twenty hands. Far larger than horses in the Human Kingdom.

Her grandparents' house was big enough to hold two families comfortably, and Fawn and her parents would live there, helping them with the ranch. She hoped the ranch didn't include mounting the horses. The thought of being atop such a towering, moving creature terrified her.

Something faint tickled her chest, as it had for months, like a whisper of foreign emotion. Her mother said the moodiness stemmed from her turning into a woman. Just something else to add to her growing list of grievances.

Something wet and slimy smacked the side of her face and slid down her cheek, making her jolt. A small piece of cake tumbled down her dress and onto the floor.

"There's something on your face, squirt," her father said casually, pointing at her cheek.

Fawn's eyes dropped to the plate in his lap, where his piece of cake had a noticeable chunk missing.

"You should be more careful when you're eating," he continued, lifting his cake for an exaggerated bite.

Her mother let out a sound between a laugh and a snort, and he wiggled frosting -covered fingers at his wife. "Would you like some, dear?"

Fawn picked up her entire piece of cake and chucked it at her father's chest. Not hard enough to explode everywhere, but enough to splatter across his torso. Her mother clapped a hand over her mouth to stifle her laughter, and her father looked down in shock.

Fawn braced, knowing what came next, and cursed herself for not keeping part of her cake for her arsenal. Her eyes slipped to her mother's lap, lamenting the empty plate.

Her father's eyes danced with mischief when they met hers, and she tried not to laugh at the frosting stuck in his mustache.

"You're laughing at your old man?" he asked, his voice full of mock hurt.

Fawn nodded through her uncontrollable giggles and screeched when a piece of cake splattered against her forehead.

"John," her mother said, trying to scold him.

"I was aiming for her mouth," he fibbed, winking at Fawn, who tried to keep a straight face.

Anytime Fawn or her mother was sad, her father did what he could to turn their mood around. Throwing food like a child in a small, enclosed space wasn't ideal, but it had the intended effect. Fawn's chest warmed, grateful that no matter how awful life seemed, she always had her parents to lift her up.

She licked the frosting around her mouth and smiled, then scooped the cake from her forehead and flung it at her father.

2

Fawn stood on a stool, methodically brushing Ivy, the fae Shire horse her grandfather had gifted her when she arrived at the ranch a month ago. The brush's bristles rasped against Ivy's thick coat, each stroke grounding Fawn in the simple rhythm of work, away from whispers and stares. The large beast had a light coat with reddish spots sprinkled all over like freckles. Her calm demeanor soothed Fawn more than anything else. She'd always been comfortable taking care of the horses but climbing onto their backs was another story entirely. The height alone made her stomach pitch.

Working on her grandparents' ranch hadn't been terrible. Aside from the cold climate and snow, she enjoyed it.

School was a different story. The word itself had become heavy; school wasn't learning, it was misery. Being the only half-human in her class made her a target, as did her teeth. She loved her mother, but why hadn't she inherited her father's looks and ears? If she had the slightly pointed ears of the fae, the other kids would have no way of knowing about her human side. A single curve of cartilage could erase her difference, could let her fade into the crowd instead of putting a target on her back.

Stupidly, she didn't think to cover her ears on her first day, and a girl with an ugly look on her face laughed outright, drawing attention to what her classmates considered a fault.

Most adult fae she'd encountered hadn't cared, though a handful looked down on her with disdain.

She sighed, gave Ivy a pat, and jumped down. The horses were too tall for her to reach their backs from the ground.

She put away the brush and stool and stepped into the cold air, glancing at the imposing palace walls. Being the main supplier of horses for the crown, her grandparents' ranch bordered the palace and while the walls were impossibly high, the palace towers rose even higher.

Fawn often wondered what the inside looked like. She'd never seen the palace in the Human Kingdom—or any other fae kingdom for that matter—and wondered if the rooms inside were as massive as the outside suggested.

"Are you done for the day?" her father's voice interrupted her thoughts.

Turning toward him, she planted her hands on her hips. "Depends on why you're asking."

He chuckled. "How about we go for dinner in the village?"

Fawn perked up. They never went out for dinner. "Mom said we could?"

He leaned down conspiratorially and whispered, "I haven't asked her yet, but if we double team her, she'll give in."

Disappointment weighed on Fawn's shoulders. "She'll say no. She always does."

Sighing, her father squeezed her shoulder. "Your mother feels out of place here."

Being human, her mother sometimes faced the same scorn

as Fawn, but whereas Fawn's hair could cover her ears, her mother's hair was too short to do the same.

Fawn's father glanced down, noticing her disappointment. "I'll tell you what. You and I will go. Your mother will be okay here with Grandma and Grandpa for the evening." He lowered his voice again. "If she tries to say no, I'll hold her down and you tickle her until she gives in."

Fawn rolled her eyes with a smile. "You really think she'll say yes?"

He nodded. "I know so. Let's get cleaned up, and we'll go."

Fawn tried not to run toward the house, but she couldn't help it. They were going to eat in the village! She skidded to a stop, remembering she'd left Ivy's halter hanging on the back fence. They'd been walking the perimeter, but Ivy grew restless, so Fawn removed the halter and let her wander for a bit. Mares could be testy, something Fawn learned quickly. It had been easier to let the girl roam than to deal with her in her ornery state.

"One second," she called over her shoulder as she jogged to the fence closest to the palace walls.

Lifting the halter and lead rope from the fence, she turned and froze. A large group of people strapped with weapons quietly stalked across her grandparents' pasture, gesturing toward the palace walls. Fawn's lungs seized, refusing to pull in air. The gleam of steel caught the fading sun, a glint that froze her lungs harder than the mountain air ever had.

What if they are rebels? Her father warned her the fae kingdoms had them, but she never thought she'd see them.

"What's taking so long?" her father's voice shouted from near the barn. Fawn drew in a sharp breath, eyes wide, as the rebels froze and turned toward her father. A man from the group looked around the pasture, spotting her still form.

Making a split-second decision, she took off running

toward her father, shouting at the top of her lungs. "Dad! Help!"

Moments later, he appeared over the small rolling hill with a bow and quiver of arrows, moving faster than she'd ever seen him run. He must have grabbed it from the barn. They kept weapons there in case they needed to fend off wild animals. Noticing the group of men, his eyes widened, and he sped up. "Get back to the house, now!"

Her legs stumbled at first, heavy with terror, before instinct took over. *Run.*

Pushing hard, she ran, cursing her lack of fae speed. Someone in the group barked out orders Fawn couldn't make out, and she looked back with horror as her father met them head-on.

Fawn screamed for her grandfather, praying he heard her in time to help. Forcing her legs faster, she begged the gods to keep them safe. Her voice cracked, raw with desperation, the sound tearing at the stillness of the ranch.

Her mother burst out of their front door as her grandfather ran around the side of the house. His eyes looked past her and widened. Grandpa disappeared into the house, emerging with a bow and quiver and a sword strapped to his waist.

Her mother ducked inside, returned with her sword, and jumped off the porch. "Get inside with your grandmother," she commanded Fawn and ran toward the open field.

Fawn's foot caught in the end of her skirts, sending her tumbling to the ground. Being summer, the ground lacked its usual blanket of snow, leaving nothing to cushion her fall. She hit the ground with a sickening crack, and black dots clouded her vision before everything faded away.

৯৯.

"You missed two questions on your exam today," Dean's father informed him. "*Two*."

Dean's mother sat quietly, eating her dinner as if her husband hadn't just spoken to her son like he'd murdered an angel.

"I had the highest grade in the class," Dean pointed out, hoping his father might congratulate him for once.

"No one will follow an uneducated king," his father said with disgust. "Our family has protected Eden for centuries, and I will not allow you to put our people at risk because you'd rather gallivant around with your friends instead of study."

Dean's hand tightened around his fork. "Has Fate shown you my demise?" he asked coolly. He knew his indifferent attitude only angered his father more, but sometimes he couldn't help himself. The daily private 'training' sessions with General Craven had changed Dean. He no longer cowered in his father's presence. He kept the peace when he could, but he no longer bothered to feign respect for his father.

The king's icy eyes pinned Dean in place. "You *will* be the king our people deserve. If I have to chain you to a table until you can recite every tome in their ancient library, so be it."

Dean shoveled more potatoes into his mouth to keep from telling his father off. Every night, Dean wished he was anyone other than the future Garden King. Maybe it was best they hadn't found Fawn yet. If his parents treated her the way they treated him, he would kill them, and he had no desire to be king yet.

"Yes, father," Dean relented, too tired to fight.

Optimistic excitement broke his morose thoughts, and he fought the urge to smile. *Fawn.*

He felt her growing excitement, and he wanted to enjoy it. Not taint it with his parents' nagging. "May I be excused?" he asked politely.

The king sighed and waved his hand. "Go."

Dean stood and quickly pushed his chair under the table.

Fawn's joy faded, and Dean's heart pounded against his chest as her anxiety speared through him.

Her terror climbed, and he gripped the chair next to him.

"What's wrong?" his mother asked, frantic, as she stood and rounded the table toward him. "Dean?" He might have laughed at her uncharacteristic display of concern if not for the panic clawing at his insides.

"Fawn," Dean managed to say. The fear disappeared as fast as it'd come. His own fear gripped him tightly, and he closed his eyes to focus on the bond.

"*Dean*," his father barked from beside him.

Dean faintly registered his mother calling for a healer and his father demanding he calm down.

"Something's wrong," he choked out. "She's hurt." He clutched at his chest and closed his eyes, reaching for the bond. "I can't feel the bond." Opening his eyes, he met his father's piercing gaze. "We have to find her."

Dean's mother awkwardly rubbed circles on his back, and his father remained quiet, scrutinizing his son like an annoying problem to be solved.

Dean straightened, helplessness engulfing him like a too-tight blanket.

Still, his father said nothing.

Fawn blinked awake, groaning at the throbbing in her head. Her bedroom slowly came into focus, and she glanced out the window into the night.

What time is it? I don't remember getting in bed.

A sob penetrated the silence, followed by a teary voice. "Fawn? Honey, are you awake?"

Pain shot through Fawn's skull when she turned toward her grandmother, taking in her disheveled state. "Grandma? Why are you crying? What's going on?"

Her grandmother sniffled and grabbed Fawn's hand. "Rebels attacked the ranch and palace yesterday," she began, her voice strangled.

Memories clouded Fawn's vision, and she sucked in a sharp breath as her mind replayed her father aiming his bow at the group of men. She tried to push herself into a sitting position, but her grandmother laid a hand on her shoulder.

"Your parents..." she began with tears streaming down her face. "Honey, your parents are gone." Sobs wracked the old woman's body. "Your grandfather managed to save you, but when he went back to help..." She hiccupped. "He was too late, and the rebels were gone." The older woman took a deep breath to calm herself. "They managed to get into the palace garden and kill the queen."

Something inside Fawn cracked, splintering her chest down the middle with a soul-crushing pain. Her grandmother whispered soothing words, crying with Fawn over their loss.

Her shoulders heaved as she sobbed in her grandmother's arms. Drawn by the sound, her grandfather joined them and wrapped his arms around them both. "I'm sorry, squirt. I tried to get to them." One of the strongest men she knew took a shuddering breath and released a quiet sob of his own. "I tried."

Later that evening as she laid in bed, a deep self-loathing filled every crack her parents' death made.

Had she not lost her temper with Robert, forcing her family

to flee to the fae lands, her father would be making her laugh at the dinner table. Instead, she'd let her emotions rule her behavior, and it aided in her parents' death.

Her lip started to tremble, and her emotions threatened to take over once again.

No.

She shoved her grief down, locking away her pain in a tight box. Never again would she allow her emotions to destroy anything else. It wouldn't be hard because losing the two most important people in her life had already killed something inside her.

Three people died yesterday, but only two stopped breathing.

Dean bolted upright in bed, clutching at his chest. He'd been staring at the large canopy above him, unable to sleep, his thoughts fixed on the silent bond.

Fawn's confusion hit first, followed by a grief so sharp it knifed through him and stole his breath. Though his mate was in distress, relief flared—she was alive—but it died quickly when, moments later, the bond faded to nothing.

Panic set in again, much like it had a few days ago when the bond went quiet. Those silent days had been hell, and he didn't know if he could survive them again. He'd stopped praying to the gods long ago—they had done nothing but allow his father to hurt him—but he prayed now.

Don't take her from me, he begged. *Please.*

Two weeks later, his father returned from the one kingdom they hadn't checked–the Human Kingdom. Humans couldn't be a royal fae's mate, and fae children had to be in the fae lands for their magic to manifest. There had been no reason to look there, but after the bond faded, the council advised a search just in case.

The grim look on the king's face made Dean's stomach plummet.

"We found her," his father said, voice softer than Dean had ever heard. "According to the birth records, Fawn was a half-human, half-fae girl living in the garden region of the Human Kingdom with her parents."

Dean absorbed the words; his mind snagged on one. "Was?" *No.*

"It was reported recently that the girl and her parents died in a carriage accident."

His mother made a sound between a cry and a gasp. "That can't be."

The king's eyes cut to the queen. "I assure you, it can. This is precisely why the mates of royals are brought to the palace when they're revealed; it's too risky to leave them unprotected." His father ranted on, calling the loss of Dean's mate disastrous—an omen that could mean Eden's downfall.

Everything around Dean faded to background noise. Nothing his parents said mattered after his entire world imploded. Dean stared out of the window at the palace gardens and let the darkness consume him.

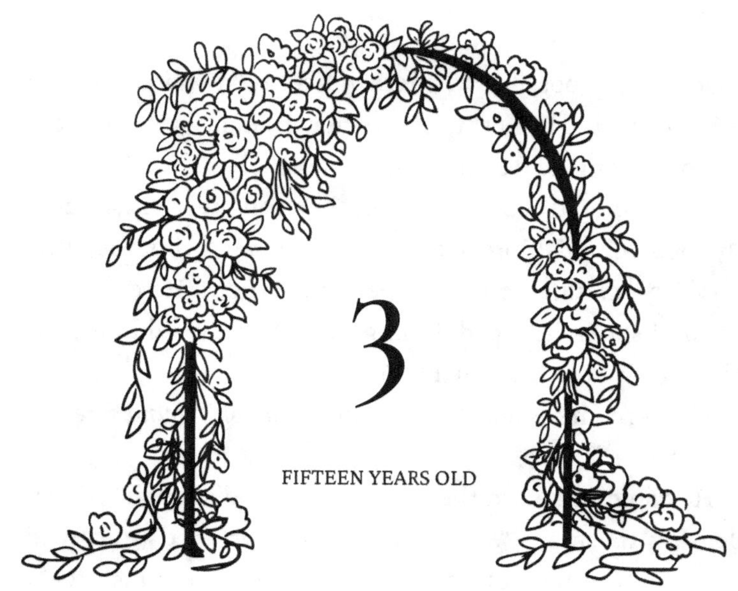

3

FIFTEEN YEARS OLD

Dean dodged another near-fatal blow from General Craven. The man's attacks had grown more vicious lately, as though he bore a personal vendetta. The whoosh of steel skimmed his ear, the air itself splitting as if it wanted to cut him open.

He stumbled back but quickly righted himself just as the general swung the butt of his sword down toward Dean's head. Air whooshed past his arm as a massive serpent struck from behind, coiling a thick, bluish-black scaled body around the general and squeezing until the man gasped for breath.

Dean stared slack-jawed, jolting when a foreign thought pierced his mind. *"Would you like me to kill him?"*

The thought slithered into Dean's mind like venom—half tempting, half terrifying.

It wasn't exactly a voice, more a knowing of what the serpent meant to say. His *familiar* had finally arrived. When a royal-born heir turned fifteen, the gods bonded them to an animal *familiar,* along with searing a tattoo of the animal into their chest. Dean had turned fifteen two days ago, and while he'd known his *familiar* would be some form of snake or serpent, it had been impossible to guess which. He'd waited anxiously, worried it would be nothing more than a small garden snake.

How wrong he'd been.

'*Yes*' tottered on the tip of his tongue. He should be ashamed for wishing death on the general, but he wasn't. Dean's eyes landed on the expectant serpent. He dropped his gaze and shook his head. Killing the general would only incite more wrath from his father. "*No.*"

The serpent hissed. "*Are you sure? You don't sound sure.*"

"*I'm sure.*"

He could've sworn the serpent looked disappointed before releasing the man. "*Suit yourself.*" She slithered toward him, lifting the top part of her body until they were face-to-face. "*I'm Cassandra.*"

Dean took in her massive form. She had to stretch at least fifteen or twenty feet long. "*Dean Hawthorne,*" he replied. "*It's nice to meet you.*"

He hadn't noticed the general charging until that moment. When the man raised his sword, Dean darted around Cassandra. "You dare harm my *familiar?*" His voice dropped into a low, dangerous register he'd never used before.

The general pulled up short, a chorus of emotions flitting across his features. "It attacked me."

Cassandra slithered around Dean and hissed at the general. "*He could have killed you.*"

"She protected me," Dean told the furious man. "Your methods go far beyond sparring, and she is duty bound to stop you. You know that as well as I do."

General Craven sighed and lowered his voice so as not to be overheard. "I am only doing as your father ordered. You know that."

Dean's anger rose. Every cut, every bruise was his father's

signature inked into his skin. And still it wasn't enough. He knew his father ordered it, but his father didn't stay for the lessons. The general didn't have to be cruel, yet he was.

"Your father is responsible?" Cassandra asked, outraged.

Dean ignored her.

"She is not allowed in my training arena again," the general informed him, as if he had a say.

Dean arched a brow with a smirk. He didn't know where his sudden surge of confidence came from—perhaps because in the last year his skill had sharpened enough that he knew it wouldn't be long before he could best the general; or maybe because he now had someone on his side who would stop the madness when it went too far.

Either way, a weight lifted from his soul, and it felt *good*.

Her speed and size aside, *familiars* couldn't die until their bonded royal did. To kill her, the general would have to kill Dean. The Royals only had one heir, and as much as Dean's father seemed to hate him, he needed him alive for the sake of the kingdom.

"I'd watch who you think you can order around," Dean told the general. "Not even my father can keep her out if she wants in. *Familiars* answer only to the gods, and they can call every animal in Eden down upon you if they wish."

The general's fury grew but Dean didn't miss the fear that flickered in his eyes. "Leave."

Dean turned on his heel with a broad smile. "Gladly."

Dean's steps echoed through the large marble hallways of the palace, toward his father's office, Cassandra slithering beside him. His *familiar* still seethed at the general's audacity. *"I will*

kill him if he insults me again," she vowed. *"I don't care what you want. I will not be disrespected."*

"If he's foolish enough to try again, I won't stop you."

They approached the king's office, and Dean drew a steadying breath. *"There's something you need to know before you meet my father."* He quickly explained his father's treatment of him through the years; how his father demanded perfection and his cruel punishments. *"He'll do whatever he deems neces- sary. If he thinks you're a threat to his regime, he'll find a way to stop you."*

Dean had an idea of how to protect her, though he wasn't sure it would work.

"I'll kill him, too," Cassandra replied matter-of-factly. *"If he's a cruel king, Eden is better off without him."*

"He is good to the people," Dean countered. *"They won't take kindly to his death."*

Cassandra lifted and turned to him. "Anyone who treats a child the way he treats you is cruel, whether he shows it to others or not. *You don't worry about me. I can protect myself."*

The words sank into him heavier than praise ever had. Someone saw him. Chose him. Defended him.

"Is your bite deadly?" Dean mused.

Cassandra's forked tongue whipped out, and she opened her mouth, showcasing two crimson fangs elongating before his eyes. *"If I want it to be. I can simply paralyze someone or kill them instantly, depending on my mood."*

Dean eyed her fangs. *"Good."* He raised his fist and knocked on the large, wooden door accented in gold. His mother's touch.

"Come in," his father bellowed. The serpent at Dean's side brought a satisfied smile to his father's mouth. "Ah, I see the gods have given you a fierce companion fitting of a king." Dean's father stood and rounded his desk, inspecting Cassandra. "It's perfect." The king's *familiar* was a large stag, dangerous in his own right, and Dean's father often said only strong royals deserved strong *familiars.*

"Her name is Cassandra," Dean said. His father opened his mouth to reply, but Dean cut him off. "I will no longer be sparring with General Craven unless I choose to do so. Cassandra attacked him today, and he insulted her in return."

The king turned slowly to Dean. "You seem to think you have a choice." He motioned to Cassandra. "This beast will obey me. I am her king."

Cassandra hissed, her blood-red fangs growing. *"The fuck I will."*

The king stepped back. "Control your beast," he commanded. "I'll not stand for disobedience."

Cassandra shot forward and wrapped around his arms and neck, choking him until he turned purple. She opened her jaws and flicked her tongue across his cheek with a bone-deep hiss.

"Father, don't move," Dean said quickly. "Her venom kills in an instant."

The king froze, and an elegant voice drew everyone's attention across the room. "You'll not harm the boy or the serpent," it said with quiet authority. Dean's gaze locked on a woman with white hair, snow white skin, and pale grey eyes, draped in a white flowing dress. *"Ever.* Harm them, and you will die soon after, dooming Eden to fall."

Dean stared at the woman, entranced. *Where did she come from?* He couldn't look away from the otherworldly woman with a tangible aura. The urge to kneel nearly dragged him down, but he forced himself to resist.

"Release him," the woman commanded softly.

Cassandra obeyed immediately, and Dean's father dropped to the ground, gasping and choking.

Dean glanced at Cassandra. *"Who is she?"*

"My name is Lilith." Dean snapped his gaze to her. "I am a Fallen Fate from the heavens," she said, answering the question he hadn't even asked. "I do not reveal myself to heirs until they ascend the throne, but you are an exception."

Cassandra remained suspiciously quiet. *What is a Fallen Fate?* Dean asked his *familiar,* still unable to address Lilith, whose power pressed down like a weight.

Cassandra moved toward Lilith and rubbed her face against the woman's cheek. *"She is Fate in the flesh."*

"The Fates dwell in the heavens," Lilith explained. "But for reasons you needn't know, I reside here in Eden to guide the Garden Kingdom royals." She moved closer. "You are a descendant of the first fae and the protectors of Eden."

"I... what?" Dean replied, feeling stupid.

"It's true," his father said from the floor. "You are too young to understand."

Lilith's tone took on a hard edge. "The prince is wiser and more mature than the children his age. Your cruelty has forced my hand."

"That's ridiculous," the king sputtered. "He must be forged into a proper king."

Lilith's unsettling gaze turned lethal. "And he will take his own life if you continue. Without his heir, Eden will fall." His father blanched, as did Dean.

"My mate is dead," Dean blurted out, the familiar stab of pain igniting in his chest. "My heir will be weaker than any royal in history."

Lilith came to stand behind him and placed a soothing hand on his arm. "You will marry and have a daughter strong enough to help the other queens defeat the darkness that will befall Eden. You *will* know happiness." It didn't escape his notice that she didn't say he'd marry his mate, and for some reason, the confirmation from such a powerful being that Fawn was truly gone gutted him.

Despite his grief over what might have been, a pulse of comfort radiated through him, even if he didn't believe her. "Okay."

"Cassandra," Lilith addressed the *familiar*. "When the time comes, never let *her* out of your sight."

The serpent hissed lightly in return and left the room with Dean at her side.

Dean looked back at the Fallen Fate and couldn't help but wonder who "her" was.

Fawn draped a blanket over Ivy and patted her side, coaxing her into the barn. The snow fell harder, and she needed to be sure every horse was sheltered and warm. "Good girl," she murmured, rubbing the horse's neck.

After checking the stalls, she trudged across the field toward the house to help her grandmother with dinner.

"Are all the horses up?" her grandfather asked once she stepped inside.

Fawn nodded and made her way into the kitchen.

"Thank you, squirt," he said. Fawn waited for the familiar nickname to stir the tidal wave of emotions she usually had to lock down, but nothing came. Grief, pain, fondness... anything. She'd spent a year pushing it all down until there was nothing left to feel.

Part of her was grateful, while the other part knew it wasn't normal, but like everything else, she couldn't find it in her to care. Living in a perpetual state of indifference beats living in pain any day.

Her subtle, inexplicable mood swings continued, but they felt like background noise.

Fawn's hand twitched, knowing if she didn't get her soggy dress off soon, she'd panic. The feeling of wet clothes against her skin created a kind of panic she couldn't control.

Her grandmother's gaze dropped to Fawn's clenched fist. "Honey, go change into something dry and warm. I'm almost finished with dinner."

Fawn thanked her grandmother. When she hit the second floor, her grandfather's deep voice stopped her. "I'm worried about her, Judith."

A pot clanged against the counter, followed by a heavy sigh. "I don't know how to help her," her grandmother agreed. "She barely speaks, and she doesn't have any friends." Fabric rustled, and a chair scraped across the floor. "What if we lose her too?" Her grandmother's breath hitched on a quiet sob.

Heavy footsteps sounded and another chair moved. "We won't let that happen," her grandfather promised. "We'll keep trying to get through to her; take her into the village more or something to keep her busy."

Her grandmother sniffled. "I'll speak with her teacher, see if he has any suggestions."

Not wanting to hear more, Fawn tiptoed to her room. She hated that she worried her grandparents. They'd been nothing but kind and loving, and she'd never leave them like they feared.

She didn't speak much because her parents had been her best friends, and without them, she hadn't much to say.

Fawn couldn't give them what they wanted in earnest, but she could fake it. With a new resolve, she dressed quickly and wandered downstairs. "What's for dinner? I'm starving."

EIGHTEEN YEARS OLD

Fawn gripped the wheelbarrow handles and pushed the muck around the barn, cursing herself for not shoveling a path through the snow first. The catch sat beyond the barn, down a slight slope, and pushing the wheelbarrow downhill would've been easy had she shoveled first. But every inch of snow fought her, dragging at the wheel like the mountain itself resented her presence.

"Need some help?"

"Thank the gods," she mumbled and set down the wheelbarrow handles to greet her grandfather. "I forgot to shovel the path."

The old man snickered. "And instead of fixing it when you realized your mistake, you thought you'd try your hand at wheelbarrow plowing?" His laughter carried through the crisp air, rich and booming, softening the sharp edges of the cold.

Fawn rolled her eyes. "I thought it'd be easy," she grumbled. "The snow isn't that deep today."

"I'll grab a shovel." He patted her on the head and disappeared around the side of the barn. Holding the shovel and a pair of gloves, he reappeared shortly at her side. "Do you want to shovel, or do you want to push?"

Fawn surveyed the hill and the wheelbarrow to calculate which would take more effort. Most might leave the easy stuff for their grandparents, but her grandfather was young at only fifty-seven, and in better shape than most men in their twenties. "I'll push," she decided.

He winked. "Figured you would. Back it up a few steps until I can clear the way."

Once she had the wheelbarrow moved, her grandfather went to work. A smart person would've waited for him to clear the whole path before following with the load.

Fawn never claimed to be smart, a fact proved when she neared him with the wheelbarrow, slipped, and hit him from behind. She watched in slow motion as her grandfather tried to catch himself but tripped over the shovel and tipped forward.

The grunt he made mixed with the crunch of the snow as he face-planted, followed by silence, as if even the birds were shocked.

She gasped and ran to his side, dropping beside him in the snow.

He raised his snow-covered face to look at her, but before she could apologize, he lightly threw a handful of snow at her. She squealed and scrambled back. His deep laughter rumbled through the quiet morning air as another snowball pelted Fawn's body.

She froze then burst out laughing and scooped up weapons of her own.

"You think it's funny to push a helpless old man?" her grandfather teased as he threw more snow.

"It was an accident," she exclaimed with another laugh.

"You expect me to believe that?" His eyes twinkled, the

lines around his eyes creasing. "You're just like your daddy." He gathered up a handful of muck from the wheelbarrow and held it up.

Fawn stopped moving, eyeing her grandfather warily. "You wouldn't dare."

"Wouldn't I?" For every step he took forward, she took one back.

"Winston, you better put that pile of shit down right now!" her grandmother yelled, startling them both. "The last time you and John threw muck at each other, I was scrubbing it out of your clothes for weeks."

Grandma approached them and grumbled something under her breath about this family throwing things at each other. Her apron was dusted with flour, hair wild from the kitchen heat, and yet she wielded more authority than any sword.

Fawn remembered years ago, on their move here, her father throwing cake at her face. To her surprise, a faint fondness warmed her. It was the first time she'd really felt anything in years.

"I'm trying to help her lighten up, Judith," he replied innocently, and Fawn wondered if his words held a hint of truth.

She'd not seen this teasing side of her grandparents before. Had they been tiptoeing around her? She hated that they thought they needed to.

"Don't let him fool you, Grandma," Fawn jumped in. "He retaliated because I accidentally pushed him in the snow."

Her grandmother huffed out a breath, planting her hands on her hips. "Winston, you—"

Fawn gawked at her grandmother's muck-covered chest and slapped a hand over her mouth.

Grandpa ran.

Braddock laid flat on his back, panting for breath. "One of these days I won't go easy on you," he warned Dean, who rolled his eyes and held out his hand to help his friend up.

Despite Braddock's massive size, he was no match for Dean's skill, strength, and speed. No one was. Not even General Craven anymore.

"Thanks for holding back," Dean deadpanned.

Braddock brushed himself off and rolled his shoulders. A piece of long, wayward hair fell in his face, and he pushed it behind his pointed ear and crossed his arms. "I'm a nice guy. It's bad form to humiliate the future king in front of his subjects."

Dean's lips twitched as he fought off a smile. "Right." The leather vest he wore stuck to his sweaty bare skin, and not for the first time, Dean cursed whoever designed their training leathers.

Cassandra slithered across the training arena, scaring half of the warriors on her way to them. *"You should let him win at least once,"* she insisted. *"You're going to give him a complex."*

Dean snorted. *"Nothing in this world could make Braddock think less of himself."* A trait Dean admired. Braddock thought he was the best, that he could do anything he wanted and be good at it, but he never once insinuated that he was better than anyone else. Braddock liked himself, *believed* in himself, and nothing anyone else thought would change that.

"I like him," Cassandra tried again. *"Let him win this once."*

Dean shook his head at the serpent. *"If I go easy on him, he'll know, and that will piss him off."*

"I hate when you guys do that." Braddock pointed between Dean and Cassandra. "It's rude to gossip in front of other people and not share."

Dean smirked. "We were talking about you."

Braddock blew Cassandra an exaggerated air-kiss. "If you want a kiss, just ask."

"Can I bite him?"

"I thought you liked him?" Dean pointed out. *"Is biting like kissing for you?"*

"I wouldn't kill him." Her forked tongue shot out at Braddock. He laughed in return, and she did it again.

"Let's go again," Braddock insisted, lifting his sword into the sparring position.

Dean complied and took up his spot across from his friend. "Last round."

They circled each other before coming together in a clash of metal. They used dull swords so as not to seriously injure the other, unlike the battle-ready blade General Craven used to use.

Around and around they went, and Dean had to admit that in another year or two, Braddock would be one of the top warriors in the battalion. He had the drive and talent, and as much as Braddock joked around, his ability to cut it off and focus made him excel at nearly everything.

Warm, fuzzy tingles built inside him, throwing him off-kilter mid-spin. The spin slowed and Braddock's sword came down on Dean's kidney. The unexpected blow sent him to his knees.

Had he not been focused on the strange but slightly familiar feeling in his chest, he might have hopped up in time. Instead, Dean ended up with Braddock's sword at his throat.

"Had to shut you up at least once," Braddock boasted. "It'll teach you to be humble."

Dean would have laughed at Braddock telling someone to be humble if he wasn't still feeling whispers of laughter.

5

TWENTY-ONE YEARS OLD

Fawn,

You're gone. I know that. Yet, you haunt me still. I can't see you, touch you, hear you, but I feel you. I stupidly told my mother I could still feel you. She said my brain was trying to cling to something long gone, like a phantom limb.

I don't mention it to anyone anymore, except the palace healer. I went to her once, after feeling you, to see if I was mistaking physical pain for foreign emotions. It sounds stupid when I write it out, but I was desperate.

She suggested writing my thoughts down every time I feel you. She's a healer for both physical and mental ailments and claims it can help people sort out their thoughts when they don't feel comfortable speaking with people about it.

She meant journals, not letters to the dead. But writing to anyone else—even myself—feels wrong. How can I miss someone I never even met?

Because you were the only proof that some part of me was still alive. The only light threaded through years of shadow.

I only felt you for a year, yet your emotions became my addic-

tion. My obsession. Now they're gone.

I felt you today. A bit of affection trickled down the bond, and I can't help but wonder if another man caused it. The thought made me blind with jealousy. I'm jealous of someone who doesn't exist.

Maybe I am losing my mind.

Maybe madness is just what love looks like when it has nowhere to go.

Or maybe you're not really gone. I can't let myself consider the alternative—that I've spent years mourning while you're somewhere out there, living without me.

I'm pathetic. It's tragic, really.

If anyone finds this, they'll lock me away until I come to my senses. I wonder if that would be best.

Tragically Yours,

Dean

Dean stared at the letter, wondering if he should burn it or tuck it away to read when he needed to realize how ridiculous he sounded. In the end, he hid it in his desk, unable to fully let Fawn go.

He existed in limbo. Not sinking. Not rising above. Rotting, his soul decaying a little more each time he felt her ghost.

Fawn laid in bed and stared at the wall. A deep longing flickered within her, but for what, she didn't know. She only knew she missed *something*. Her soul ached for it, and she wondered if the void would ever be filled. Since the day her grandfather threw muck at her grandmother, she had the occasional break in the bleak numbness in her chest.

This differed from those instances. The whisper of foreign

emotions she often felt confused her. She usually ignored them and refused to let them rule her actions.

But tonight, she'd allow herself to wallow.

Fawn nodded to the guard at the palace gates, thankful to be off work. Last year, she got a job as a maid at the palace. The time had come to move out of her grandparents' home. They'd insisted she stay, but at twenty-three, she needed to venture out on her own.

Needing to be independent, she decided to find a new job. She couldn't do much beyond cook, clean, and work horses, so she applied at the palace. To her surprise, they'd hired her.

Most of the staff were kind and helped her adjust. The job came with room and board if needed. Not having to pay for food and a place to live was a huge bonus.

After her shift, she usually retreated to her room or visited her grandparents, but tonight a festival in town drew her out.

A few maids had invited her to join their group, but she declined politely. Fawn didn't keep many friends by design. Most people didn't know she was half human; she kept her ears hidden, though the constant concealment exhausted her. She couldn't risk confiding in anyone, fearing they might tell others.

As an adult, she'd come to realize most fae didn't care she was half-human like the children did. But Fawn's magic was no match for that of a full-blooded fae. She could seldom see through a fae's glamour, and the power imbalance terrified her.

Vendor carts lined the streets, a small band played, and people laughed and danced on a sectioned-off floor in the road. Colored lanterns swayed overhead, casting the snow-pale streets in a kaleidoscope of red and gold. The air smelled of roasted nuts and spice, thick enough to taste on her tongue. A smile ghosted across her lips at the lively scene. Against all odds, she found herself liking life in the fae kingdom. Things were brighter here. The foliage in the fae lands burst with a myriad of colors, a rainbow compared to the simple greens and flower-accents of the human lands.

Even in the Mountain Kingdom covered in snow, the needles on the pine trees glistened all different colors in the sunlight. The grass, when not blanketed in white, shined a pretty pink.

A gorgeous woman and man caught Fawn's eye. The front of the woman's dress cut low, almost exposing the top of her nipples. They stood at the entrance of the pleasure house, speaking to people who passed. They moved with a sensual ease that drew Fawn in, pulling her across the street for a closer look.

Every shift of their bodies was deliberate, as if gravity itself bent to their rhythm. Desire clung to them like perfume, and Fawn inhaled without meaning to.

Fawn had always been curious about the pleasure houses but never went inside one.

The woman spotted her first and smiled. "Hello, sweet-heart. Can we interest you in a complimentary visit tonight?"

The man, sensing Fawn's inexperience, moved closer,

dropping his voice into a sensual caress. "Have you experienced a show before?"

"No," Fawn admitted and fought the urge to fidget.

The woman's eyes lit up. "Everyone should experience a pleasure house at least once. We have stage performers in different rooms, private boxes where you can watch the shows, and lounges where you can watch and *play* with others," she explained. "You don't have to do anything you don't want to. We have guards throughout that will come to your aid if anyone makes you uncomfortable."

Fawn had experienced sex before but couldn't help but feel like she was missing a piece of the puzzle. There had to be more to sex for everyone to go on and on about it, and if there was anywhere to find out, it would be a pleasure house.

"I'd love to," she replied finally.

The couple smiled, and the man ushered her inside, speaking to a guard inside the foyer. Another woman met her at the entrance to guide her through the building until she felt comfortable enough to be on her own.

The rooms were dark, lit only by candlelight. No windows dotted the walls to allow outside light in, and it gave a sensual ambiance. Plush red couches and chairs filled the first room, facing a large stage.

Two men and a woman filled a large bed. The slapping of their bodies against each other as they filled the room with deep moans shocked Fawn to her core. She didn't know what she expected really, but a group display wasn't it.

They stirred nothing in her sexually until she wondered what it would be like to be on stage, taking their pleasure with her as their visual guide.

That she responded to.

Heat coiled through her, wetness gathering between her thighs.

The woman showing her around sported a knowing smile. "Shall we continue with the dancers?"

Fawn's cheeks heated. "I'd like that." She couldn't wait to see the rest.

From that night on, Fawn was entranced. An obsession took root—the idea of becoming like the men and women on display.

What would it be like?

She didn't think she could fuck in front of that many people, but dancing she could do.

From that night on, she returned often, studying every movement of the dancers. Foolish didn't begin to cover how she felt, practicing alone in her room before a mirror to imaginary music. But after a few months, she was confident enough to audition.

They hired her on the spot, and within weeks, dancing became her lifeline. Two or three nights a week was enough to satiate the need that kept growing inside her.

The atmosphere was thick with desire, amplifying her own. It seeped into her pores, an intoxicating thrum that left her humming long after she left. For once, emotion wasn't danger. It was freedom. Not strong enough to lose control—she never allowed that—but strong enough to let her enjoy herself for the first time in years.

A heady rush of lust and satisfaction surged through Dean, making his cock twitch. *Fuck. Not here.* Lately, flashes of desire attacked him out of nowhere. Sometimes the culprit was obvious—like women at the lakes, swimming in barely-there scraps of fabric.

But more and more, it didn't matter where he was or who

he was with; need would slam into him, and he had no way to sate it. Stroking his cock or fucking someone never took the edge off, and he couldn't figure out why.

Tonight, he stood with Braddock and a few others from their circle at a local alehouse. Being royal, Dean's glamour worked on non-royal fae; only other royals could see through it.

It let him shift his appearance and enjoy a night out without being bombarded.

Heat coiled through him, and he had to restrain himself from panting. He wore a fitted short-sleeve button-down with tailored trousers, yet it felt like he was sweltering under seven layers of coats.

He gulped his ale and nudged Braddock's shoulder. "Is it hot in here?"

"My body doesn't get hot," Braddock said, crossing his arms. "It stays at the perfect temperature at all times." Dean stifled a groan. He should've asked someone else.

Dean couldn't make sense of what he felt. It was almost as if the urges weren't his own. His mother's words flickered through his mind: *A phantom limb.*

He blew out a breath, shook his head. "I'm fine. Must be the crowd."

A pretty girl with long blonde hair, light beige skin, and an inquisitive smile caught his arm. Her touch sent tingles scattering across his skin. "Do I know you?" she asked, tipping her head slightly.

"Not likely," Braddock said with a smirk. "He's not from here."

The blonde ignored him, trailing her fingers across Dean's skin. His cock pressed painfully against his trousers. He already guessed how this would end, and smirked at her. "My friends call me D."

A coy smile curved her lips. "I'm Anna."

Dean didn't know when she'd moved closer, but her body pressed against his. Fucking Anna wouldn't completely alleviate his need, but it couldn't hurt either. Sex scratched an itch, but not completely, and he didn't know what was missing. *Partial relief was better than none.*

Anna bit her lip, an act of seduction he found ridiculous but effective nonetheless now he wondered what those lips would look like wrapped around him.

He leaned down and lowered his voice. "Do you want to grab another drink and find somewhere quiet to talk?"

Dean lounged in the chair across from his father's desk, leather creaking under his weight. He sprawled like a man with no crown waiting on his head just to watch the vein in his father's temple throb. "What can I do for you today, Your Highness?"

His father's jaw ticked, as it always did when Dean needled him. Every smirk, every careless quip was a small rebellion, the only blades he dared slip between his father's ribs. He trusted Lilith's protection, but he also knew his father, and until Dean took the throne, he kept himself in check.

Except for meetings with the council to train Dean to take over the throne in a month, his father ignored him. His mother sat by and watched his father treat him like shit his entire life, and now she wanted to mend their relationship. He pretended to be open to the idea, but deep down, he'd never forgive her.

"It's time for you to learn more about Lilith," his father gritted out. The name alone tightened the air, a ghost whispering in the corners of the room. Dean straightened despite himself.

He'd not seen Lilith since the day she revealed herself. But he carried her shadow everywhere—her nearly translucent eyes, her voice like prophecy curling around his nightmares. The Fallen Fate crossed his mind often, wondering what other secrets she held.

"You will meet with her regularly from now until you pass the throne on to your daughter and her mate," his father continued.

Daughter. Knowing the sex of his future child before conception unsettled him even now. The idea of a Fate walking among them was inconceivable—and yet true.

"Additionally," his father went on, "it is time for you to take a wife."

Dean's spine stiffened. "No."

His father fucking smiled. "Lilith has informed me of this herself. You can ask her." He grabbed a sheet of paper with a few names jotted down and held it out. "The council has put together a list of suitable women from noble families."

He'd known this day would come, but he'd hoped he'd have more time. "Implying that I must marry someone of noble birth is disgusting. Any woman, high born or not, is suitable. I'll need time to find a bride."

To Dean's surprise, his father nodded. "Their lineage has nothing to do with suitability, but a woman raised in a noble family is familiar and comfortable with court etiquette. It took your mother years to adjust to court life. Your bride will not have the luxury of adjusting. She will be queen in a year."

Dean hated that his father had a point. He picked up the paper and scanned the list. Most of the women were familiar, but one stuck out more than the rest.

Cali Galla. Braddock's cousin.

He tucked the paper away in his pocket and stood, gesturing for his father to lead the way.

To Dean's surprise, his father led him to the dungeons and

through a hidden door into a massive cave. A pool of crystal-clear water filled the middle of the cavern, and the walls sparkled with crystals. The cavern breathed with its own heartbeat, droplets echoing off jeweled walls while the pool shimmered as if lit from beneath.

Lilith appeared from around one of the cavern walls. Her pale lips pulled into a smile that calmed Dean instantly. The sight of her unraveled something inside him, a tether snapping between fear and awe. He hated how easily she rattled him. "I've been looking forward to this day." She glanced at the king. "You may leave."

Dean's father glared at him and left, leaving Dean and Lilith standing in silence.

"You have many questions," she stated.

"You have no idea." He grimaced. She knew, of course she did. A Fate knew everything. It didn't make it any less unsettling.

She smiled kindly and motioned for him to follow her. "Come. We have much to discuss."

He followed the mysterious woman through a corridor into a simple sitting room. He'd expected someone as regal as a Fate to live lavishly, but he couldn't be more wrong. A couple of oversized chairs sat in a corner with a table and lantern between them, and three plush couches formed three sides of a rectangle with a table in the middle.

Dean paused on the various paintings of landscapes and people, some which he'd seen in other paintings around the palace. "You keep pictures of past heirs?"

Their painted eyes seemed to follow him, centuries of kings and queens staring as if weighing whether he was worthy of their place on the wall.

She appeared beside him, and he jumped. Lilith snorted; a

sound so mortal it confounded him. "Not all, just the ones I counted as friends."

Dean smirked. "I don't see my parents on your wall."

Lilith's face darkened. "No, you don't."

One painting caught his eye. A man with golden hair, blue eyes, and a mischievous grin. Something about this painting was different somehow. "Who is this?"

Lilith's eyes flashed, and her throat bobbed. Interesting. "Cain. He's a god, as you call them here. His father, Adam, created Eden and sent Cain and three other gods to oversee Eden after creation to ensure things went smoothly. The high king of the heavens insisted I accompany them."

Dean stared at the painting with wide eyes. No one knew what the gods looked like, and it amazed him that he stared at one now. "Why did you not return to the heavens with them?"

Lilith left his side and sat in one of the oversized chairs. He turned to her expectantly, and his face fell at her expression. Dean knew the look well. Heartbreak.

"Cain had an affair with a human," Lilith said softly. "She bore the first fae—half god, half human."

Dean's stomach lurched. The gods weren't holy—they were liars with lust like men. Fae had been born from betrayal. His chest tightened.

Lilith's gaze flickered with pain. "That birth infused the Garden Kingdom with powerful magic."

Dean swallowed hard. "So, all of Eden was built on treachery?"

"Yes," she confirmed. "The other three gods followed suit, taking human lovers and creating the other three kingdoms." Lilith's voice quieted. "Then they left, and someone had to stay and deal with the aftermath."

Dean stared at her, speechless. He wanted to ask if she and

Cain had been lovers before he betrayed her with a human but couldn't bring himself to.

"Thank you for telling me," he said eventually.

Lilith's expression shifted to one of calm and smiling. "Let's move on to more important things."

Dean leaned back in the chair. "Father tells me I'm to take a bride."

"You are," Lilith confirmed. "You must betroth yourself to a woman before you take the throne, or Eden will fall."

No fucking pressure at all.

"Is there a war coming?" Just what he needed: a war to break out when he takes the throne.

"Not for many years." Lilith gazed off, her eyes glazing over. She blinked, and they returned to normal. "The Mountain heir will have a daughter, the most powerful fae to be born."

Dean's brows raised. "How powerful?"

"At only three years old, she will break the barrier that binds the royal fae heirs to their kingdoms."

"Shit," Dean muttered. Too bad she hadn't been born before him. "What does this have to do with me getting married?"

Lilith pinned him with her terrifying gaze. "If you are not betrothed by the time you take the throne and married before you are twenty-seven, you will have no heir." The words didn't fall like suggestion. They landed like shackles, each syllable locking tighter around his future. Her eyes pinned him. "The Mountain Princess cannot defeat the coming evil without your daughter's help."

Dean's brows furrowed, and Lilith raised a hand. "Do not ask more questions. I am only allowed to tell you so much."

"When you tell me, could you be less cryptic?" Dean joked lamely.

Lilith smiled. "Fae and humans have free will. I can nudge

you in certain directions, but it is up to you if you take the advice or not."

Free will, she called it, but to Dean it felt like being shoved down a corridor lined with locked doors with one narrow path masquerading as choice.

"How do I know you're not lying?"

Lilith shrugged a shoulder. "You don't."

8

TWENTY-FIVE YEARS OLD

Warren kissed a spot behind her ear, and she recoiled. It should have turned her on, but his face and breath on the side of her neck only made her want to shove him away.

He yanked back and murmured, "I forgot."

"It's okay," she lied. It irritated her that he still forgot things that bothered her, even after months together. How many times had she told him? The fact he still forgot left her wondering if he ever truly listened—or if he only wanted the pieces of her that pleased him.

She pushed her frustration down and told herself the good with Warren outweighed the bad. They'd be married soon anyway.

Fawn warmed at the reminder, feeling genuinely happy for the first time in years. The thought wrapped around her like borrowed sunlight—fragile, fleeting, but enough to thaw her chest for a heartbeat. They'd met at the feed store when her grandparents sent her to check an order. Warren, new behind the counter, struck up a conversation. He was half human, half fae too, once running a horse ranch in the Human Kingdom before moving here.

They'd been together ever since. She'd built her life around him brick by brick, meticulously setting the foundation for their life together. Her grandparents thought she should wait on the wedding, but Warren made her feel alive, and they loved each other. Why wait?

Once they realized she wouldn't change her mind, they brought Warren on to work at the ranch to "keep it in the family."

Warren turned her over to look at him. "Good morning, gorgeous."

She smiled wide. Cruel kids in school had killed her confidence, but as her mother promised, she'd grown into her teeth, and working at the pleasure house boosted her self-esteem. Having people desire her enough for a mere dance would do that.

Warren didn't like her side job and had demanded she quit on a few occasions, but it was one thing she couldn't give up. At least not yet. His disapproval always lingered like smoke, clinging to her skin even after she'd scrubbed herself clean.

He leaned in and kissed her slow and deep. "What do you think about taking a getaway trip to the Human Kingdom before we get married?"

Her smile faded. She'd love to visit the Human Kingdom. Neither had been back since moving here, and there were certain foods and places she missed, but going before the wedding was an odd request. "Wouldn't it be better to go on our honeymoon after the wedding?"

Warren sighed. "I wish but we have the stable masters from the palace coming a few days after the wedding and I need to be there."

Why would Grandpa schedule the meeting so close to her

wedding? "I understand." A pre-wedding honeymoon sounded better than nothing.

Strong arms pulled her close and Warren kissed her again. "Good. I arranged for us to leave today." She jerked back to argue but he shook his head. "I already spoke with both of your jobs and your grandparents. They helped me keep the surprise."

Her heart softened, even as unease pricked sharp beneath the sweetness. Surprise and losing control felt uncomfortably alike sometimes.

Her heart melted. "You did that for me?"

His brow dipped. "Of course I did, gorgeous. I'd do anything for you."

Her fiancé released her and slid out of bed to gather his clothes. Warren buttoned his pants and grabbed his shirt from Fawn's desk chair.

She admired him as he dressed. Warren was handsome with long, dark blond hair, light beige skin, and bright green eyes.

She sat up and pulled the sheet around her body. "I wish you could stay for breakfast."

His face softened and he bent over to brush his lips against hers. "Me too, but I need to get things ready for our trip. Meet me at my house at lunchtime."

"Alright," she lamented and flopped back on the bed.

About thirty minutes later, Fawn rolled out of bed to get dressed, and then noticed the sunlight streaming through her window reflecting off something on the floor.

The hilt of Warren's favorite dagger peeked out from under her bed, and she bent over to retrieve it.

She'd see him in a few hours, but he carried his dagger

everywhere; said he felt naked and unsafe without it. Fawn tapped the scabbard against her hand and decided to take it to him now and help him prepare for their early honeymoon.

An hour later Fawn climbed Warren's porch steps and heard a woman yelling on the other side of the door.

"Are you fucking someone?" the voice demanded.

"You think I'd do that to you?" Warren returned. "What are you even doing here?"

"Are you kidding me?" the woman shrieked. "I came here to surprise you last night and you were gone. Then you come stumbling in this morning smelling like sex. How could you?"

Fawn couldn't move or breathe as her heart beat out of her chest. The words slammed through the walls, each one cracking her ribs until it felt like her chest would split open.

The voices were slightly muffled. Perhaps she misheard.

"Naomi," Warren tried to placate the hysterical woman. "You wouldn't understand. This is crown business." *Crown business?*

"Then explain it to me." The underlying hurt in Naomi's voice would have made Fawn feel sorry for her if her own life wasn't imploding. "You moved us to the Garden Kingdom to fight in their battalion, and then immediately take off on *business*. I came to surprise you and found you like this."

The world tilted. *Us.*

The Garden Kingdom? Battalion? Fawn's heart stopped completely, hovering in her chest before shattering as the implications of Naomi's words set in.

A long pause followed.

Warren started talking again just as Fawn slammed open the door and hurled his dagger at him. Her hand shook with rage, but the throw cut the air clean, fueled by every ounce of betrayal lodging like glass in her throat. Luckily for him, it was sheathed, and it landed halfway between them. Unluckily for her, she caught the tail end of his sentence too late. "...take Fawn to the Human Kingdom to kill her."

The words echoed, hollow and endless, carving her name into a death sentence she hadn't been privy to. It took her brain a moment to wade through the hurt and absorb his words. "...*take Fawn to the Human Kingdom and kill her.*"

Warren and a beautiful human woman, if her ears were any indication, jumped and spun to face the door. Naomi stood stunned, and Warren cursed under his breath. "Fawn?"

"You were going to take me on our *'early honeymoon'* to fucking *kill me*?" she choked out, unable to grasp the reality of her situation. It dawned on her then that he might try to kill her now and she'd stupidly stuck around to yell at him.

Fawn spun on her heel to run but only made it a few feet before Warren lunged and snagged her around the waist. He slammed her against his chest and tightened his hold. The air rushed out of her lungs; his arms, once a comfort, became iron bands of betrayal.

"Warren what are you doing? You can't kill someone!" Naomi screamed.

Fawn twisted and tried to jab her elbow into his face, but he dodged the blow. "Stop struggling," he commanded and dragged her inside.

"Let me go!"

"Calm down," he snapped, "or I'll snap your fucking neck."

He's going to kill me, and I'm too weak to stop him. Dancing kept her body strong, but not in the way that would help her fight off a desperate man.

Naomi sobbed somewhere behind them, begging him to stop.

Warren tried to say something else, but his words were cut

off by a sickening squelch and a gurgling sound. Hot liquid sprayed the back of Fawn's neck, and his arms slackened around her.

They fell away, and Fawn stumbled forward. She spun around to find Warren on the ground with a dagger sticking out of the back of his neck. The man grasped at his neck until his movements slowed and stopped altogether.

Fawn's wide eyes met Naomi's hysterical ones. The woman stood in shock, holding her bloody hand away from her body. "I killed him," she whispered. "I-I killed him."

Fawn stood stunned, looking from Naomi to Warren and back again. She didn't know what to say as Naomi sobbed harder and wailed, "I'm a murderer."

Once her shock wore off, Fawn scooted around Warren's lifeless body and wrapped her arm around the woman who saved her life. "You did it to save me," Fawn reminded her.

"W-what if they don't believe us?" Naomi stammered. "What if they think we did it because he cheated on both of us?"

Fuck. The woman might be hysterical, but she had a point.

Fawn guided Naomi down the hall. "We need to clean ourselves up and then we'll figure out what to do."

Naomi blubbered the entire way to the bathroom, and as they wiped themselves down, Fawn tucked her hurt and fear away, smothering them deep.

"It's going to be okay," Fawn assured her. "Did you bring a heavy cloak with you?"

Naomi sniffled and nodded. "It's hanging by the door."

"Good." Fawn grabbed it and draped it over the woman's shoulders. "Keep it closed while we walk so no one sees the blood on your clothes."

The trek to her grandparents' ranch from Warren's cottage took about an hour on foot. In times like these, Fawn wished riding a horse didn't scare the shit out of her. As they followed the path, Naomi explained that she and Warren were set to be married next year. A few months ago, he moved them from the Human Kingdom to the Garden Kingdom to join their battalion. He wasn't half-fae, he was fully human. The deception reached far deeper than Fawn could have imagined. Everything he'd told her was a lie. Why her?

Once at the farm, they followed the path around the house to search for her grandfather. "Grandpa," Fawn called out once inside the barn.

Grandpa stepped out of a far stall and grinned. "Hey, squirt." He looked to a crying Naomi and his smile fell. "What's wrong?"

Fawn blew out a long breath. "We need your help to hide a body."

A long silence followed as her grandfather studied her face. "Did one of you kill them?"

"Yes," she answered truthfully.

He scrubbed a hand down his face. "Why?

"He tried to kill her," Naomi answered first.

Grandpa gave a curt nod. "Then let's get started."

Fawn,

Is it unfaithful to keep writing you while betrothed to another? It feels that way. I haven't fucked anyone since I agreed to the marriage arrangement with Cali. I won't humiliate her like that, but I can't give you up.

It's sick.

I can't find it in myself to love her, but as of late, a warm feeling often fills me. It's difficult to identify the emotion. I've never felt it before. The closest thing I can compare it to was how I felt when I felt you, just not as strong—like a faint echo.

The strangest part is that it's there, but I don't think it's my own.

On more than one occasion, I've wondered if it's you. I keep reminding myself you're gone, that it's not you, but my soul won't listen.

I'm king now, but I feel like a fraud. I never wanted the position, but I'll do right by my people and rule them the best I can. The upside is I can now leave my kingdom. I've not mentioned my plan to anyone, but two heirs will be taking the throne two months before my wedding, giving me the perfect excuse to travel.

I'm going to look for you myself before I marry. I don't trust my father, I never have, but he knows the importance of the mate bond. Without it, the royal bloodline will weaken, putting the safety of our kingdom at risk. His obsession with protecting Eden wouldn't allow him to risk it.

Even a Fate told me to marry Cali, and yet...

I'm an asshole for looking. I've told Cali I hold no affection for her; I'd never be so cruel as to lie to her about that, but if she knew I was chasing a ghost, the woman I truly want, it would break her heart.

Hope outweighs my guilt, and not even the Fates could stop me from looking for you.

I know my efforts are futile, but if I don't do this, I'll never stop wondering, what if?

Tragically Yours,

Dean

Dean replaced his quill and sat back, tipping his head to stare at the ceiling.

"What am I doing?" he muttered.

A soft knock on his door pulled him from his self-loathing, and he shoved the letter in his drawer.

"Come in," he called and immediately wish he hadn't when Cali strolled through the door.

She smiled wide. "Hello, handsome."

His guilt spiked, and for a moment, he considered calling off the wedding. She deserved better.

"Good morning," he greeted her and stood. "To what do I owe this pleasure?"

Her words drowned into background noise as his heart tried to break his ribs. What the fuck? The anxiety rose swiftly and crashed just as hard, replaced by a painful ache. He clutched at his chest, trying to work out what was happening.

Hurt and betrayal, he recognized, but they weren't his. He knew the full force of Fawn's emotions all too well. They had been seared into his soul at the age of thirteen.

His lungs seized as pure unadulterated terror gripped him. *Screaming.* Fawn was screaming. He grabbed at his hair, not knowing what to do or how to help her.

The screaming stopped, and the fear faded. *Confusion. Worry. Relief. Determination.* The latter lingered, a slight pulsing deep within him. Whatever scared her, she survived.

He faintly heard Cali calling his name, and her gentle hands guided him back into the chair. Slowly, the last remnants of Fawn winked out, as they always did.

He rested his head in his hands, feeling insane. Was his brain pulling this shit because marrying Cali would sever the bond? *If it still existed.*

If a mate married someone else, the bond broke. No one knew much beyond that because it'd never happened before, but it's stated plainly in the ancient texts.

"Fuck," he cursed.

"Dean, you're scaring me," Cali said, squatting in front of him. "Talk to me."

A few months ago, he'd confessed to Cali that he'd occasionally felt the mate bond. He'd wanted to be transparent with her, but she'd gotten upset and left. They never brought it up again.

"I'm fine, sweetheart," he lied. "Just something I ate trying to burn its way up my throat."

Her healer training kicked in, and she stood to leave. "I'll ring for licorice root tea."

"Wait," Dean stopped her, knowing what he had to do. She faced him expectantly. "I need to speak with you."

Her lips pursed, turning the skin around her mouth white. "That sounds ominous."

Dean stood and met her halfway. "Cali, I can't marry you without searching for Fawn first."

Cali jerked back like he'd slapped her. "What?" She shook her head. "Fawn is dead."

He looked away, unable to face her—coward that he was. "You know I still feel her sometimes. I can't marry you while pining after another, wondering if she's out there somewhere."

A resigned sigh drew his attention back to her. "Oh, Dean." She patted his arm. "If this is what you need. But promise me something." He waited silently for her to continue. "When you return home without her, I need you to let her go. For both of our sakes."

He hated himself. "I promise," he lied.

PART TWO
TRAGIC BEGINNINGS

Cali squeezed Dean's middle in a bone-crushing hug, her arms wrapped tight as if she could anchor him in place. "When will you be back?"

He awkwardly patted his fiancé's back, the gesture stiff and unconvincing "I don't know. Weeks, at least."

She stepped back and looked away, her gaze darting away. The pain she tried to hide needled at him, but he couldn't marry her—not without confirming for himself that Fawn was truly dead. First, he would attend the Mountain Prince's coronation. Afterward, he would demand access to the Mountain Kingdom's birth records. If his mate wasn't listed, he'd move on to the Human Kingdom. If a death certificate existed, he needed to see it with his own eyes.

He'd written to the other royals once, years ago, asking if they had a record of her. Each reply had been the same: no. Still, his soul would not rest until he saw the records himself. Foolish? Probably. But he *needed* to do this.

"I wish you'd see reason," Cali whispered, her voice frayed at the edges.

"If I don't do this, you and I will never be happy together," Dean explained gently. The lie that they'd ever have a chance at happiness burned in his chest. He doubted he'd be happy with anyone other than Fawn, but he could pretend.

Tears shimmered in her eyes, catching the light. "Because you refuse to let go. We've been together for over a year, but you won't touch me. You won't even try to form a connection past friendship."

He gave himself a moment to respond before answering, steadying his breath so he wouldn't snap. "Don't ask me to let go of something you don't understand."

"You think I don't understand wanting someone who's isn't here?" she demanded, her voice incredulous. "I love you, Dean, but your heart isn't *here*. You're miles away, pining after the idea of someone you've never met."

Dean recoiled, stunned. "*Love*? You don't know me well enough to love me."

Cali's expression hardened, her jaw tightening. "Don't tell me what I feel. You think I don't know you?" She let out a sharp, bitter laugh. "I know you love radishes on your salad and ask for extra."

His brows shot up. He hated radishes. Once, Braddock had told the cooks they were his favorite, and ever since his salads had come piled with them.

"I know you only fuck in places you'll get caught," she continued before he could cut in. That was true at least.

"And I know your favorite color is blue."

It wasn't. He wore it because it was the Garden Kingdom's royal color.

Cali wasn't cruel. She wasn't even unkind. She was simply... Cali. Sheltered, adored among the nobles, coddled by her parents, and rarely told no—even when she should have been.

Instead of correcting her, he played along, letting a sardonic smile twist his lips. "That is stalking, sweetheart, and I don't appreciate you violating my privacy."

Cali bristled. "I'm observant, you ass. I don't *stalk* you. I pay attention. Don't tell me I don't know you or that I don't love you because I do."

His amusement thinned into something hollow. "You don't, Cali," he sighed. "If you knew the part of me I don't show, you'd run."

"Let me in and I'll decide for myself."

Dean twisted the gold ring on his finger—a family heirloom he had always intended to give to Fawn. His mother had brought it to him to give to Cali, but he didn't think he could put it on her finger. It belonged to his mate and no one else. Instead, he would purchase Cali a breathtakingly expensive replacement, and she would be none the wiser.

"Nothing you say can change my mind about looking for Fawn," he stated plainly. "I told you because I refused to deceive you but make no mistake—I *am* doing this."

Cali swiped at a wayward tear, her chin tilting in stubborn resolve. "Then I'll be here waiting."

Fawn had never had a real friend outside of her parents, but burying a body with someone forged an unbreakable bond.

After Warren's betrayal, she hadn't thought she'd trust anyone again. Yet somehow it had been surprisingly easy to open up to Naomi. They had both grown up in the Human Kingdom and hated (and buried) the same man. Turned out they didn't need much more in common than that.

Fawn's grandparents decided it best for Naomi to move out to the ranch with them instead of returning to a fae kingdom on her own. The last thing they needed was whoever hired him to come sniffing around, asking questions.

To think that a murder attempt led her to this moment was almost enough to make Fawn thankful for it. Almost. Naomi's booted feet swung wildly as she tried to throw herself over Ivy's back. Fawn knew the proper steps to mounting—she'd seen her family do it countless times—but her brain refused to accept the logic of putting all her weight on one stirrup without the saddle rolling sideways.

Grandpa had explained it more than once. Didn't matter. The only way she'd ever end up on horseback was if someone slung her dead body over the saddle.

"Help me!" Naomi squawked. She'd gone at it all wrong and used her upper body to heave herself across the saddle instead of her leg. One foot hung in the stirrup and the other flailed helplessly as her torso draped across Ivy's back.

Fawn considered helping but had already warned her not to try riding without Grandpa there to supervise. Naomi had ridden a handful of times, sure, but not enough to risk it with only Fawn watching. The fae Shire horses were generally gentle in temperament but it wasn't uncommon for a mare to fuck with someone for the fun of it. They'd never hurt Naomi, they were too well trained for that, but they would put her through it.

Right on cue, Ivy pranced to the side, robbing Naomi of the mounting block, and the frightened girl shrieked. "Fawn, help me!"

Ivy dipped her head to scratch an itch against her front leg, utterly unbothered by Naomi's plight. Meanwhile, Naomi fought to yank her foot free of the stirrup, hands scrabbling at the saddle. "Grab the saddle horn with both hands," Fawn instructed, tone patient but dry. "Push yourself upright with your left leg." Naomi mimed the motion slowly, hand wrapping the horn as she straightened. "Good. Keep your weight on your left foot and hoist your right leg over the saddle."

Naomi threw her leg in a clumsy arch and let out an unladylike grunt. "I did it!" she hollered. She lifted both arms in triumph, then wobbled dangerously and clutched the horn again. "I can't wait to tell Grandpa."

Fawn snorted. "He'll kill you for trying without him." She circled Ivy, laying a steadying hand along the mare's flank before moving toward her head. She flashed Naomi a thumbs up. "You did great, *killer*." Her friend scowled at the morbid nickname.

"Ivy, bite her," Naomi commanded. The mare ignored her and instead nuzzled into Fawn's arms, searching for a treat.

Fawn laughed and pulled a horse muffin from her pocket. She couldn't bake worth a damn, but over the years she'd perfected treats for the horses. They didn't care what they tasted like.

Ivy happily devoured the treat from Fawn's flattened palm and immediately nosed for more. "You should sell those," Naomi suggested, petting Ivy's mane. "The horses love them."

Fawn waved her off. "Baking all day? Not my idea of fun. I only started because I was bored as a teenager. Now I keep it up because the horses are spoiled." She ran a hand down Ivy's velvety nose and cooed. "Isn't that right?"

A rough-legged hawk screamed overhead, startling Ivy. The horse jerked and moved in a nervous dance. Naomi, being the seasoned rider she was, screamed and clamped her legs tight. The mare bolted.

Naomi's scream echoed across the pasture as she clung to the saddle horn. Her hair flying behind her like a banner. If she hadn't looked terrified, it might have been a beautiful picture.

Fawn sprinted after them, lungs burning. "Relax your body!"

"I can't fucking relax!" Naomi screeched. "I'm going to die!"

Grandpa appeared over the hill, eyes wide as he glanced from Naomi to Fawn. Fawn doubled over, hands braced on her knees, breath ragged, while Grandpa dashed for the barn.

Ivy loped gleefully around the pasture, clearly in it for the sport. Fawn had a sneaking suspicion the mare was screwing with Naomi at this point. Grandpa flew from the barn, bareback on Raider, his black stallion, and cut across the field in a straight line toward Naomi.

Within minutes Grandpa had both horses stopped and Naomi safely on the ground. His voice carried all the way back to the barn, scolding her about safety, supervision, and the importance of turning a runaway horse into a tight circle.

Naomi trudged behind him, cheeks flushed, hair sticking out at wild angles. "I'm sorry, Grandpa."

Fawn reached for Ivy's reins, but her grandfather shook his head. "I'll put them up for the night. You take Naomi inside." He glanced at the frightened woman. "Horses aren't playthings. You could have been hurt."

"Yes, sir," she mumbled. Fawn hated the defeated look on her face. If her father had been here, he'd have known how to soften the sting without excusing the mistake. Without thinking, Fawn scooped up a snowball and let it fly. It splattered across Naomi's face, cold and wet.

# 10

Fawn wished Naomi could be here with her, walking across the dais of the royal dining hall in front of the entire palace staff. Fawn tried not to look nervous walking to her assigned seat. Amelia had invited Fawn and another maid, Birdie to her secret wedding to the king. They didn't know her well, but according to Amelia, Birdie and Fawn were kind to her when no one else was.

The wedding had been shock enough, but then Amelia asked the two maids to dine at the royal table with her, King Rennick, and a handful of the king's closest friends.

Fawn and Naomi couldn't believe it. *A half-human maid dining with royalty?* Unreal.

A young man in a server's uniform pulled out a chair and gestured for Fawn to sit. "Here you are."

Fawn nervously scanned the other high tables as her stomach knotted. Other royals and council members sat around her, while the rest of the palace staff filled tables on the main floor below.

A childlike giddiness filled her as she slid into the seat

beside Birdie. A few curious glances slid her way, and she lifted a hand to check her hair, making sure her ears were covered. Amelia displayed her round ears proudly, but as the king's mate, no one dared look at her sideways. Most people didn't know Fawn's secret, and she'd intended to keep it that way.

She covertly looked down at her dress. It wasn't befitting a royal celebration, but it was the nicest she owned. The warm blue wool clung to her arms and torso with a plain square neckline, and the heavy skirts covering her practical boots. Sitting where everyone could see her suddenly felt like a very bad idea.

As royals and council members from other kingdoms continued to fill the tables around her, a flash of blue caught her attention. A quick peek at the approaching man nearly dropped her jaw. His jacket marked him as one of the kings, and he was *beautiful*.

His straight nose and smooth, chiseled jaw made for a stunning profile. His hair—not quite brown, not quite blond— fell perfectly into place, like a faerietale prince come to life. She wanted to see the color of his eyes, but they scanned the room as his hand absently rubbed his chest.

An elbow nudged her side, and she turned to Birdie. "You're staring."

Birdie's lips quirked into a knowing smile, and Fawn's cheeks burned. "Did you see him?" Fawn whispered, sneaking another peek over her shoulder. "It should be illegal to look like that."

Birdie chuckled into her wineglass. "Royal-born fae have always been otherworldly attractive. You'd think they descended from gods."

Fawn bobbed her head. King Rennick was handsome in a rugged, warrior kind of way, and the new Desert King was terrifyingly gorgeous. She hadn't yet seen the Tropical rulers, but she imagined they were more of the same.

Soon their table filled, and the conversation picked up. The king's friends were witty, and Fawn found herself enjoying the evening. "Nice haircut," Echo, Amelia's guard, said to Finn, King Rennick's best friend.

Finn's warm brown cheeks reddened as he ran a hand over his bald head. "Maybe I'll dye your hair blond in your sleep. You'll have to shave yours too."

Fawn pressed her lips tight to hold back a laugh. King Rennick had decreed that every blond, male-presenting person in the Mountain Kingdom shave their heads, all because Amelia had once said she liked men with blond hair.

Echo took a swig of ale and swiped the back of their hand over their mouth. "Try it and see if I don't dye your other hair blond. Let's see if the king still lets you keep your precious jewels."

The table erupted in laughter.

Dean sauntered up to the new Mountain King wearing a lazy smile. The man looked ready to tear apart every man who so much as greeted the blonde woman beside him.

"Rennick," Dean drawled, extending his hand. "It's nice to finally meet you in person. Apologies for not coming sooner."

"Think nothing of it," Rennick replied, his voice gruff. He gestured to the woman at his side. "This is my wife, Amelia." Dean noted the shape of her ears. The Mountain King had taken a human mate? His mind jumped to Fawn. Would her ears have been round too?

Grief rose sharp and sudden, but he tamped it down. He

needed to see the Mountain Kingdom's records as soon as possible.

He flashed the Mountain Queen a practiced smile and lifted her hand to his mouth. "A pleasure to meet you." He kissed her hand and smirked when Rennick stiffened. "Dean."

Rennick yanked Amelia protectively to his side. "Careful how you look at my wife," he warned.

Dean chuckled low in his throat. "Easy, Mountain King. I only meant to greet her properly." He winked at Amelia before strolling off. He understood Rennick's possessiveness. If he had his mate, he'd kill any man who tried to take her from him. But he couldn't resist riling the new king up.

Dean headed for the dais reserved for the kingdoms' elite. He hadn't brought his council members like everyone else; he didn't need them questioning why he insisted on traveling to the other kingdoms afterward.

A giddy excitement not his own tickled his chest as he climbed the stairs, and he surveyed the large room. *Is it her?* Sensing her didn't mean she was here, but he couldn't shake the restlessness inside him.

He took his seat beside the Tropical King and Queen, Felix and Sarah. Their son, Roman, wouldn't turn twenty-five for another few months. One of Roman's friends were currently visiting the Garden Kingdom and staying at the palace. Queen Sarah had written to Dean a few weeks ago, explaining the woman was taking a trip through Eden and asking if he could offer her protection while visiting.

"Dean," Sarah greeted, smiling warmly. "We can't thank you enough for welcoming Violet into your home."

Dean lifted his glass of wine. "Think nothing of it, sweetheart. Any friend of yours is welcome in my home." She blushed at the endearment he used on everyone. Felix's eyes narrowed his way, and Dean hid his smile behind his drink.

They made small talk, and he nearly laughed when Sarah threatened to cut out her husband's tongue for teasing her. Felix whispered something back with a heated stare, and Sarah's cheeks flamed.

A pang of jealousy struck Dean square in the chest. He wanted that. Badly.

A round of rowdy laughter rose nearby, and he didn't just hear it—he *felt* it, as if it were his own. His heart leapt to his throat as he scanned the tables, his gaze landing on a woman with ash-brown hair and a breathtaking smile. She turned her face toward a young server who stared at her adoringly. *It's her.*

All rational thought fled, and he was across the dais in a flash, ripping the man away from her. His mate screamed and scrambled from her seat, her terror coiling inside him so sharply his knees nearly buckled. He tried to steady himself, not wanting to frighten her further, but a sick part of him basked in her fear. Her fear confirmed what he already knew: he'd found his mate. *Fawn.*

"I thought you were dead," he rasped, scooping her into his arms.

Fawn kicked and thrashed. "Put me down!"

He begrudgingly lowered her to the ground, but his eyes never left her. She was fucking beautiful, just like he'd always known she would be. "You're stunning, Fawn."

She tried to retreat but bumped into her chair. *Good.* He wouldn't have let her get far anyway. "How do you know my name?" Her voice wavered a bit.

Every eye in the room was on them, but Dean didn't care. He'd found her.

Calm down, he warned himself. *She has no idea why you charged across the room like a wild animal.*

How could he explain himself without sounding insane? If she'd grown up in the Human Kingdom like his father claimed, she might not know much about fae—but if that was true, why was she here?

"I've known your name since I was thirteen," he said. "My father had men searching the four fae kingdoms for you." *Supposedly*. His voice softened. "But when we were fourteen, I felt agony, followed by deep sorrow." Fawn trembled under his intensity, and he tried to rein himself in. "And then I felt nothing at all."

Callum, Rennick's father, rose and approached. "Let me take you two somewhere private where you can discuss things without prying eyes."

Fawn transformed before his eyes, and the bond in his chest shifted too. She slipped a mask of cool indifference, her emotions fading into a whisper. Her control would've been impressive if it didn't hide her from him.

"You're his mate," Amelia soothed. "He won't hurt you."

Fawn thought he'd hurt her? A groan rose from the boy on the ground, and Dean turned to stare down at him. *Oh.*

"I'm only half fae," his mate blurted, wincing. "There's been a mistake."

One truth his father had told. Dean reached out, brushing her cheek in the hope of calming her. She might play indifferent, but he felt the ghost of her fear. "There is no mistake, darling."

Amelia sighed dreamily while Rennick scowled at Dean.

Dean's hand slid to the side of Fawn's neck, his thumb grazing her slightly elevated pulse. "You are mine, and I am not leaving here without you."

She shied away from his touch. *Too much, idiot.*

"Come," Callum said, wrapping his arm around Fawn's shoulders. Dean wanted to rip his arm off, but it would only frighten Fawn more.

11

Fawn silently followed Callum in a daze, the imposing and beautiful king trailing behind her. She didn't know his name or which kingdom he ruled—only that he thought she was his mate.

Callum stopped at a door in the guest quarters and gestured for the king behind her to open it. *It must be the king's room*, she thought.

"Thank you, Callum," her supposed mate said, shaking the older man's hand.

Callum turned to Fawn, who fought to look unaffected. "Dean is a good man, and you are his mate. He won't hurt you."

Dean. "Allegedly," she muttered.

Dean frowned at her, bid Callum goodnight, and ushered her inside. Like any other royal guest room, the sprawling space boasted ornate rugs and furnishings with scrollwork and gold detailing. Utterly gaudy, in her opinion.

"If you think this is ridiculous," Dean said with a wry grin, "wait until you see the Garden Palace. My mother's taste in decor makes this place look plain."

"You're from the Garden Kingdom?" At least she knew his name and kingdom now.

"I am," he confirmed. "Have you ever been?"

She walked further in, feigning interest in anything but him to collect her thoughts. "No, but I grew up in the garden region of the Human Kingdom."

She stopped, heat blooming at her back. Tilting her head back, she arched a brow at the Garden King. "Do you always stand this close to people?"

He grinned down at her. "Is it too much?" Dean stepped back half an inch. "Better?"

She chuckled despite herself and spun to face him. "I think there's been a mistake. I can't be your mate."

He cocked his head to the side. "Why?"

Sighing, she tucked her hair behind one ear and pointed at the rounded tip. "I told you earlier that I'm half-human."

Dean reached forward and traced the top of her ear, sending tingles across her skin. "I know. Why would that matter?" Fawn opened her mouth and closed it. Opened it again. The Garden King tapped his chest. "There's no mistake. I can feel your stronger emotions when you don't shut them off. I felt you laugh earlier, and I can feel your confusion now." He dropped his hand and studied her face. "You are remarkable at hiding how you feel. I'm not sure how much you know about the royal fae and their mates, but the gods told me your name when we were thirteen."

Then why hadn't he claimed her? "You didn't come for me," she stated, keeping the accusation minimal.

"My father looked for you," he assured. "He checked the birth records in every fae kingdom but found nothing."

There'd be no record of Fawn in the fae kingdoms because

she'd been born in the Human Kingdom—but so had Amelia, and Rennick had found her.

Sensing Fawn's skepticism, he added, "There had never been a human mate in the history of Eden until now, and all fae children are raised in the fae lands to harness their magic. My father had no reason to check the Human Kingdom's records."

Anger not her own prickled Fawn's insides, matching the storm brewing in the young king's grey eyes. "When we were fourteen, I felt grief and agony, then the bond went quiet. My father decided to travel to the Human Kingdom for lack of other options. The other kingdoms had once again denied having any record of you." Dean swallowed hard. "They showed him your death certificate and informed him you and your parents died in an accident."

Fawn stared at the floor. That didn't make sense at all. Did someone think she died in the rebel attack? But that was in the Mountain Kingdom. "My parents died," she confirmed. "But that wasn't in the Human Kingdom. It was here."

Dean looked ready to murder someone, and his anger simmered in her chest. It felt strange to think of the foreign sensations as his, but since meeting him, they'd matched his demeanor, and with each passing second, she believed his outrageous claim a little more. "You're angry," she observed.

His light grey eyes met hers. "I am, but not at you."

Not knowing what else to say, she spotted a pair of plush chairs in the corner and sat. "Is there a way to confirm I'm your mate?"

Everything made too much sense to be wrong but being mated to a king sounded too good to be true, especially one who looked like Dean. Fate hadn't exactly been kind to Fawn, and she needed every assurance she could get.

He dropped into the chair across from her and lounged back. "What day is your birthday?"

She rattled it off quickly and his lips tipped up on the side. "That's my birthday too. The gods whispered your name into my mind when I turned thirteen, and I can feel you when you let your emotions slip." He'd said as much, but it didn't hurt to double check.

Holy shit, I'm the Garden King's mate, she panicked inwardly. *Now is not the time to lose control, Fawn. Calm the fuck down.*

He leaned forward and rested his elbows on his knees. "Do you not feel me?"

His question doused her panic, leaving only foolishness in its wake. How could she be so stupid as to not realize she had felt *someone else's* emotions all these years?

Fawn's thoughts drifted back to that day when she'd worked up the courage to ask her mother for help. It was shortly after she'd turned thirteen.

"I don't feel like myself," she'd told her mother. *"Sometimes I think I feel two different ways at the same time. Is there something wrong with me?"*

Her mother hadn't asked for an explanation; she had merely laughed and smoothed Fawn's hair from her face. *"No, sweetie. It means you're about to start your monthly courses soon. It's part of growing up."*

"If feeling like a mess means growing up, I don't want any part of it," she'd declared sullenly.

Her mother was human, and humans weren't taught much about fae. Fawn's father wanted his daughter to know about her other half and would tell her stories at night before bed. Her mother never stayed for his lessons, calling it "father-daughter time." Fawn had assumed her mother already knew the ins and outs of fae, but what if she hadn't? The woman had always been wary of fae, even more so after they moved to the Mountain Kingdom. It was a miracle she'd married one.

Dean's voice pulled Fawn back to the present. "Did I lose you?"

"I can feel you, but it's faint," she said slowly. "My mother said it was what happened to teenagers."

"Faint?" He stared off, running a hand along his jawline. "When a mate feels something strongly, the other can feel it clear as day."

Fawn considered his words. "That's not what this is. Right now, I feel a confusion that's not my own, but it's not strong or clear. It's like an afterthought." She recalled something Amelia said the first day they met. "Amelia said she couldn't feel Rennick's emotions at all because she didn't have fae magic." She pointed to herself. "My magic is almost non-existent."

Dean ran a hand through his hair, mussing up the perfectly styled locks. "Consider yourself lucky. There wasn't much good to feel for most of my life."

Memories of the somber loneliness sometimes flooding her surfaced. The hatred. The hopelessness. As she aged, the loneliness and hopelessness stayed, but the hatred faded, replaced with laughter and... *oh gods*. Every drop of blood drained from her face when she realized if she could feel his arousal, he could feel hers.

His head jerked up, his eyes narrowing. "What are you thinking about? I can feel your mortification."

Fawn couldn't speak. She loved displaying her body for others to enjoy because it made her feel powerful. It also turned her on. Did he feel that every time she danced? Every time she fucked?

She gaped. All the times she'd feel flickers of arousal for no reason... hell, she'd even come a few times from the unexpected attacks. If possible, she whitened even more. Had she been feeling him fuck someone else?

She didn't know why the thought pissed her off. They didn't know each other, and she'd been far from innocent. Still, the thought of feeling him fuck another person made her want to tear him apart.

"Fawn." Dean's voice snapped her out of her spiral. His large body kneeled in front of her, and his large hands encased both sides of her face. "What's wrong?"

Taking a deep breath, she shoved everything down.

"Stop," he snapped. "Don't hide yourself from me. We're in this together, and I can't help you if I don't know how you feel."

Fawn removed his hands from her face. "You could take cues or ask like a normal person."

"Fine," he conceded. "I don't need to feel your emotions to see your pretty face is the color of death. What's wrong?"

She cursed inwardly. If they truly were mates, and at this point she had no doubt they were, they would marry and have a child anyway. Forever was a long time to keep secrets from one another.

Fawn cleared her throat. "What exactly can be felt through the bond?"

Dean's large hand rested on her knee and his finger tapped as he thought. "Any strong emotional response."

Is being aroused a physical response, emotional response, or both? Shit, she didn't know.

"Fawn?" His knuckle lifted her chin, forcing her to look into his amused eyes.

The words burst out of her before she could stop them. "Can mates feel each other fuck?" Of all the ways she could have asked, she picked the worst fucking one.

Dean froze, and Fawn briefly wondered if she should jump

out of the window to avoid the rest of this conversation. Sex didn't embarrass her, and she danced naked for strangers often, but feeling his interactions against his will felt invasive.

Knowing someone felt hers... well, with the initial shock worn off, the more she thought about it, the more she liked it. Having someone feel you isn't much different than having them watch you. She squirmed a little, and Dean's hand on her knee tightened.

She focused on his emotions inside her. *White-hot rage.*

Pinned in a chair with him on his knees in front of her, she couldn't escape. "I can't control whether I feel you or not," she defended herself. He had no right to be mad at *her* for it. "I didn't know what it was. I just thought I was hypersexual," she babbled on. "I mean, I am, I love sex, don't get me wrong, but—"

"*Enough,*" he hissed through his teeth.

"Don't speak to me that way," she snapped. "It's not my fault I can feel your private moments. At least I can't feel them full force, then you'd *really* feel violated."

His head jerked. "You think I feel violated because you felt me fuck someone else?"

She hiked a shoulder. "I don't know why else you would be pissed off."

He stood abruptly and took a step back, running his hands through his hair again. "I'm pissed off because I don't want to think about my mate with someone else." *Oh.* In that case, she had information he really wasn't going to like. "To know that I fucking *felt* it?" His arms dropped to his side. "I want to kill something."

"I'm good at burying bodies." The joke slipped out before she could stop it.

The silence between them stretched on forever, broken only when Dean threw his head back with a loud laugh. His eyes twinkled when they met hers, and a small dimple appeared in his right cheek. She pressed a hand to her chest, his laugh vibrating through her stronger than anything she'd felt before. It was as though her soul could *hear* it, warm and rich and perfect.

"You really are my mate," she whispered, unable to temper her awe. She hadn't realized until that moment that a small part of her still doubted.

His smile widened. "And you are my queen."

❦

Fawn's face drained of color. "Queen?" she whispered.

Dean shrugged off his royal coat and tossed it on his bed. She looked ready to bolt, and he'd need full range of motion to catch her. "Yes, darling. When you marry a king, you become queen."

She looked like she might faint. "I can't be queen of an entire kingdom."

Dean approached her in slow, measured steps. "What are you afraid of?"

Her face slackened. "Everything! I'm a *maid* who grew up on a *godsdamned* horse ranch." She stood motioning to her plain clothes. "This is the nicest dress I own. I don't know anything about politics or fighting."

Her rising panic clawed through Dean's insides, twisting into something horrible. *I have to do something.* He yanked her to his chest, hugging her tight, rocking her back and forth. Braddock's husband, Monroe, always said hugs calmed people down and made them feel better.

Fawn's body stayed stiff in his hold, but her breathing began to slow. Though that might've been because her face was smashed against his chest and she couldn't breathe. He gently guided the top of her head until her cheek rested against his chest.

"You're crushing my ribs," Fawn croaked, wiggling a little.

Dean cursed and loosened his hold. "I'm trying to calm you down."

Fawn's shoulders rose with a deep breath. "I'm okay." He didn't move. "You can let go now." There had to be a reason to keep holding on. "*Dean.*"

With great reluctance, he unwound his arms from her body and led her to a large settee in front of the fireplace. "I don't like you working yourself up over baseless fears." She tried to argue, but he held up his hand. "It doesn't matter if you grew up with wolves or dressed in rags. Whatever you need to know can be taught, and you now have unlimited funds at your disposal to buy whatever clothes you want. Parade yourself around in the cheapest tarp or the grandest cloth. I don't care."

He sat beside her and wrapped her hand in his. "The only thing we need to focus on right now is getting to know each other."

Fawn's mouth twisted to the side. "Easy for you to say. You were raised to be king."

"I was raised by a man who had a war general beat me for punishment," Dean said coolly. "Being born wealthy and powerful doesn't mean a damn thing. Even gold melts in hell."

He waited for her pity, but she offered none. Fawn stared at him for the longest time then nodded. "So what happens next?"

Dean ran through the logistics of their travel home in his head. At a normal pace with ample rest, the journey home took about a week. If they stopped minimally and rode hard, they could make it in less. "I'll speak with the stable and my men about travel," he thought aloud. "We'll be on the road by morning."

"Like hell we will." Fawn folded her arms across her chest. "I have a family. A job. I can't just leave."

"I'm certain your job already knows you won't be back," Dean pointed out, but his mate averted her eyes.

Oh fuck. Does she have a partner? She couldn't be married or the bond would've broken, but some people chose not to wed. If she was attached, he'd have to stage her partner's death, but if she had children... would they accept him as their father? He'd buy them whatever they wanted if that's what it took.

Thoughts of Cali slammed to the forefront of his mind. She would be heartbroken when he broke the news. His fiancé—*ex-*fiancé, had been sure he'd come home alone. How would Fawn take the news of his betrothal to another? If she got to know him first, would she take the news better?

She watched him wage an internal war expectantly. Fawn still guarded herself, and he couldn't bring himself to risk her shutting him out completely. The thought of the bond going quiet again slicked his palms with sweat.

No, he'd send a missive to Braddock, explaining his situation. His friend would keep Cali out of the palace until Dean returned and called on her to end their engagement. Then he would tell Fawn. If the engagement had already ended by the time he told her about Cali, she'd understand the other woman was no threat to her.

Before they left, he'd have Rennick send a messenger post haste. If they rode hard, they'd arrive to the palace before Dean and Fawn. With that settled, he braced himself and asked, "Do you have a partner?"

Fawn burst out laughing. It wasn't the warm, sunny laughter he loved—it was disbelief. "Gods, no."

"You're single?" he clarified.

Another chuckle. "Yes. I'm completely unattached, except for this pesky bond tying me to a too-tall fae king."

He scowled. "I'm only six foot three." Maybe six foot four. It'd been just under a decade since they'd measured him.

Fawn held her hand level with the top of her head. "That's nine inches taller than me. I'll need a running start to kiss your lips without a stool."

The implication sat heavy in the air between them. He wanted to devour her, but not yet. They needed to get to know one another first. Fawn wasn't a quick fuck in the back of an ale house. She was his mate, and when he buried his cock inside her for the first time, he wanted it to be the last thing bringing them together, not the first.

"I'd like to know about your family," he said earnestly.

If the subject change surprised her, she didn't show it. She only smiled at him, stealing his breath. "Grab your riding boots, pretty boy. We're going to the ranch."

12

In hindsight, they should have waited until morning to visit the ranch. The carriage door opened, and cold, snow-flecked air burst inside. Fawn burrowed deeper into her cloak and accepted Dean's proffered hand to descend the steps.

Her mate's royal carriage outshone any she had ever seen. Its grandeur embarrassed her, and her only reprieve was that Dean seemed to dislike the gaudiness as much as she did.

"You can redesign anything you'd like," he had said, catching the distaste she tried to hide. *"I, for one, will welcome the change."*

"Why haven't you changed it?" she'd mused. *"You took over as king last year, didn't you?"*

"I did." He had assessed the gold interior, then shrugged. *"I decided to let the next queen change it as she wished. If not, I would have gutted the entire thing myself."*

The next queen. Who would he have married if they had never met? She didn't want to consider it for reasons she couldn't name. She barely knew him. Why did she care if he had another woman lined up?

Fawn knocked on her grandparents' door before entering, not wanting to startle her family. It wasn't terribly late, and she knew they would still be awake. Sure enough, Grandma and Naomi sat by the fire in the front room, mending clothes, while Grandpa appeared from the hallway.

"Hey, squirt. What brings you by?" Grandpa asked. Dean stepped through the door behind her, and the room fell quiet.

"This is Dean. The Garden King."

No one spoke. Dean stepped forward and offered his hand to Grandpa. "Dean Hawthorne."

Grandpa shook Dean's hand and darted a glance at Fawn. "Peter Whitman." He gestured to his wife, who approached with Naomi. "This is my wife, Judith, and Fawn's best friend, Naomi."

Grandma extended her hand, and Dean kissed her fingers. He did the same to Naomi, and the woman mouthed, *"Oh my gods,"* when he looked away.

"I think we'd better sit down and talk," Grandpa said.

"I'll make tea while everyone gets settled." Fawn hurried into the kitchen, her hands shaking with nerves.

The teapot whistled, and she placed it on a tray with their cups, sugar, and milk. "How do you take your tea?" she asked Dean.

"I'll make my own." He reached for the pot, but she popped his hand.

"It's rude for a guest to serve themselves," she chided. "How do you take your tea?" Dean chuckled, flashing that infuriatingly handsome smile, and heat crept up Fawn's neck.

Naomi stared open-mouthed, while Fawn's grandparents exchanged a long look.

"Two sugars, no milk." His eyes never left Fawn as she poured. When she sat down, he caught her hand and squeezed. "I met Fawn at the Mountain King's coronation," he started. "She's my mate."

The other three started talking at once.

"What?"

"How is this possible?"

"You're marrying a sexy king?" The last came from Naomi.

Dean's deep laugh moved through Fawn like a light breeze. He waited for the others to calm down and said, "I'm sure you all have questions."

"Why did you not claim her earlier?" her grandfather demanded. "Royals retrieve their mates as soon as they're found."

Dean leaned back in his seat, still holding Fawn's hand. "We tried, but no record of her existed in the fae kingdoms. A year later, my father traveled to the Human Kingdom where they told him Fawn died alongside her parents, and on my end, the bond had gone quiet." He'd not asked Fawn specifics of that time in her life, but she could tell he wanted to.

Her grandmother huffed in indignation. "That's not true."

Fawn snorted, and Grandpa mumbled, "Obviously, Judy." Grandma swatted him with a glare.

Naomi looked lost. "Why would someone tell your father that?"

Dean's hand tightened around Fawn's. "I don't know, but I intend to find out."

Deep lines carved Grandpa's forehead as he turned toward her. "Have you felt his emotions this entire time?"

She rubbed her palm against her skirt and instantly regretted it. The scratch of the material against her skin almost made her gag. "I've always felt faint emotions that didn't match my own. They weren't strong, but they were there. I asked Mom about them. She said it was puberty."

"Fawn's magic is almost non-existent, making the bond weak on her end," Dean explained. "I don't know why. Mate bonds are supposed to be the most powerful magic in our world, but the same thing happened with the Mountain King's human mate."

"You're going to be a queen," Naomi breathed. "Holy shit." *Holy shit is right.* Fawn deliberately avoided thinking about being queen, otherwise she'd faint or throw up.

Grandma reached over and tugged Naomi's ear. "Language."

Dean brushed his thumb over Fawn's. "I know it's sudden, but everyone in the Mountain Palace knows Fawn is my mate, and the safest place for her is the Garden Kingdom where my personal guard will protect her with his life."

"And you?" Grandpa pressed. "Will you protect her with your life?"

"Yes," Dean answered before Grandpa finished his sentence. "I don't plan on letting her out of my sight, but in the event that she is, Braddock will be there."

She filed Braddock's name away for later.

Grandpa gave a curt nod. "Good. We still don't know who sent Warren to kill her."

Dean went still. "What did you say?"

"I haven't told him," Fawn hissed at her grandfather.

"It's important he knows," her grandfather countered. "How can he protect you if he doesn't know?"

She pinched the bridge of her nose, trying to ease the tension behind her eyes. "Nothing has happened since Warren. I've been diligent. Whoever sent him probably thinks he's still trying to drag me to the Human Kingdom."

The king hadn't moved, and worry pricked at her. Would she feel it if he had a heart attack? "Dean?"

"Someone explain." Two words were cold as ice. Fawn focused on his emotions, and a dangerous rage flickered down their bond.

She and Naomi quickly recounted what they knew about Warren. They both hesitated to tell him about Naomi killing the bastard and the entire family burying the body.

Dean listened patiently, asking questions here and there. When he discovered Warren fought in his battalion, Fawn thought he might explode. "Where is he now?"

"At the bottom of my manure catch. Naomi stuck a knife through his neck." Apparently, her grandfather had no qualms outing them. Fawn shuddered at the memory. They'd dug through the manure until they hit the bottom, then they dug a grave, tossed Warren in, and covered everything back up.

Naomi looked ready to faint at Grandpa's confession. Everyone held their breath, unsure how the king would take the news. Dean's body eased a fraction. He released her hand and slid his arm around her waist to pull her close. The action made butterflies erupt in her stomach. *It's been one day, Fawn. Calm the hell down.*

Dean's fingers gripped her side, anchoring her against him. "I owe you all a tremendous debt. Whatever you need, it's yours."

He released Fawn and stood. "It's important we return to our kingdom at once. Getting Warren into my battalion without going through years of training takes political power not many possess. I need to find out who they are and mount them on the front gates as a warning to anyone who thinks they can touch their queen and live."

Fawn couldn't stop her nipples from hardening or the fire heating her blood. His commanding tone did something to her. Dean's knowing eyes slid to her and his lips twitched. *Oh, hell.*

"If Warren managed to join your battalion, what makes you think you can trust any of them to protect our girl?" her grandmother demanded.

The muscle in Dean's jaw feathered with tension. "I trust Braddock with my life. He'll not leave her side *if* I'm not around, but I don't anticipate that happening until this person is caught."

Grandpa stood and clapped Dean on the shoulder. "I hope you're a good man." He stepped back, crossing his arms. "Because if you're not, I'll have no problem burying you beneath a pile of shit where you belong."

After long conversations, decisions were made. Naomi would return to the Garden Kingdom with Dean and Fawn, but her grandparents would stay on the ranch. They'd lived in the Mountain Kingdom their entire lives, and Fawn didn't want them to leave everything they'd ever known.

Dean assured them anytime they wanted to visit, he'd take care of everything.

While Naomi packed, Fawn bid her grandparents goodbye. She hadn't cried in years, but she wept against her grandfather's chest. "Thank you for everything."

Grandpa held her tight. "You're everything to us, Fawn. There's nothing we wouldn't do for you."

Fawn hugged her grandmother next, and after another tearful farewell, she moved to Dean's side.

"When will you wed?" her grandmother asked.

Fawn stiffened. "We just met." She knew everyone expected her to jump at the opportunity to be queen, but what if she and Dean hated each other? What if he chewed loudly?

Fawn started to sweat under the weight of everyone's gaze.

"I know this is scary, dear, but you don't have a choice." The calm in her grandmother's voice did nothing to soothe her.

"Yes, she does," Grandpa barked at the same time Dean said, "She'll always have a choice." He lifted her hand and kissed the inside of her wrist. "My job is to convince her to choose me."

❧

"I think that's everything," Fawn declared and closed the lid to the last trunk. She paused, then flipped it open again. "Let me double check."

Dean was too occupied glaring at the flimsy lock on Fawn's bedroom door in the palace to remind her that she'd "double checked" three times already. Anyone could break in with that pathetic excuse for security. The thought of someone trying to hurt—no, *kill* Fawn enraged him beyond anything he'd ever known.

She'd recounted the story as if reciting a faerietale. Had Naomi not sounded petrified, he'd have thought they were joking. He admired her strength. Not when she downplayed attempted murder, but any other time it was a very admirable quality.

In the morning, they had a meeting with Rennick and Amelia on their way out. Fawn wanted to say goodbye, and Dean needed to speak with the king about a few things.

As his mate dug through her trunks, his mind wandered to ways to woo her into loving him. He already knew he'd fall fast, and it'd be nice if she was close behind.

"What's your favorite hobby?" he asked her.

Fawn poured herself a glass of water and set the pitcher on her side table. "I don't really have any."

He brushed a piece of loose hair from the back of her neck.

She grimaced and an uncomfortable feeling slid down the bond. Did she not like him touching her neck? Filing the information away for later, he pushed on. "Everyone has something they like to do in their downtime."

She set down her glass and plopped on the bed. "Not everyone has a hobby."

Dean lowered himself beside her. "Reading?" She shook her head. "Puzzles?" No again. "Cooking? Sewing? Hunting? Horseback riding?"

She chuckled and laid back. "No to all. Especially the last one. You couldn't pay me to mount a horse."

Dean laid back and rolled to his side, propping himself up with his elbow. "You grew up on a ranch," he pointed out.

She gazed up at him, amused. "I've never ridden a horse in my life. They're too tall."

"They have these wonderful things called mounting blocks," he teased. A pillow whacked him in the face, and he plucked it out of his assailant's hands. "That wasn't very nice."

He bopped her on the face with the pillow and warmed when she giggled. If you'd told him five minutes ago that Fawn Whitman would giggle, he'd have called you a liar. It transformed her face, and he would hit her with a pillow every day if it meant he could see her like this.

"I don't like being up high," she confessed. "Even the calmest of horses spook, and it's a long way down."

He tossed the pillow aside and turned to her fully. "I wouldn't let you fall."

She reached up but curled her fingers into a fist and dropped her hand. *Touch me,* he silently urged. Instead of granting his wish, she sat up. "We need to finish packing and go to sleep."

Groaning, Dean hoisted himself to his feet and held a hand out to help Fawn stand. "One last look then we're done," Dean said. She grumbled under her breath as they both did a full sweep of the room for anything they might have missed.

Dean opened the last drawer in her dresser and found a thin piece of red silk nestled in the corner. He lifted it into the air and maneuvered the strips of fabric until he realized what he held. His mouth dried and his cock jumped to attention. A pair of underwear made entirely of silk strings and a tiny triangle stared back at him.

Fawn snatched the undergarment from his fingers and shoved it into one of her trunks. "Thank you." She busied herself fussing with the crown-provided bedding and dusting the furniture.

"Fawn." Dean's voice came out rough. He didn't know what he wanted to say, but he knew what he wanted to see. He kept his mouth shut and willed the image of Fawn in barely-there silk out of his mind. Clearing his throat, he took the dusting rag from her. "Grab your nightclothes and toilette."

She looked him up and down. "Why would I do that?"

His brows bent downward. "You are welcome to wear something of mine to bed and use my things. I only thought you'd want your own."

She planted her hands on her hips and lifted a smart brow. "What do you think is about to happen, Your Grace?"

"In the Garden Kingdom, they call us Your Highness," he corrected her. Growing up he never thought much about why the Garden King royals had a different title. He now knew that Cain demanded his bloodline be held in higher regard. They were the first fae, and the strongest. The other kingdoms didn't know that, and Dean thought it best to keep it that way.

"You're sleeping in my chambers tonight," he continued. She tried to argue, but he clamped his hand over her mouth. "I'm not going to ravish you, but nor will I let you out of my sight."

He lowered his hand and Fawn trudged to her trunks to gather her things. "Fine." Dean bit back a triumphant smile and opened the door. She blew past him with a bag slung over her shoulder and quipped, "but I'm not fucking you."

Dean chuckled and shut the door. "Yet."

13

"Warren Landry is still missing, sir," General Craven reported to Samuel, one of the wealthiest and most powerful nobles in the Garden Kingdom.

"And the girl?" the older man demanded.

"She's still working at the palace and the pleasure house," the general said.

Samuel never told General Craven who Fawn Whitman was or why he wanted her dead, but he had a guess. The king's mate had been named Fawn, but Dean's father, Henry, claimed the girl died years ago.

It no longer mattered. The new king hadn't claimed the girl as his mate, which freed General Craven from any allegiance to her. Even if she *was* the king's gods-blessed mate, she wouldn't be for long. Once he married Cali Galla, the bond would be broken.

Samuel slammed his fist on the desk. "I want her fucking *dead*. Now."

General Craven nodded. "I will send—"

"No," Samuel cut him off. "Do it yourself and do it now before the king sees her."

The general furrowed his brow. "How would the king notice a palace maid in the Mountain Kingdom?" Realization struck him. "He's in the Mountain Kingdom for the king's coronation." Samuel nodded grimly. "We might already be too late, sir."

A calculating glint lit Samuel's eyes, and the sight raised the hairs on the general's neck. "We're not too late until he marries the little bitch. Even then, accidents happen."

Samuel's words confirmed the general's suspicions. General Craven wasn't a good man, but he honored his oaths —especially the one he'd sworn to the crown. Once the king publicly claimed Fawn Whitman as his mate, the general couldn't—wouldn't—touch her.

Samuel studied him, gauging every flicker of his expression. "I'll pay you more. Whatever you want, I'll double it."

Years of discipline kept the general from balking. Samuel already paid him enough to set up his family in luxury for generations. He couldn't fathom what to do with more, but money equaled power in their world, and General Craven always wanted more.

14

Bland foliage in shades of green and brown blurred past the window of the royal carriage as it bumped along a snowy road in the mountain region of the Human Kingdom. The Mountain Kingdom capital lay close to the Human border, and the magical barrier separating the two kingdoms took little time to cross. It'd been years since Fawn had seen the Human Kingdom. She once thought she missed it, but now it struck her as dreary and lifeless.

Naomi sat across from Fawn and Dean, peppering the king with questions. He answered each one with practiced patience, indulging the excitable woman.

She asked a lot of things about the Garden Kingdom. Even though she'd lived there for a time, Warren had advised her not to venture out much because she was human.

Fawn couldn't imagine how betrayed Naomi felt by the man she'd loved for years. She put on a brave face, but Fawn sometimes caught her staring off, eyes glazed with unshed tears. You couldn't turn love off just because the other person shit on it.

The fact that he'd slept with Fawn while engaged to another woman made her want to resurrect him just to kill him twice.

"I don't know if our cottage is still available," Naomi admitted. "I never went back or paid rent after coming here."

Dean waved a hand dismissively. "You'll have a set of rooms in the palace." Naomi made a choking sound, and he chuckled. "Did you think I wouldn't protect you too? You saved Fawn. Anything you want or need is yours."

Fawn's heart pounded against her ribs. This powerful fae king wanted *her*, a half-human with nothing to offer him in return. She'd made an effort to open herself up to him as he asked, but she kept her heart guarded. He *needed* her for the bond to keep his bloodline strong, not because he *wanted* her as a person.

They'd only known each other a day, and every time he showed a piece of himself, she liked him more. Did he like the pieces of her she allowed him to see?

Naomi stared out the window, lost in thought, and Dean leaned over, his lips hovering near Fawn's ear. "What are you thinking?"

She'd rather eat a fist full of rocks than admit her worries to him. "Whether or not your family and friends will accept me." *Not a complete lie.*

Dean pulled back and gently forced her to look at him. "My friends will love you. As for my family, they don't even like me. Their opinion doesn't matter."

Naomi hummed to herself, preoccupied with the passing scenery. Fawn lowered her voice so as not to be overheard in the spacious carriage. "Why don't your parents like you?"

Dean straightened, and his fitted shirt pulled across his muscular biceps and chest. "They expected perfection, and I fell short."

Fawn searched for the right words. What kind of parents told their child they weren't good enough? "No one is perfect."

His hand flexed against his thigh. The subject upset him, but if they were to marry, she needed to know everything about him.

"My father expects excellence, demands it. His punishments were harsh when I was young, but turned brutal when I hit my teens." The king's eyes glazed over, lost in a memory. "When I turned fifteen, a family friend stepped in. From that day forward, the punishments stopped."

Fawn laced her fingers through his, and he glanced down at the contact. "I don't know you well, but from what I've seen, you're a good man."

His mouth lifted on the side. "I can't promise you'll like everything you learn about me, but I swear I'll do whatever it takes to make you happy."

Fawn leaned her head on his shoulder, feeling the truth in his words. "I know you will. I'd like to make you happy too."

He kissed the top of her hair, melting the ice around her heart a little more. "You already do."

She lifted her head and met his piercing gaze. "You know next to nothing about me."

Dean's eyes bounced between hers. "You have no idea what you did for me when we were young." Fawn tried to make sense of his declaration. She'd never seen him a day in her life before yesterday. "Around the time our bond snapped in place," he started to explain, "the worst of the punishments started. Those were dark days for me, and you were my only source of happiness. I'd be locked in my rooms, sinking into darkness, and then you'd laugh." He placed his hand on his chest. "I held on to the feeling, knowing one day I'd get to hear it too."

Words evaded her. She remembered the feelings of desperation and loneliness that would flicker in and out. Had she known a boy suffered on the other end of a magical bond, she'd have done whatever she could to enjoy herself and send him everything she had.

"When I thought you'd died, so did my hope at a happy life. My soul was long gone, following yours around the after-life, while the gods trapped me here in an empty shell. I wanted to join you, wherever you were, and begged the gods to let me. Then I felt you laugh on that dais, and I knew that for once, they'd answered my prayers."

Silent tears tracked down Fawn's cheeks, and across the carriage, Naomi sniffled and fanned her face. "I wasn't trying to eavesdrop," she sniveled, "but you two are loud."

Dean continued to watch Fawn, gauging her reaction. There weren't enough words in the world to express how she felt. It killed her that he'd yearned for someone who'd had no idea he'd existed. She didn't know if she could push anything through the bond, but she tried to flood it with as much affec-tion as she had. Leaning into him, she whispered, "I'm glad you stayed."

Dean leaned against the carriage and connected with Cassandra while the women relieved themselves outside. He usually closed his eyes to connect, but he refused to take them off his mate. Each woman held up a cloak to block the other while they took their turn, but that was as much privacy as he'd allowed.

Through the serpent's eyes, the brightly colored rainbow leaves and flowers of the palace gardens surrounded him and he blocked out her vision to keep his own clear. *"Cassandra."*

"Dean," his *familiar* greeted. *"How was the coronation?"*

He considered Cassandra the closest thing he had to a sister, and he couldn't hold in his news long enough to entertain her small talk. *"I found my mate."*

He felt the serpent's shock through the bond. *"Are you sure?"*

"I'm positive. Father's information was half-right. She is half-human, and her parents died when we were fourteen, but Fawn lived."

"Your parents saw her death certificate," she recalled.

"I'm neither an idiot nor stupid, Cassandra," he snapped. *"Either my father lied, or he was lied to. I'll find out later, but right now, there are more pressing issues."*

"You are an idiot sometimes," she needled.

He ignored her taunts and pushed urgency through the bond. *"Someone in the Garden Kingdom hired a man to assassinate Fawn months ago."* He felt Cassandra go on high alert. *"The assassin's name was Warren Landry—a human. According to his former fiancé, someone in our kingdom hired him as a warrior and immediately sent him to the Mountain Kingdom on business. She came to surprise him for a visit, and he confessed his plans to kill Fawn."*

"Where is the man now?" she demanded.

"Dead. His fiancé killed him when he attacked my mate."

"Good for her," approved Cassandra. *"Do you know who hired him?"*

"No." Dean scanned the forest around the girls to ensure no one came close. They were in the middle of nowhere, but he'd not let his guard down. *"I need you to keep your ears open for anything suspicious."*

"I don't have ears," she deadpanned.

Dean couldn't tell if she was joking or not. *"Really?"*

"I told you that you were an idiot," she quipped. *"Serpents and*

snakes do not have outer ears that hear. We have an inner ear that detects vibrations."

"Still an ear," he muttered. *"How do you understand people speaking to you?"* She'd replied in Dean's mind to things others have said.

Cassandra's amusement and exasperation set Dean's teeth on edge. *"We're mind linked in each other's presence. I hear what you hear. Have you never noticed that you hear nothing on my end?"* When they mind link, they can block out the other's sight and hearing so they're not seeing and hearing double if they want. *"You're always in the gardens or the forest away from everyone. You said you hate people."*

"I do hate people—they annoy me." She hissed. *"Do you not find it strange there are no sounds around me?"*

Dean concentrated on Cassandra's senses. Complete silence. *Huh.* *"That would have been nice to know eleven years ago when we met."*

"It doesn't matter that I can't hear people when you aren't around."

"It matters now," he said pointedly. *"Can you read?"*

"I'm going to break your ribs when you return home. No, I cannot read." Dean smirked when she added, *"Idiot."*

"Keep your eyes sharp and call me the second you see anything suspicious, snake."

Cassandra mentally bristled. She hated being called a snake, claiming serpents were superior. *"Goodbye, idiot."*

Dean cut the connection and dragged a hand down his face. Without Cassandra's help, he'd have to wait to start his investigation when he returned.

Fawn and Naomi started toward the carriage, but Naomi tripped, her arms windmilling on her way down. His mate burst out laughing as she tried to help her friend up, and Dean felt his world narrow to only her.

No one would take her from him, and if they tried, they would arrive in hell one piece at a time.

❧

Naomi took Dean's outstretched hand and exited the carriage. "Can we *please* stay the entire night?" she whined. "I'm exhausted." He'd explained to them that each night they'd only stop for a handful of hours, and neither woman had been happy with the news.

He needed to meet with Braddock and smoke out whoever wanted Fawn dead before they tried again. *"Aren't I in more danger in your kingdom?"* Fawn had asked. The fact that she had to question her safety in her rightful home was enough for Dean to exterminate everyone in it.

"You're in danger everywhere that I'm not," he'd replied. *"The sooner we are home, the sooner I can eradicate our kingdom of the suicidal person who decided to harm their queen."*

He needed to speak with Lilith, too. She *knew* Fawn lived and told Dean to marry another. Could a Fallen Fate die? He wasn't sure, but he'd find out. "No. We leave in four hours."

Both women moaned and grumbled the entire way into the small, quiet inn in the tiny roadside village.

After getting their room keys, Dean led the girls upstairs and unlocked one of the doors. "Naomi, you're in here." He handed her an overnight bag and pushed open the door to a small, single bedroom. "Here are your things."

"Thank you," she mumbled and trudged inside, shutting the door in his face.

Fawn yawned behind him, and he led her to the next door and opened it to usher her inside. She looked between the two single beds. "Why are there two beds?"

Dean hadn't told her they'd be sharing a room, and he

didn't know how she'd respond. Setting their bags down, he turned to her with all the innocence he could conjure. "We can push them together, darling. You need only ask." He pretended to inspect the small bed. "If you'd rather share one, you'll have to be on top."

Color flushed her pretty cheeks, and her slightly crooked front teeth dug into her bottom lip. "Why are we sharing a room?"

He opened her bag and dug around for the things she'd need to bathe and get ready for bed. "Someone tried to kill you." A shift nightdress made of fine silk and bordered with lace unfolded as he pulled it from the bag. His blood heated at the short length and thin material. *For fuck's sake, how am I supposed to sleep next to her in this?*

Fawn snatched the nightdress from him and put it back in her bag. "That's not an answer."

Dean's brain battled between answering her question and asking her to put on the sexy shift. Logic prevailed, and he grabbed fresh, fitted undershorts from his own bag. "When I said I wouldn't let you out of my sight, I meant it."

She retrieved a smaller bag and a bundle of fabric and searched the room, stopping on the bathtub and sink next to a slim door. "Why are those not in the bathroom?"

Dean crossed the room to open the small door to reveal a toilet. "This is just a water closet." He closed it and turned back to her. "It seems our room *is* the bathroom."

The look of shock on her face shouldn't amuse him as much as it did. Noting his enjoyment, she scowled and pointed to the main door. "Stand in the hallway so I can bathe."

He nodded to the window behind her. "I'm not leaving you alone in a room with a window."

Her head whipped around to the window and back to him. "I'm not going to jump out!"

"You're not going to be able to stop someone from climbing in, either," he retorted. "I'll turn my back."

With a huff, she stomped to the large, porcelain tub, turned on the faucet, and waited for him to sit on the bed with his back to her. Knowing his mate stood naked on the other side of the room tortured him more than he'd realized it would. Stepping into the hall would've been better, but he couldn't bring himself to be away from her.

"Tell me about your friends," Dean said conversationally. Anything to drown out the small splashes of water against her bare skin.

"You met Naomi," Fawn responded. "She's really the only one I have." Another small splash. "Amelia was a friend of sorts," she added, "but we didn't know each other long. I think she just needed someone who wouldn't judge her for her rounded ears."

"She genuinely likes you," Dean attested. "The morning we left, she was upset to see you go."

"I hope so. I liked her."

"You'll see her again soon," he promised. "We can travel whenever you'd like, and if we don't see them before, we'll see them at the Tropical Prince's coronation in a little less than a year."

The sound of water cascading off her body as she stood was a test of Dean's strength. He wanted nothing more than to see his darling bride in all her glory. *Not yet.*

A minute passed, then, "Your turn."

He gathered his things in his hands and turned around. She may as well have taken a battering ram to his chest with how hard his breath expelled at the sight of that thin silk sticking to her damp body.

He closed his eyes and muttered a hurried prayer for

strength. Fawn's hand lay on his arm, and his nerves lit up like a lightning storm. "Are you okay?"

I'm trying not to break my cock against its enclosure. "I'm fine." Dean forced himself to open his eyes, keeping them firmly on her face, "There's a chill in the air, and you should get under the blankets quickly. I don't want you to fall ill."

He could tell she wanted to argue, but she mercifully relented and climbed into bed.

Dean removed his shirt, tossed it to the ground, and started to unbutton his pants. He saw the instant she registered the scars littering his torso. Fawn made a choking sound and climbed out of bed. "What happened?" She crossed the room and held out her hand to touch them, but stopped. "Gods, Dean. Is this from training?"

His tight smile didn't go unnoticed, and her face fell. "In a way. They're from my father's idea of punishment."

"Your father deserves to be run through with a sword." Her eyes caught on his serpent *familiar* tattoo. "This is beautiful." She did trace the dark lines on the left side of his chest. They trailed down and ghosted over a few scars. "I hate him."

Most would say that in solidarity, but she meant it. He felt her hatred and her empathy made him fall a little more.

"Those days are long over, darling." He covered her hand with hers. "One day I'll explain it all, but for now, I want to bathe dust and grime off of my spectacular body."

His mate chuckled, and she returned to her bed. He unbuttoned his pants, but she twirled around. "Wait!" He dropped his hands and lifted a brow in her direction. "I forgot to drain the tub and wipe it out. Let me do it so you don't have to stick your arm in my dirty water."

He glanced back at the full tub and grinned wickedly at her. "You think your bath water bothers me?" Trying to keep a straight face, he added, "I'll just bathe in it to save time."

The look of absolute horror on her face broke his resolve, and he barked out a laugh. She huffed and walked to his side. "That's not funny."

"It's a little funny." *That you think I wouldn't gladly drink your bath water,* he silently added.

Fawn leaned over the porcelain, but he held her back with one arm and grabbed the drain topper with his other. *"Dean,"* she admonished.

He set the drain stopper on the shelf next to the soaps. Looking her dead in the eye, he scooped a handful of water and brought it to his mouth.

Fawn yelped and threw herself at him, spilling his precious cargo. "That's disgusting!"

"But darling, I'm thirsty," he purred and grinned, trying to scoop more, but she caught his arm.

"Stop trying to drink my dirty bath water or I'll drown you in it," she threatened.

The water disappeared from the tub, and he looked ruefully at the empty porcelain. "That drained faster than expected."

Fawn's breath came hard like she'd done something strenuous, though restraining a fae king couldn't be easy. "What in the hell is wrong with you?" She grabbed a clean cloth from the stack on the shelf and wiped the inside of the tub. He wanted to stop her, but figured she'd try to strangle him if he didn't let her do this.

"If you think I'm bad, you're in for a hell of a surprise when you meet my friend Braddock," he told her instead.

She straightened to dispose of the dirty cloth, then said, "Tell me about him."

Dean turned on the water to refill the tub and replaced the drain stopper. "I've known him since we were learning to walk. His father is a nobleman and friends with my father." Braddock's father wasn't on the council, but his brother was, and they were both friends with Dean's father. "Braddock's father often brought him to the royal nursery. The rest is history."

Fawn's mouth tightened. "Noblemen? I thought they were from storybooks and novels."

Dean stopped the water and gripped the waist of his pants to push them down. Fawn spun around and hurried to her bed, earning a laugh in return. "Unfortunately, they're real." Freed from the confines of his clothes, he stepped into the warm water, lowered himself, and lounged back. "Only the Garden Kingdom has them. They're descendants of the oldest families in Eden."

Fawn burrowed under her blankets and turned on her side to face the wall. "If no other kingdom cares who comes from what family, why does yours?"

"Ours," he corrected. "There is a lot about our kingdom you'll learn with time. I don't want to overwhelm you with everything at once. I'd rather get to know you better first."

A brief silence, then, "Braddock isn't like the others." Not a question.

"No." Dean grabbed the soap and a cloth from the shelf. "He was my friend because he wanted to be, not because of my title. I hope our child has a friend like that."

She yawned, and the blankets rustled. "Do you want children, or do you feel obligated?"

"I want children," he said instantly. "I wish we could have more than one." Dean wanted to be the father he never had.

"We can adopt more," she suggested, and he couldn't internally contain his excitement. "You like the idea."

"I like the idea of raising children with you, biological or not," he admitted. "You're everything I've always wanted. The joy you used to bring me is something I want our children to experience, too."

"I'm not that person anymore," she whispered, her words a little broken.

"Then let me be the one to bring you out of the darkness, Fawn. Let me in so I can make you happy." The quiet felt heavy, and he held his breath.

"Okay," she replied finally, and Dean felt hope trickle down the bond.

Fawn stepped out of the carriage, groaning at the ache in her back. Dean had forced a grueling pace, refusing unnecessary breaks to stretch their legs. Nights meant no more than four hours of rest, and days blurred as she and Naomi drifted in and out of sleep in the swaying carriage.

Dean sat stoically beside her or rode alongside them, staying close enough to see her through the window. She'd have liked to have spent their trip getting to know each other better, and they did to an extent, but they were all so exhausted from lack of sleep that conversation felt impossible.

She tipped her head back, staring at the Garden Palace in all its blinding golden glory. It was huge with large domed towers accented in gold, and white marble steps leading to the front golden entrance. "The Garden royals really love gold," Fawn muttered.

Dean stood impossibly close, his heat making her sweat beneath her heavy wool dress. "It's obnoxious," he agreed.

Naomi bent her head back to take it all in. "It looks really nice." She plucked at the front of her dress. "I need to get out of this dress before I die."

Fawn fanned herself. "I second that." All their clothes were designed for the Mountain Kingdom climate, not the warm air of the garden climate. Fawn's shoulders dropped. "I don't have anything lighter."

"You can wear one of mine," her friend offered. "I have a few dresses from when I lived here."

Fawn looked from Naomi's tall, very slender body to her own. "I don't think they'll fit."

Dean moved out from behind her but left his hand on her lower back. "I have a robe you can wear until your dresses arrive."

Her brow furrowed. "What dresses?"

He guided them down the wide stone walkway toward the golden entrance. "The ones you two are going to order. I'll have a modiste sent to our rooms."

Fawn dug her heels into the ground, forcing them to stop. "*Our* rooms?"

Dean's eyes narrowed. "We've been over this. We stay together at all times."

"*Dean*," boomed the deepest voice Fawn had ever heard from the palace steps. A massive man with warm, light brown skin, wavy shoulder length brown hair, and a heavy brow strode down the cobblestone walkway. Dean's grin split wide as he met the man halfway.

Naomi looked at Fawn and shrugged. "Let's go meet your boyfriend's friends."

Fawn huffed. "He's not my boyfriend."

Naomi bumped Fawn's shoulder, playful as ever. "He's your mate. I don't know much about them, but from what Grandma and Grandpa told me, you're going to get married and become queen. That makes him your boyfriend." She moved her head side to side as she thought. "Or fiancé."

"Dean!" a feminine voice cried out, followed by the pitter-patter of light footsteps against stone.

Fawn watched as Dean turned to a pretty woman seconds before she launched herself into his arms and kissed him on the lips.

Everything slowed as Dean peeled the woman off him and set her on her feet. He patted her awkwardly on the arm. "Sweetheart, we need to talk later." *Sweetheart.* He wasn't speaking to Fawn; he was speaking to the woman who had just kissed him.

Sweetheart. The word hammered in her skull, over and over.

Naomi's gasp turned into a snarl. "That fucking bastard."

What the fuck? How had she managed to agree to marry *two* men already involved with other women?

What the fuck is Cali doing here? This couldn't be worse. His eyes darted to Braddock, who looked as lost as he did. He must not have received the letter. *Fuck.*

Dean spun away from his betrothed that *shouldn't be here* and stalked toward his mate. Fawn's inner turmoil made his anger rise, and he wanted to throw Cali in the dungeon for putting her lips on what belonged to his mate.

He reached for Fawn, but Naomi shoved him back. He didn't budge, though her strength impressed him. A weaker man would have stumbled. "It's not what it looks like," he swore.

"What it looked like was another woman jumped into your arms and kissed you," Naomi snarled.

Godsdammit. "That's not what I meant. Cali is—"

The woman in question appeared beside him and tried to twine her arm through his, but he shook it off and moved closer to Fawn. Cali's breath hitched. "Dean? What's going on?"

He couldn't ask Braddock for help because no one knew he'd found his mate.

"Who are you?" Naomi asked Cali before Dean could explain the situation.

Grabbing Fawn's hand, he gently tugged her away. "I need you to come with me."

He watched in horror as Cali stepped forward and crossed her arms. "I'm Dean's fiancé, Cali."

Fuck my life.

Fawn ripped her hand from Dean's and stumbled back. "You're engaged?" His perfect mate tried to keep her voice even, but he heard the slight tremble.

The acrid feeling of her sense of betrayal soured his stomach before it fizzled away. "No, don't do that," he pleaded. "Don't shut me out again."

"Fine," she spat. Her pain and anger slammed into him, forcing a grunt.

Dean cupped both sides of her face, forcing her to focus on him. "Fawn, it's not what you think. Please let me explain before you run."

Cali sucked in a sharp breath. She echoed Fawn's name, her heartbreak evident, but he refused to look away from the brown eyes holding him captive. He had to convince Fawn not to leave, otherwise he'd be forced to lock her in their rooms.

His mate extracted herself from his hold and stuck out her hand to Cali. "I'm Fawn, Dean's mate."

Dean finally looked at Cali. The woman's tear-streaked face twisted into something ugly as she slapped Fawn's hand away.

Dean snatched her wrist. "You lay a hand on her again, and I'll kill you."

Everyone fell silent until Braddock approached the group. "Let her go. It's not her fault you bombarded her with this news in front of everyone."

"I don't care if she's upset." Dean released her with a warning glare. "I'll not stand for anyone disrespecting their queen."

Cali's tears fell faster. "You can't truly believe she's your mate. Your mate died years ago. It's time you accepted it. I don't know how this woman convinced you otherwise, but you need to see the facts in front of you."

"He approached me," Fawn snapped. "Scared the shit out of me and claimed I was his mate." She pointed at her chest. "I've felt him here half of my life. I didn't understand what it was then, but now I do." Her hand dropped into a fist at her side, and for a second, he thought she might swing. "I'll not let some woman I've never met accuse me of something she knows nothing about."

Pride swelled in Dean's chest. His mate was a force to be reckoned with. "You insult my intelligence and that of your queen," he stated, placing his hand on Fawn's lower back to stop her if she tried to lunge. *Or run away.* "Braddock, take Cali inside. I'll deal with her after I've settled Fawn and Naomi."

Braddock said nothing and guided Cali toward the palace. She protested the entire way, and Dean watched until they disappeared inside.

"You never mentioned an engagement," Fawn accused. "We've been together for almost a week, and you hid this from me?" She jerked, but his grip on her side kept her pinned. "You thought what? That I'd be okay gallivanting around with a taken man?"

"I'll kill you for what you've done," Naomi vowed. "I don't care if you're a king or a god descended from the heavens."

She tried to attack him, but Cassandra appeared out of nowhere and wrapped her large body around the furious woman. She looked down and froze, as did Fawn at the sight of the large serpent.

"What did you do?" his *familiar* asked, amused. *"I'm tempted to let her go. I think she was going for your throat."*

"She's Fawn's best friend," he said tightly, wishing he'd handled things differently. *"With everything going on, I forgot about Cali, and she met us outside."*

"Dean," Fawn whispered in a panic. "Help her."

Cassandra uncoiled herself and slithered to Dean's side. *"Is this her? She's commanding you already* and *her friend wants to kill you. I like her."*

Dean glared at the serpent. "This is Cassandra. She's my *familiar*, and I swear she'd never hurt either of you. In fact, the wench almost let Naomi attack me for fun." Naomi shot Cassandra an appreciative look, and Fawn bit back a smile.

Dean pinched Fawn's side, coaxing the reluctant smile free. *That's a good sign, at least.* He tipped his head toward the palace. "Please come inside and let me explain."

She glanced at him and nodded once. "This explanation better be good, or we're gone by morning."

No, darling, you're not.

੬

Fawn followed Dean into a large study with Naomi close behind. She'd never been more thankful for her friend than she was when she'd stuck up for her. Well, maybe when she saved her life, but her protectiveness was a close second.

He closed the door and led her to a cushioned settee in the

middle of the room. The study lacked the palace's grandeur; she guessed it was the one place he'd redecorated for himself.

Naomi sat in one of the large chairs adjacent to Fawn, and Dean took a seat beside her on the settee. "First, I want to make it clear that there never has been and never will be a romantic relationship between Cali and me."

A flicker of relief eased the unease twisting of Fawn, but she'd listened to the rest of his explanation before she made her final decision. If it weren't for the bond revealing his truth, she would have left already.

"I can't say the same for her," he went on. Naomi's eyes slitted. "She thinks she loves me, but I've never given her a reason to." After only a few days with Dean, Fawn understood how a woman might fall for him. "I've never been in a romantic relationship with anyone," he continued, "and after I took the throne, I was forced to pick a wife."

Hearing the truth, Fawn couldn't fault him, but an ugly twist of jealousy still crawled over her skin.

"They gave me a list of women they deemed suitable. I'd only met Cali in passing, but she is Braddock's cousin and a good person."

Fawn hated hearing him praise the woman who he'd chosen to replace her. *Not his fault*, she repeated to herself. Perhaps shock had made Cali lash out—perhaps she really *was* a good person. The thought made Fawn feel worse.

"I've never touched her intimately." His eyes bore into hers, imploring her to believe him.

"That's bullshit," Naomi interjected. "We saw her kiss you."

A storm fell over Dean. "That was the first time, and she had no right to put her lips on mine without permission." He slid his hand over Fawn's. "That right belongs to you and no one else."

A thousand butterflies took flight, putting Fawn in an internal uproar. What did she say to that? *Thank you? Good? Touch her again and I'll let Naomi slit both your throats?*

Naomi sat back in her chair and crossed her legs. "I believe you."

Both Dean and Fawn snapped their heads in her direction. Naomi no longer looked ready to string him up by his neck. Her playful demeanor returned instantly, and for a beat Fawn wondered if her friend was actually insane.

A few months ago, Naomi bawled her eyes out with the guilt of killing a bad man, but when it came to the king, she had no issue trying to separate his head from his body.

Dean huffed out a laugh and thanked her, then turned to Fawn. "And you?" His chest stopped moving with anticipation.

There was one thing he didn't explain that she needed to know. "Why didn't you tell me about her?" She wouldn't marry a man who lied by omission any more than she would a man who lied with falsehoods.

It surprised her when his neck flushed red and crept into his cheeks. "Because I'm a foolish man." She said nothing, waiting for him to continue. He scratched his jaw, muttered something to himself, and sighed. "I sent a message to Braddock before we left to keep Cali out of the palace until we returned. I'd planned to settle you in, break off my engagement with Cali, and tell you everything."

"You thought, what? That I'd be grateful you left me in the dark until you were single?" She hadn't meant to sound so harsh, but men were fucking morons.

"I thought you would take the news better if I were no longer engaged when I told you. You have to know she means nothing to me."

She felt his sincerity and remorse, but it still pissed her off. Would she have shut down had she known he was still engaged? Probably. Did she deserve to know a man she shared a bed with, if even innocently, was engaged to another? Absolutely.

Dean looked so forlorn, Fawn pushed her annoyance aside for another day and decided to put the man out of his misery. Fawn flipped her palm up and gripped his hand tightly. "I believe you, but don't withhold anything from me again. I won't be so forgiving the next time around."

Air whooshed out of his lungs, and he hung his head for a moment. Lifting it again, he stopped her heart with his intensity. "I won't lie to you—I feel guilty for what I've done to her. We were meant to wed when I returned, and she'll be humiliated. But you're more important than she ever was, and I'd cut her down a thousand times over to keep you."

16

Dean handed Fawn another dress, eyeing the heavy wool fabric, worried she'd collapse from heatstroke if she wore it again. Tomorrow, he'd take her shopping for clothes that wouldn't suffocate her.

"Why are you glaring at my clothes as if they've personally offended you?" she snipped and yanked the dress out of his hands. "If they don't live up to your royal standards, too bad. I like them."

She'd been curt with him ever since the mess with Cali. He thought they'd gotten past it after he explained everything, but he'd thought wrong. "I don't care what they look like." Plucking another dress from her trunk, he unfolded it and held it out for her to hang up. "They're inappropriate for our weather. You'll overheat."

His mate snatched the dress without meeting his gaze. "I have to wait until I can go into town and buy something cooler."

"I'll find you a dress to wear into town." He reached inside and pulled out one of her enticing shift nightdresses and bit back a groan.

Fawn snatched the silk from him and shoved it into a drawer. "I can be hot for one day while I shop."

"No you can't," he argued. "You'll overheat."

"This isn't the Desert Kingdom," she said over her shoulder. "It's warm here but not sweltering. I'll live."

Dean closed the empty trunk and opened the next. "I'm not chancing it."

She made an indistinguishable sound and picked a pair of shoes to stow on one of the shelves. "We'll see."

"You're still mad," he said, sitting on one of the benches in the middle of the room.

Fawn turned to him and pushed her hair behind her ear, revealing her heritage. She realized his attention caught on it and covered it again. He furrowed his brow. *Why did she do that? He liked her ears.* They were smoother than the sharp, pointed ears of the fae.

"Wouldn't you be?" She sat beside him, shoulders slumped. "It took a lot for me to open up to you, but I did, only to find out you kept a huge secret from me."

Cassandra was right; he was a fucking idiot. "If I could take it back, I would. I thought it'd be better to tell you I *used* to have a fiancé instead of telling you I still had one."

She fanned herself and he slitted his eyes at her long sleeves. "I understand your thought process, but I don't agree with it. I forgive you, but I'm having trouble forgetting. Oh!" She jumped up. "I have something for you. I'll be right back."

Curiosity piqued, he waited with restless anticipation for her return. What could she possibly have gotten him? His face dropped. *I didn't get her anything.*

She rushed back into the room with her hands behind her

back. "Close your eyes." He obeyed, and the swish of her skirts got closer. "Open your mouth and stick out your tongue."

His tongue flicked out, long and teasing, and Fawn's lust-filled surprise hit him square in the chest. He grinned and pulled it back into his mouth. "You'll reap the benefits of it later, darling. I promise."

"Nevermind," she mumbled. "Put your tongue back in your mouth but hold it open."

He grinned but obliged and something solid hit his tongue. Fawn placed a hand on the top of his head and another on his jaw and pushed.

His teeth sank into the foreign object and the taste hit him. He tried to open his mouth but she pushed harder. "Lick it," she commanded.

Dean jerked his head from her grip and spat out the bar of soap. As if she'd anticipated it, she shoved a soap covered toothbrush in his mouth and scrubbed. She jumped on his lap and straddled him to keep him in place, but he stood easily, placed her on the ground, and careened around the bench to put a barrier between them.

He gagged and tried to scrape the soap from his teeth and tongue. "What is wrong with you, woman?"

She pointed the toothbrush at him like a sword. "You called her sweetheart."

"What?" His mind couldn't catch up, too preoccupied by the film in his mouth.

"Cali," she snapped. "You called her sweetheart, and I want that word washed out of your mouth."

He stopped his futile efforts to remove the thick soap from his mouth and stared at her. "That's what this is about? Darling, I call everyone sweetheart. It's a habit."

"Not anymore you don't." She rounded the bench and he darted to the other side. "How would you feel if you heard me call another man a pet name? Warren called me babe. Maybe I'll try it out around the palace."

She had a point; the thought of her using a term of endearment on anyone but him made him feral. "I'm sorry," he apologized. "You're right. I didn't think, and it won't happen again." He'd never admit it to her, but seeing her jealous made his cock hard.

"Good," she said with a curt nod.

"I'm going to rinse out my mouth." He pointed to the toothbrush. "Put that thing away." The little minx tried to hide her smile but he saw it.

Right as he finished getting the disgusting mess out of his mouth, someone barged into the sitting room without knocking. Dean stalked out of the bathroom to see which idiot was bold enough to barge into his rooms uninvited.

Braddock filled the doorway, his mountain frame shadowing the room, with Monroe at his side. "We need to talk."

Dean ignored his friend and addressed Monroe. "It's good to see you. You look lovely today."

Monroe twirled, his light-blue floor-length dress floating around him. He was a short, plump man with blond hair shorter than Dean's, suntanned beige skin, and an infectious smile. "It's new. Brad said it matches my eyes." Braddock glared at his husband, and Monroe instantly dropped his arms. "Don't compliment me when I'm trying to be upset with you."

"And what great offense have I committed now?" Dean drawled, though he already knew.

"Cali didn't deserve the way you treated her today," Braddock stepped in. "You blindsided her and then punished her for reacting."

"I sent you a letter ahead of our convoy explaining everything," he replied as Fawn exited their dressing room to join them. "You were supposed to keep Cali away until I could speak with her. I did everything I could to prevent this."

Braddock crossed his arms. "No one gave me a letter, otherwise I'd have kept Cali away, if for no other reason than to save her the humiliation."

"It's unfortunate what happened, and I'm sorry she found out the way she did, but she had no fucking right to slap Fawn's hand away." Dean stepped forward and Braddock stiffened. "I meant what I said. If she touches Fawn again, I will kill her."

Monroe's jaw hung open. Dean waited for the man to berate him for his treatment of Cali. The two were friends, and he'd been more excited for the wedding than she was, but he surprised them all when he turned to Braddock. "Would you kill someone for hitting me?"

Braddock frowned down at him. "That's all you got from that?"

The shorter man lifted a sharp eyebrow. "Well? Would you?"

Fawn's eyes widened and she sputtered out a laugh.

"I wouldn't have to because no one is stupid enough to touch you," Braddock stated with the same confidence he'd possessed since childhood. "They know I can beat anyone in a fight."

Fawn snuck a glance at Dean, and he smirked. Monroe harrumphed and turned away. "You didn't say yes. Dean would kill his own fiancé and you won't even kill a hypothetical person."

"Ex-fiancé," Dean corrected him.

"You missed the part where I said no one would touch you to begin with," Braddock grumbled, "but I'd kill anyone if they tried."

"Then why are you mad at him?" He pointed at Dean and winked. The sly little fox backed his husband into a corner.

Fawn burst out laughing and Monroe beamed. "I'm Monroe," he introduced himself. "This big oaf is my husband, Braddock."

"I'm Fawn." She hiked her thumb in Dean's direction. "I'm his mate."

"I've been dying to meet you," Monroe told her. "The whole palace has been buzzing about you since the scene in the courtyard." Braddock shot his husband a silent warning, and his husband mouthed back, "It slipped."

All the blood drained from Fawn's face, and Dean tucked her into his side. "Don't worry, darling. It's all good things." *It better be.*

Monroe and Braddock exchanged a long look and Fawn pressed herself closer to Dean. "What are they saying?" she asked the couple.

Monroe smoothed his billowy dress, and Braddock sighed, shaking his head.

"Spit it out," Dean barked. What the fuck could they possibly have to say about his mate?

"Most are excited you've found your gods-blessed mate," Monroe said slowly, still fidgeting with his dress. "Others think you're lying and pushing Cali aside for a human whore."

Dean's vision bled red.

❧

No one moved or spoke for the longest time. "I'm going home," Fawn announced, and Monroe placed a hand on his chest, his eyes full of remorse.

She felt Dean's fury mix with ice cold fear. "You're not going anywhere."

"I won't stay here and be treated like shit." She stormed to the dressing room to pack her things. "I lived my entire teenage years being treated less than for being weak. I'll not subject myself to it as an adult."

Her fingers brushed the hair over her ears. *Still covered.* So why did people think she was human? Dean followed her into the large dressing room. "If you put anything in those trunks, I will redden your ass."

Fawn whirled around and narrowed her eyes. "I'd like to see you try."

"Me too!" Monroe called from the bedroom. Braddock said something too low for Fawn to hear, followed by Monroe's giggles. "We're going to give you two some privacy." Seconds later a door shut.

"I mean it, Fawn," Dean warned. "Don't even *think* about leaving me."

Without breaking eye contact, she grabbed a pair of boots and tossed them into a trunk.

Dean's jaw clenched, and she opened a drawer, pulled out her undergarments, and threw them in next. "That's two," he stated, his voice taking on a dangerous edge.

Two what? She ignored him, yanked open her stocking drawer, and flung them in.

"Three."

"Are you practicing your arithmetic?" she mocked and pulled down a few dresses to add.

"Four." His voice deepened with each number.

She added one thing after another, periodically glaring at him.

"Five."

"Six."

"Seven."

She reached for more things, but strong arms encircled her

from behind and his warm breath caressed her cheek. "I said you're not leaving."

She wiggled in his hold, hating the way her body responded to his commanding tone. "You can't stop me."

A smooth chuckle. "Yes, darling, I can."

"Dean," the most melodic voice Fawn had ever heard said from the dressing room door.

They both turned, Fawn still trapped in Dean's arms, and an ancient looking woman with snow white skin and hair to match, stood patiently in the doorway, staring at the king. "I need to speak with you."

Did women show up everywhere he went? Already in a foul mood after learning of her reputation, Fawn couldn't help taking a shot at Dean one last time. "Are you his fiancé too?" she asked dryly. "He likes to collect them."

Dean tightened his arms and murmured, "Eight."

"No. You will be the one to marry the young king and give him an heir, but first I must speak with him." Were witches real? *If they are, this woman leads the clan.*

The woman smiled. It looked like she didn't know how and was trying it out for the first time. "My name is Lilith, and you will learn more about me after you are queen. Dean, meet me in my chambers."

Fawn's brows shot to her hairline. "Are you his mistress then?" she joked.

"Nine," Dean whispered in her ear, then spoke louder for Lilith. "Whatever you need to say to me, you can say in front of my mate. We have no secrets."

"Except your fiancé," Fawn muttered under her breath.

"Ten."

"I must speak with you alone," the witch said. Fawn decided she didn't like Lilith. Or witches.

Lilith disappeared through the door, and Dean released a tired sigh. "I need to meet with her."

"What you need is to start locking your door," Fawn quipped. He released her, and she gave him her back to assess the mess she'd made. Tossing clothes into her trunks without folding them had left nothing but chaos. "I need to finish packing anyway."

Dean left without another word. She hated to admit it disappointed her that he didn't try harder to make her stay. Not that she would, but it would have been nice if the man who wanted to marry her had fought a little more.

She could hear him shuffling around in the bedroom while she packed. A door opened in one of his rooms, accompanied by the low murmur of voices. Dean appeared in the dressing room doorway with a maid in tow.

He led the older woman in and pointed at Fawn's trunks. "These need to be unpacked."

Fawn slid in front of her things and crossed her arms. "No, they do not."

"Come here, darling," Dean beckoned with his hand.

Fawn pretended he didn't exist and went on about refolding the things she'd haphazardly packed.

A firm shoulder bumped against the front of her hips and the world turned upside down. She yelped and grunted as Dean threw her over his shoulder like a sack of grain. "Put me down!"

"I gave you the chance to come on your own accord." He squeezed the back of her thigh. "You forced my hand."

"That's not what forced means," she shot back. "Forced implies you had no choice. You *chose* to manhandle me like a brute."

He tossed her onto his ridiculously comfortable bed. "Agree to disagree."

Scrambling into a sitting position, she crawled to the other side of the bed. "You're insane."

A large hand wrapped around her ankle, stopping her. "I'm going to give you a choice."

She flipped over to her back and sat up. "I don't think that word means what you think it does."

Ignoring her, he looked over his shoulder at the bedroom door. Cassandra slithered inside, stopped next to Dean, and raised the head end of her body into the air.

"You will stay in this bedroom with Cassandra without trying to escape."

She waited for him to give her the other choice, but he just watched her expectantly. "What's my other option? You said I had a choice. Maybe you need to pick up a dictionary and brush up on your vocabulary."

Cassandra turned to Dean, and he glowered back. "If you *choose* to attempt escape, Cassandra will let me know, and I will tie you to the bed until I finish my meeting."

"That's not a choice!" she protested.

"Sure it is," he returned with a straight face. "You get to choose to be tied up or not."

Fawn blinked, struggling to understand how anyone thought this man sane enough to rule a kingdom. "Neither." She leaned toward Cassandra and stage-whispered, "Has he been diagnosed with insanity?"

The serpent moved her head up and down and Dean poked the side of his *familiar's* body. She hissed at him and red fangs extended from her large mouth. Fawn tried to jump back but making a fast escape on a bed proved to be difficult.

Dean and Cassandra seemed to share a silent exchange before he bent and pressed a kiss to the top of Fawn's head. He straightened before she could shove him away. "Be good, darling. I'll be back as soon as I can." He turned to leave but stopped in the doorway. "Oh, and Braddock is in the sitting room. He'll let the maid out when she's finished unpacking your things."

"This is kidnapping," Fawn yelled after him.

17

Fawn sat on the edge of the bed, staring at Cassandra. The serpent never blinked, and she couldn't tell if it was a reptile thing or if Cassandra was simply a staring contest champion. *Familiar*s only spoke to their bonded, but earlier the serpent had sort of nodded at a yes -or -no question.

Fawn decided to give it a go. "Do you live in the palace?" Nothing. "Do you help the king kidnap people regularly?" Cassandra ignored her, slithered to the door, and coiled into a neat pile.

"She can't hear you," Braddock called through the door. "Snakes don't have ears." If they did, would Cassandra bite him for calling her a snake instead of a serpent? It seemed insulting.

Fawn hopped off the bed and opened the door. The serpent moved faster than a lightning strike and wrapped around her like a rope. Fawn screamed and struggled against the *familiar*'s crushing hold.

Braddock waved his hand in front of Cassandra's face to get her attention and gestured for her to let Fawn go. The *familiar*'s forked tongue flicked out. I'm going to be squeezed to death. Braddock signaled again, and the serpent reluctantly released her.

Fawn scurried closer to him, never taking her eyes off Cassandra. "Why did she do that?"

"She thought you were trying to escape." He eyed her. "Were you?"

"No, I was coming to talk to you," she said, exasperated that she had so little freedom she couldn't even walk from the bedroom to the sitting room. "It's hard to hear through a closed door."

Braddock thought for a moment. "Everyone wants to talk to me. You couldn't help it."

"I'm sorry your cousin found out about me the way she did," Fawn said. She could tell that Dean hurting Cali hurt Braddock too. The two must be close, but if Dean said he sent a letter ahead of time, he did. "His fiancé was a surprise to me too."

Braddock grunted. "Figures. For someone smart, he can be a dumbass."

"People are really calling me a whore?" Despite her anger-induced fit earlier, she wouldn't actually leave Dean. She knew him well enough to know he'd never let her. A secret part of her she'd never admit felt a thrill at the prospect of someone wanting her desperately enough to chase her to the ends of the world.

Braddock shook his head to toss his hair over his shoulder. "They won't be for long."

"Telling someone the truth doesn't make them believe it," she lamented. "They'll say what they want if it's juicy enough."

"They won't be saying much of anything," he muttered under his breath.

The fabric of her dress tickled the inside of her elbows. She growled with frustration, knowing the feeling would only get worse if she didn't find something else to wear. It didn't matter that she'd been wearing this dress all day or that she'd worn it a million times. She needed it off before she ripped holes in it with her bare hands.

"I need to see Naomi." She could help Fawn take the sleeves off without ruining the dress. Plus, Fawn wanted to make sure she'd settled in okay.

Braddock shook his head. "Your mate will lose his mind if he comes back and you're gone."

That sounded a bit drastic. "I'll be quick," she promised. "I need help with my dress. I can't wear this." She held out her arms.

Braddock walked to the dressing room and emerged seconds later with a dress. "Here."

Another wool dress with long sleeves wouldn't help. She'd never had this happen with her dresses, but right now the sleeves were intolerable. She'd struggled with sensory issues all her life. Different textures and certain sounds set her on edge, and it felt like she would burst out of her skin. And sometimes something that never bothered her before made her skin crawl for no reason. And she fucking hated it.

"I need Naomi's help taking these sleeves off," she explained. "No one is going to hurt me if you and Cassandra are there."

He nodded thoughtfully. "You're right. Everyone knows I'd win in a fight." Nudging Cassandra with the toe of his boot, he indicated that they were leaving.

Cassandra wrapped around Fawn tighter than before. The confinement only heightened the need to be free of her dress. She struggled against the serpent's hold. "Let me go, please."

Braddock grabbed Cassandra's neck and the *familiar* hissed, her fangs extending. He motioned for her to let Fawn go again, and to Fawn's amazement, she did. "What are you, a snake charmer?"

Braddock puffed out his chest. "All animals listen to me. It's a gift."

Fawn doubted it, but Braddock's confidence still impressed her. She wished she possessed that level of self-assuredness.

"We need to be quick." He led Fawn down the hallway and around the corner to Naomi's rooms. Dean had set her up on the royal floor, and it endeared Fawn to him more.

No one answered when Braddock knocked the first time, so he tried again, the sound echoing down the empty halls. "She might have gone to eat dinner," he guessed.

When did I eat last? She'd have to rip her sleeves off herself, and silently mourned the future loss of her dress. It was her favorite, and she had little hope it would come out unscathed. She'd wanted to save it for visits to the Mountain Kingdom, and Naomi's sewing skills far outweighed her own. "I'm hungry too."

Braddock steered her back toward Dean's rooms. "We can ring for a maid."

So much for getting out of the rooms for a while.

Dean sat across from Lilith in her cavernous home, scanning the paintings on her walls. "I'm hurt I'm not up there yet."

Lilith floated across the room to her favorite chair and took a seat. "You will be with time." She waved her hand. "Ask your question."

Dean leaned back and rested his ankle across his opposite knee. "Why tell me to marry Cali when you knew Fawn was alive?"

Lilith tutted, the sound befitting the older woman she disguised herself as around non-royals. "I never said that."

Dean scoffed. "You told me I had to get engaged so I could live a happy life."

"I did," she agreed. "I never said you would marry your betrothed."

Damn her and her riddles. "Stop being cryptic and tell me why."

"Because you need Cali, or your mate will die."

Dean shot to his feet. "What the fuck did you just say?"

Lilith's expression rarely changed, but her nose twitched with annoyance. "Don't speak to me that way. I understand you are upset, and I'm sorry I cannot tell you much." To her credit, she sounded sincere. "You cannot make Cali leave."

His jaw dropped. "I'm not staying engaged to her."

Lilith dipped her head in a slight nod. "Correct, but nor can you ask her to leave the palace. You need her here."

"I'll lock her in the dungeon if she so much as looks at Fawn with disrespect."

Lilith shook her head. "You cannot."

Dean scrubbed his hand through his hair. To hell with his appearance. "I'll have to tell Fawn who you really are to explain why my ex-fiancé gets to keep living in our home."

Lilith's eyes glazed over for a few seconds. "You cannot. Do not allow Cali to disrespect Fawn, but do not hurt her either. She stays, and your mate cannot know about me. You need to think of a reason to placate Fawn."

"I won't lie to her, Lilith. That's a shitty way to start out a relationship."

"You're a good man, Dean, and you don't deserve the terrible things you've endured. But if you don't do as I say, Fawn will die."

Dean stared at the floor. How in the fuck would he navigate this?

"I have something for Fawn." Lilith stood and disappeared into another room and returned shortly with two dresses. "She needs these until you can get her more."

Lilith's cryptic ways and indifference irritated the shit out of Dean, but he sensed she had a good heart and that *she* didn't deserve the hand life had dealt her either.

He accepted the clothes and bowed slightly to the Fate. "Thank you."

༄

Dean walked into his sitting room and froze. Braddock should have been guarding the bedroom door, but the space stood empty. "Braddock?" He threw open the door to their bedroom and felt his heart rate kick up. *Where are they?* "Fawn?"

His chest heaved, and he dropped the bundle of dresses on the floor. *What if something happened?* The person trying to kill her could have sent another assassin and overpowered Braddock and Cassandra. The only thing keeping him from completely losing his shit was that there were no bodies.

Rushing into the hall, he yelled Fawn's name, praying she'd... what? Walked up and down the hallway for fun? Air sawed in and out of his lungs as rage battled fear. *Cassandra.* He closed his eyes to connect with his *familiar* when the sweetest voice he'd ever heard interrupted him. "Dean?"

Fawn stood at the end of the hall looking beautiful and unscathed with Braddock and Cassandra at her side. Dean ran forward and scooped her into his arms. "Fuck."

She slid her arms around him and hugged him back. "I'm okay," she soothed, sensing he neared the edge of insanity. "I went to see Naomi."

Still clutching his mate tight, his icy grey eyes stared daggers at Braddock and Cassandra. "I said she couldn't leave. I thought—" He stopped to calm himself. "I thought another assassin had been sent."

Braddock crossed his arms. "There would have been bodies on your sitting room floor if they'd tried."

"*I wouldn't have let anything happen to her,*" Cassandra added. "*You cannot hold her prisoner while you are away.*"

"I won't chance her safety," he replied out loud for all to hear, then to Fawn, "I'm sorry, darling. I shouldn't have left."

"What makes you think she's safer with you than me?" Braddock huffed and Cassandra added, "*I'm insulted.*"

Dean hugged Fawn tighter, terrified she'd vanish if he let her go. "I'm stronger than both of you combined. I can glamour her invisible if need be." As a royal, his glamour worked on non-royal fae. If he wanted them to see nothing but air, they would. Non-royal fae's glamour only worked on humans and animals.

Fawn wiggled until he loosened his hold enough for her to tilt her head back. "Braddock told me no one can beat him." She quirked a smile just for Dean like they shared an inside joke. "You can't keep me locked away. I'll go crazy."

He knew she was right, but his brain couldn't let the fear go. "You won't leave my side again."

"That's not logical," she countered. "There will be times you're needed that I can't follow."

"No there won't," he countered. "I'm not leaving you, and that's final."

Braddock and Cassandra stayed quiet, letting Dean and Fawn battle it out. The stubbornness in his mate's eyes made him proud. He liked that she stood up for herself... or he would if it didn't impair her safety.

"And if Lilith calls you again?" She lifted a sharp brow. "Or if I need to use the bathroom?" He smirked and she playfully swatted his back. "Dean Hawthorne, you are not watching me relieve myself."

"I'll stand outside the door," he suggested. "You'll not win this one, darling."

Braddock and Cassandra had slipped away while Dean and Fawn had their little spat. Fawn blew out a long breath and Dean grinned over the top of her head at the annoyance and affection swirling down the bond. She might not like the idea, but she couldn't deny she liked that he cared.

"I need to eat," she said, changing the subject. "Naomi didn't answer. I think she's at the dining hall."

"That's where I planned on taking you when I returned." Dean planted a kiss on the top of her head, wishing it were her lips instead. "I'd like you to meet our guests from the Tropical Kingdom as your first diplomatic duty."

Fawn groaned. "I can't. I need to get out of this dress, and I don't have any others without sleeves."

He let her go and threaded his fingers through hers, needing constant contact. "Lilith sent me some dresses for you."

"That's nice of her." Fawn's brow wrinkled. "She must have figured I only had heavy wool." *Something like that.*

He led them to their rooms, retrieved the crumpled dresses from the floor, and handed them to his mate. "Get dressed, darling. It's time to introduce you to your staff."

18

Fawn smoothed the white, lightweight fabric of the dress Lilith had given her. It draped across her chest, cinched at the waist with interwoven ropes, and the long, flowing skirt brushed the floor. It looked silly with her boots, but Dean promised they'd buy sandals soon.

"What are their names again?" she asked him as they neared the dining hall.

"Violet, Ares, and Griff." Dean nodded to the guard opening the dining hall door. "Ares and Griff are guards escorting Violet on a trip around Eden."

The room wasn't as large as she expected it to be. It must be the royals' private dining room where they hosted intimate dinners with friends and family. She scanned the table quickly, unable to tell who was who from the doorway. It hadn't occurred to her until then that Dean's parents might be there.

Fawn grabbed Dean's arm and pulled him back into the hallway out of sight. "Are your parents here?" She tried to peek around the door without being obvious. Her anxiety spiked at the thought of meeting the cruel king. What would he say about a half-human being queen?

"Hey." Dean's hand started to cup the side of her neck but stopped and moved to her jaw. "They're not here. They left for the Desert Kingdom days ago. The Desert King killed his father, and they are attending his funeral."

Fawn paled. "Why did he kill his father?"

Dean pressed his lips into a hard line. "The former king was rumored to be cruel, especially to women. No one knows exactly what happened, but I expect the man deserved it. He and my father had been close, so my parents insisted on paying their respects."

"Who else is here?" Without his parents in attendance, her nerves ebbed, but not completely.

He traced a soothing line along her jaw, steadying her. "As far as I know, Braddock, Monroe, and the guests from the Tropical Kingdom."

Fawn blew out a long breath. "Okay, I think I'm ready."

Dean leaned down and brushed his lips over hers. "I'll be right beside you the entire time."

Fawn's breath hitched. Did that count as their first kiss? Would he pull away if she yanked him back down and kissed him again?

He placed his hand on the small of her back and guided her into the room. The table held ten to twelve seats at most, and the room—like the rest of the palace—dripped with opulence and gold.

Dean led her to the head of the table next to Naomi and pulled out a chair for her to take a seat. Naomi reached over and touched the fabric of Fawn's dress. "I like this."

"I'm glad you're here," Fawn whispered back. "I went looking for you earlier."

Before her friend could answer, Dean turned to the prettiest woman Fawn had ever seen in her life. The woman's tan skin and long, dark auburn hair complemented her light eyes perfectly. She wore a dress similar to Fawn's, paired with jewelry of stones and shells.

"Violet," Dean said a little too loud, drawing everyone's attention. Fawn kept her gaze on her mate and waited to follow his lead. She didn't know the royal etiquette. Did she introduce herself first or did she wait to be spoken to? The only royal dinner she'd been to in the Mountain Kingdom was after the coronation, and it wasn't an intimate affair. "I would like you to meet my mate, Fawn."

The pretty woman froze and glanced at the man sitting across from her. He had warm russet skin, shoulder length black hair, and lean muscles. His eyes slid to the other end of the table. *Cali.*

Gods, why is she still here? After that morning, Fawn thought she'd leave.

Cali looked pissed, her eyes willing Fawn to die on the spot. The silence felt endless, but only a few seconds passed before Violet smiled brightly at Fawn. "Hi!" She pointed to the two men sitting across from her. "That's Griff." The man she'd shared a look with earlier tipped his head. "And that's Ares. We're from the Tropical Kingdom." The other man did the same.

The girl's sweetness seemed genuine, and Fawn matched her smile. "It's nice to meet you. I've always wanted to see the Tropical Kingdom. I've heard it's beautiful."

Violet lifted her hand and tilted it side to side. "It is if you don't mind feeling like someone wrapped a wet cloth around you the second you step outside."

"And insects," Ares added. "They're everywhere."

Violet shushed the man. "Don't listen to him. They're not that bad."

Dean sat beside Fawn, resting a comforting hand above her knee. The contact calmed her even more and she covered his hand with her own in thanks.

"I see you found a dress," Braddock said from a few chairs down.

"The material looks soft," Monroe added. "Where did you get it?"

Fawn glanced down at the dress, thinking it looked like everyone else's. They must be trying to ease the obvious tension between her and Cali. "Thank you. Lilith gave it to me."

"Is it from the Human Kingdom?" Cali questioned from the other end of the table, her voice deceptively sweet. "You're half-human, aren't you? You grew up there, didn't you? I've heard your foliage is dull." The woman sitting next to her shrank in her chair, glancing at Cali warily.

Everyone fell silent. It was obvious she sought to embarrass Fawn, but being half human was nothing to be ashamed of. She had hidden her ears most of her life to avoid being taken advantage of, but she had never been ashamed.

Fawn straightened her shoulders and kept her voice polite. "I am. I liked growing up there, but I do love the bright colors in the fae lands."

"Her kingdom is the Garden Kingdom," Dean cut in, his words as smooth and calm as his outward demeanor, but Fawn felt his fury. "She is your queen."

Violet nibbled on her lip, looking between both ends of the table, Ares and Griff tucked into their food, and Monroe shot a smug smile at Cali. His obvious defense of Fawn endeared her to him more. She'd ask Dean if he could join them tomorrow in the village to get to know him better.

"Oh, did you already marry?" the woman next to Cali asked

innocently. She sounded genuinely curious, but her question settled uncomfortably over the group.

The tension in the room thickened to unbearable. Dean's facade held firm as he gave the two women a boyish smile. "Not yet, but I don't need a ceremony to call her my wife."

Violet visibly swooned, Griff choked on his food, and Monroe preened as if Dean had been talking about him personally. Cali's friend looked remorseful for bringing it up, and Cali's eyes watered. Fawn would feel bad for the king's ex-fiancé if she hadn't tried to humiliate her.

Where is our food? If she had food, she wouldn't have to make small talk. It wasn't that she didn't want to conversate with the others, but she feared Cali would find a way to take shots at anything she had to say.

On cue, two plates were set in front of Dean and her, and she nearly slumped with relief. The steak on her plate looked delicious, and she immediately dug in, sawing off a piece and shoving it into her mouth like a starving dog.

Dean scowled at her. "You should have told me you were this hungry. I would have had food brought to the room earlier."

Fawn swallowed a bite and scooped a dollop of potatoes. "We were unpacking and it slipped my mind."

He sighed. "I should have thought to feed you. It won't happen again."

They managed to survive the rest of dinner with polite conversation—excluding Cali and the woman beside her, who were lost in their own whispered conversation.

Fawn liked Violet and her two guards. They were traveling all over Eden for Violet to study the different fashions in each kingdom, and her enthusiasm made Fawn wish she cared about something half that much. She thought back to Dean asking her about hobbies, and it struck her how half-lived her life had been.

She pushed the morose thoughts away, and by the end of dinner, Fawn felt excited about her future.

Dean had asked Lilith how long he had to keep Cali around, and she'd said he would know when the time came. How? Right now, he wanted to exile her from the entire kingdom. He understood her hurt to an extent, but she knew returning with Fawn was a possibility, not to mention, *he* hurt Cali, not Fawn. Fawn was an innocent bystander who was blindsided too.

Emi, Cali's sister, didn't have Lilith's protection, and he had half a mind to banish her on principle. She was a nice girl, but if he took away Cali's confidant, maybe she would leave on her own.

Emi's innocent question had brought to his attention that there may be those who wouldn't view Fawn as their queen until they married, and he needed to rectify that sooner rather than later.

"Stand here with Cassandra while I speak with that woman over there," he told his mate and pointed at the royal seamstress who made the warrior's fighting leathers. After telling the seamstress what he needed, she assured him she would have it done before morning and delivered to his rooms as soon as possible. He thanked her and returned to Fawn.

"What would you like to do?" he asked her. He wanted nothing more than to take her to their rooms and get to know her better, but her escape earlier proved she needed an outing.

"I don't know what there is to do here." She shrugged. "You pick."

He tried to think of something she'd enjoy. "Would you like to see the horses?"

Riding was his favorite pastime. He'd never had time in his younger years outside of riding lessons, but in his adulthood, he found it relaxing. She said she didn't ride, but he hoped to convince her otherwise. "Would you like Naomi to join us?"

She beamed at him. "I'd like that very much."

Fawn and Naomi stared open-mouthed at the horses in the Garden Kingdom stables. "Did you breed them with monsters?" Naomi asked.

Fawn agreed. The fae shire horses in the Mountain Kingdom were large, but these were massive, even by fae standards. "I think their tail alone could kill someone with one swipe."

Dean patted the solid black horse on the side of its neck. "The magic in our lands is stronger than most, and our fae animals are bigger." Every fae land had a mixture of animals from both the fae lands and from the human lands. The latter wandered over before the gods returned to erect the barrier protecting the humans and had managed to stay alive.

Her father never told her the Garden Kingdom had more magic than the others and were it not for the beasts in front of her, she wouldn't believe it.

Naomi tried to reach the horse's back and failed. "Have you ever broken a bone falling off?"

Dean had no issue scratching the stud at the base of his mane. "I'm offended you think I've fallen off." The king stood well over six feet, and his wide wingspan allowed him to reach the top. The horse's head dropped and tilted, and Fawn grinned. Ivy liked that spot too.

"I'm still learning to ride," Naomi told him. "Is there an instructor here to continue my lessons?"

A handsome man with cool dark-brown skin and long black braids tied at his nape approached from one of the stalls. "I'd be happy to teach her, if it's alright with you, Your Highness."

The man had a kind smile and Fawn liked him instantly. Some people gave off an aura that drew others in, and he had it. "I think that's an excellent idea," Dean agreed. "Naomi, Fawn, this is Jeremiah. He owns a ranch of his own and provides the palace with horses, like your grandparents."

Jeremiah stuck out his hand for each girl, and they introduced themselves. He turned his charming smile on Fawn. "Your grandparents own a ranch?"

She nodded. "In the Mountain Kingdom."

"Do you two live in town? I'd be happy to collect you both and take you riding at my ranch. I can have you riding in no time," he said to Naomi.

Dean moved closer to Fawn. "Fawn is *my mate*, and Naomi is her close friend. They live in the palace."

Jeremiah couldn't hide his surprise, and he bowed to Fawn. "It's an honor to meet you, Your Highness."

Dean stepped even closer, and Fawn side eyed him. "I appreciate the offer. I don't ride, but Naomi has been trying to learn recently."

Jeremiah scratched his jaw. "You grew up on a ranch and don't ride?"

Fawn shook her head. "I like being around them, but riding isn't for me."

Naomi remained suspiciously quiet, and Fawn noted the blush spreading across her cheeks. Her friend *liked* Jeremiah. "I don't want to take away from your lessons," Fawn replied. "Naomi, you don't mind going alone do you?"

Naomi's eyes widened and she smoothed her dress. "No. That sounds fun."

Jeremiah and Naomi discussed times to meet the following day, and Dean whispered in Fawn's ear, "Are you playing matchmaker?"

His mate shrugged. "She likes him and he's nice. If they happen to hit it off, so be it."

He ran his fingers through her hair and down her back, sending a sensual chill across her skin. "Is there anything I can do to convince you to ride with me?"

She met his searching gaze. "I don't like being high up."

"Even if I swear not to let you fall?" Did he enjoy riding or was he trying to help her overcome her fear?

"Do you ride often?" she queried, praying he said no.

To her dismay, his mouth tilted into a crooked smile. "Almost every day. I guess you could say it's a hobby of mine."

Oh hell, I'll have to ride with him. If he refused to let her out of his sight, he'd skip his daily ride to make her happy. Overcoming her fear would take time, but for him she would try. It might help if she wore a blindfold and didn't see the ground from high up. She gulped. "Okay."

His brows shot up. "Darling, I can feel your apprehension. If it bothers you that much, we won't do it."

"I want to," she fibbed. She didn't want to ride, but she wanted to make him as happy as he made her.

He dipped down and kissed her lightly for the second time that day and a thousand butterflies took flight in her stomach.

19

Fawn slipped out of the bathroom while Dean showered. He'd insisted she stay in the bathroom with him, but his overbearing need to see her at all times had to be squashed.

No sooner had she stepped into the bedroom than a strong arm banded around her waist and yanked her against a wet, hard chest. "Are you trying to give me a heart attack?" Dean rumbled.

How could he expect her to answer with his naked body pressed tight against hers? Her thin shift was a poor barrier between her lower back and his cock. His shaft hardened against her, and she wanted nothing more than to press her hips back.

Dean had been the perfect gentleman, but Fawn wished he'd ravish her at least once. She hadn't had sex since Warren, and her lust flared with the knowledge that only a scrap of silk separated her pussy from his cock.

He cursed behind her and pressed his hips against hers on reflex. "Stop."

She slid her hand over his, trying to push it lower. "What if I don't want to?"

Dean jerked back like she'd burned him, and she spun around to protest, but her breath caught in her throat. He looked wild and fucking gorgeous. Water trailed down his scarred chest, and Fawn's gaze followed it straight to his erection. "Holy shit." Her breath caught. There had been men of all sizes performing at the pleasure house, but none as big as the king.

He covered his cock with his large hand, but it only blocked a portion from her view. "Stop staring at me like that," he warned, his voice thick with want.

"Why?" Fawn stepped closer, but he backed away. "It's clear you want me too."

He closed his eyes and took a few deep breaths before opening them again. "When I have you, I want all of you. I don't want it to be just sex."

It hurt a little that he thought she wasn't his. "I might not love you yet, but I thought we had a relationship beyond friendship. Do you not feel the same?"

"Fuck, Fawn." He scrubbed a hand down his face. "You've been more to me since the moment I heard you laugh from a table away, but I don't think you're ready to be mine in every way."

In a few steps she stood in front of him and ran her hand up his taut chest. "I'm ready."

Dean's breaths came fast, and he threaded a hand through her hair and tugged. "Just this morning you were packing to leave me," he rasped. "You're not ready."

"I wasn't really going to leave," she insisted. "I threw a fit like a child, but I wouldn't have left. I *couldn't* have left you."

He dropped his hand and flexed it at his side, looking away

from her. Finally, he turned back. "I won't take you yet, but I'll take this."

He crushed his lips to hers in a hungry kiss, and she melted against him. *Yes.* His other hand snaked around her and pulled her close, but that wasn't good enough for her. She broke the kiss, clutched the top of his shoulders, and jumped. Realizing her intent, he grabbed her thighs and lifted, helping her twine her legs around his waist.

"Gods damn, you really are trying to kill me." He dove in for another kiss, licking at the seam of her lips, begging entry. Their tongues moved together in a sensual dance, and she rocked her hips against his abs. He whispered her name like a prayer and carried her to the bed.

He laid her on the edge of the bed and kissed his way down her jaw. "Is there anywhere on your neck I can kiss?" His question surprised her, and he added, "I noticed you don't like part of your neck touched."

If she thought she wanted him before, that feeling had nothing on this. "The front is okay and a little of the sides."

His tongue instantly went to the pulse point on her neck and sucked. Her nipples hardened, and she moaned, rocking her hips against his. "I won't fuck you, but I need to taste you."

The length of his cock pressed against her throbbing center, and she rubbed against him like a cat in heat. "Please."

Working his way down her chest, he sucked a nipple into his mouth through the fabric. The hot slide of silk against her sensitive skin drove her fucking crazy, and she grasped his hair to hold him in place.

He chuckled and slowly moved to her other breast. The warmth of his breath caressed her through the fabric, and she wondered if someone could come from nipple stimulation alone.

Once he'd had his fill, he moved down her body and

kneeled at the edge of the bed. Lifting her dress, a low shuddering breath ghosted across her center. "You've been bare this whole time?"

Fawn propped herself up on her elbows. "Yes. I don't like wearing anything to bed."

"Fuck, baby, you're perfect." He grabbed her hips, dragged her to the edge, and hooked her legs over his shoulders.

His tongue ran the length of her lips, and she dropped back on the bed with a long moan. "Gods."

She'd forgotten about his impressive tongue until she jerked with a cry as it plunged deeper. "Oh fuck, Dean."

His hand moved from her hip to her center and flirted with her clit, his tongue still fucking her with fervor. He curled the tip of his tongue inside her, and she couldn't handle the tingling that spread through her body. "You have to stop," she whined, and he withdrew immediately. She started to protest but he attached to her clit, sucking and caressing it with his mouth.

She'd heard the performers at the pleasure house sob before, but she thought it was performative. Now she understood because her impending orgasm bordered on unbearable. She cried out again when he slid a finger inside, pressing the sensitive spot that drove her wild.

He pulled his face back and met her gaze, his mouth glistening with her arousal. "Come for me, darling."

Oh gods damn. He licked her clit faster and added a finger, moving in time with her hips. "Dean," she begged, but she didn't know what for. "Oh gods."

Fawn screamed, and her back arched as her muscles twitched. *It's too much.* She tried pushing against his head, but he resisted and moved faster. Her pussy spasmed, and every muscle in her body seized as she screamed obscenities loud enough to wake the palace.

Dean leisurely licked her from entrance to clit until she melted into the mattress, trying to catch her breath. "Where the fuck did you learn that?" she breathed. "Don't answer that. I don't want to know."

He laughed lightly and unfolded his long body until he towered over her with a cock harder than iron. Fawn sat up and reached for him, but he caught her wrist and shook his head. "If you touch me, I won't be able to hold back."

That's what she wanted, but she'd respect his wishes. If he wanted them to wait for the full experience, they'd wait. He wiped his fingers across his mouth to collect the juices there and rubbed them on his thick shaft. "Lie back, darling. I need to get something."

Leaning back, but keeping her eyes on him, she watched with curious eyes. He took two fingers and swiped them across her entrance, gathering her cum to wipe on his cock. He repeated the motion until he'd cleaned her as best he could, using her slick to work himself.

Slowly, his hand moved across his veiny cock from base to tip and squeezed his head. He moaned and dropped his head back, stroking himself with practiced movements. Fuck, she wanted to be the one who made the cords in his neck strain.

Dean's breaths quickened and his arms flexed with each stroke. Fawn squirmed on the bed, needing him inside her, aching for him to fill her.

He snapped his head forward and crowded her until she laid back again. "Lift your dress," he ordered gruffly, slowing his movements.

He rested a knee on the bed beside her hips and moved his hand faster until he groaned her name and coated her stomach and pussy with warm cum. It kept spurting from his tip, and she couldn't help wondering if bigger dicks produced more cum.

Dean crawled over Fawn and lowered his body to capture her lips. "You're fucking beautiful."

She ran her hand along his smooth jaw. "So are you."

Dean watched his mate sleep, enthralled by everything about her. Too tired on their journey home to admire her, he drank her in now. He couldn't believe he'd caved earlier, but it was impossible to resist the need pulsing down the bond.

Climbing quietly out of bed, he retrieved the box the seamstress had left for him while they'd been at the stables. Opening the package, he pulled out the long piece of leather and inspected it with a satisfied smile. This should do nicely.

He closed the lid on the box, knowing he had a fight on his hands, but he'd do anything to keep his mate safe.

20

The next morning, Dean and Fawn started to leave for breakfast, but he stopped her by the door and picked up a box from a side table. "I've got something for you."

The box was too large for jewelry—unless it held a crown. If he thought she would wear a crown around like a pretentious fool, he was sorely mistaken. "What is it?"

"A surprise," he answered cryptically. "Close your eyes and hold out your left arm."

A bracelet of some sort? How big could it be to need a box that size? He looked too excited for her to protest, so she held out her arm, closed her eyes, and waited.

The snap of the box opening and closing spiked her anticipation. She'd never received much in the way of gifts, other than from her grandparents. Something soft cinched around her wrist, fastening with a loud clink.

More rustling and then, "You can open your eyes."

It took a minute for her to process what she saw. There was no fucking way he'd locked a leather cuff with an attached leash to her arm. She tugged at the cuff, but it wouldn't budge. "Dean, what the hell is this?"

Her mate slid his right wrist through the loop at the other end of the strap, smiling. "It's to ensure you don't leave my sight again."

She blinked at him. This had to be a joke. "Very funny. Unlock it."

"No." He opened the door to the hallway and gently pushed her forward. "We're going to be late."

His cool demeanor pissed her off and she yanked on the leash. "I'm not moving until you take this off me," she seethed.

"You can either come willingly, or I'll carry you," he said casually. "It's your choice."

"Again, I don't think you know what that word means." She tugged at the leather cuff, trying to tear it. "I'm not walking in there leashed like a dog!" Her anxiety spiked, the leather tingling against her skin.

He bent to kiss her head as he often did, and she put up a palm to block him. "Don't kiss me right now or I'll strangle you with this." She snapped the strap at him in warning.

A hurt look crossed Dean's face. "I only want you to be safe."

"This isn't keeping me safe," she said softer. "It's insane behavior."

Dean's lips quirked. "Some people enjoy being leashed. Let's test it out."

"I don't," she snapped. "Take this off of me *right now* or I'm not going to breakfast."

He sighed. "Very well." Fawn's relief was short-lived because seconds later, he hoisted her over his shoulder. "We'll do this the hard way."

"Dean!" She swatted at his back. "Let. Me. *Down*."

He popped her on the ass. "I gave you a choice."

"No, you didn't, you psycho." She tried to wiggle enough to force his hand, but he held strong and headed toward the dining room.

The only thing more embarrassing than wearing a leash in front of other people was wearing a leash *and* being carried in over the king's shoulder. "Fine," she grumbled. "I'll walk, but after breakfast you're taking this off of me."

He gently set her on the ground with a triumphant smile. "Good girl." His tone was smug enough to make her see red.

She considered punching him. "I'm going to kill you."

Dean wiggled his eyebrows. "That's foreplay, darling."

They entered the dining room, and Fawn tried to look nonchalant, as if wearing a leash was a normal occurrence, but if the looks on everyone's faces were any indication, she failed.

Violet's gaze snagged on the cuff and traced up the strap to Dean's wrist. Her two friends traded a look, and Monroe clamped his lips together with dancing eyes. *Gods damn it.* At least Naomi had riding lessons with Jeremiah this morning or else she would have asked about it immediately. "Take this off of me," she hissed low enough that the others couldn't hear.

Dean ignored her, and she decided to strangle him with the strap when they were out of prying eyes that could testify against her.

The king pulled out her chair and she lowered herself into it, averting her eyes from the rest of the table. The cuff bit into her skin, already close to unbearable.

Between Violet and Monroe, the conversation kept moving. Violet explained that her friends Lydia and Victoria lived in the Garden Kingdom and had arrived in the capital the night before to visit her before she leaves for the Human Kingdom. It was a pleasant meal and conversation, if you ignored the fact that one of the breakfast guests was shackled to another.

Fawn was thankful for Cali's absence. She couldn't bear her seeing her in her current condition. The feel of the leather against her skin had escalated, and she needed it off immediately. The others excused themselves as they finished their meal, and Monroe told her he'd meet them at the front entrance in a couple of hours for their shopping excursion. With a last glance at Fawn's wrist, he giggled and left the room at Braddock's side.

Only a few staff remained, and Dean spoke with one of the waiters about something Fawn couldn't concentrate on enough to hear. Thankful for his distraction, she took her knife and tried to carefully slip it under the cuff to saw it off. The leather molded against her sweaty skin, feeding her frantic need to escape.

Dean's hand went to his chest, and he whipped his head around to look at her just as she stuck the tip under the material and yanked. The blade sliced through the leather, but she hadn't expected it to on the first try, and the knife snapped free, her arm going forward with the momentum.

Dean tried to turn and grab her wrist, but he wasn't quick enough. "What are yo—" Fawn watched in horror as she stabbed Dean in the side. He grunted, eyes wide, and red bloomed across his pale blue shirt. "Darling," he ground out, examining the knife jutting from his side. "You never told me you liked blood play."

Fawn's hands flew to her mouth. "I'm so sorry! I didn't mean to stab you, I swear." Tears gathered in her eyes. "I just needed the cuff off and the knife slipped."

"You did say you'd kill me," he teased, his voice tense. Turning to the stunned server, he ordered him to bring a healer. "It's alright, darling." He retrieved a key out of his pocket and handed it to her. "Who knew you were this blood thirsty?"

In a daze, she accepted the key and removed the leather shackle. "I did help bury a body," she tried to joke, but the words were strangled. "Shit." She apologized profusely, and Dean used his left hand to pinch the end of her chin. "Stop apologizing. I pushed you too far because of my own fears. I see that now. We'll talk about it later, but for now, I need you to remain calm. Your emotions are crashing through my chest."

Fawn nodded and breathed deep, doing what she did best and locking her inner turmoil into a box. She bit back another apology and to her utter mortification, Cali hurried into the room with a large bag in her hand.

"What happened?" she gasped at the knife and blood. "Oh my gods!"

"I'm alright, swe—Cali. Just a bit of foreplay gone too far." He winked at Fawn.

Cali turned hate-filled eyes on Fawn and spat, "You attacked your king?"

"Her mate," Dean corrected her. "Call it a love tap."

"Move," she snarled at Fawn. "I need space to work."

"Cali," Dean warned. "Do not speak to her that way."

Cali bit back a scathing remark and positioned herself at his side. Her voice softened into an affectionate murmur. "I just hate seeing you hurt, D."

Fawn gritted her teeth at the nickname. She tried to give the woman grace in the beginning, but that grace just flew out the window for good.

"We need to take off your shirt." Cali started to unbutton his shirt, and her fingers brushed against his skin. Fawn's worry for Dean overrode her raging jealousy. The sight etched itself into her memory, destined to haunt her later.

She watched helplessly as her mate's ex-fiancé patched him up and saved the day.

❧

Dean should've been angry that his mate stabbed him, but all he could think about was the fear in her eyes. *She cares about me.* He grinned.

"This isn't funny," Fawn huffed. "I could have killed you."

He lay stretched across the bed, torso bandaged, while his mate hovered with furrowed brows. "Nothing in this world could take me from you, not even your murderous rage."

"I didn't try to kill you," she said for the hundredth time. He laughed, the sound bubbling up too easily these days, then groaned. Pain lanced through him, but it was worth it.

He'd laughed more in the week since meeting Fawn than in his entire life. "If you say so, little assassin."

She growled, frustration spilling out as she thunked a tray of food onto the side table. "Sit up. It's time to eat."

"Will you feed me, pet?" he teased, his grin sharp.

"Don't call me that," she snapped. "I haven't forgiven you for putting me on a leash."

"You can't stay mad at me after trying to kill me." He tapped the bandage. "You delivered your revenge."

"If I'd tried to kill you, you wouldn't be here to tease me about it," she shot back.

"If I die before you, make no mistake, I'll find my way back to you and haunt you until you're ready to join me in the after-life." He pushed himself upright, wincing but steady. "I thought I lost you once. I won't do it again."

Her expression softened, affection slipping through the cracks in her anger. He beckoned her closer, and when she sat beside him, he reached for her hand. "I want to apologize for the cuff."

"You mean the leash." She brushed his hair from his eyes. "You're forgiven. But you can't control me, Dean. I'll never be happy in a cage."

He encircled her wrist and pressed a kiss to her palm. "I'll try to do better," he vowed. "I'm terrified of someone taking you from me."

Her voice quieted, but her words landed like a vow. "What makes you think I wouldn't find my way back to you, too?"

A knot tightened in his throat at the promise she didn't quite name. It had only been a week—ridiculous, even reckless —but he couldn't deny it. He had fallen in love with her long before, back when he was fourteen and she'd kept his head above water.

21

The next day, Dean crossed his arms stubbornly. "Why can't I go?"

Naomi studiously looked everywhere but at him, Monroe smiled like a cat who caught a juicy mouse, and Fawn rubbed her temples. "Because you don't like shopping."

Damn Monroe for telling her. Didn't he know Dean liked anything that had to do with his mate? Even shopping. "You're letting Braddock go." He'd promised not to keep Fawn chained to his side, but he hadn't expected she'd want to leave him the very next day.

"Because Braddock isn't hurt." She shot a pointed glance at his side. "And you said if I went anywhere without you, it had to be with him."

"I didn't mean for you to leave me willingly," he argued. "That was for emergencies."

"Getting stabbed is an emergency situation," Monroe added unhelpfully.

Dean flashed his teeth at his friend. "You're right and stabbing someone is punishable however the crown sees fit."

Fawn harrumphed. "Is the punishment that I must spend every waking moment with you?" What was so bad about wanting to be around someone every minute of the day and never leaving their side? Why did everyone keep acting like that was strange?

Her voice softened a touch, and she laid her hand on his arm. "As much as I'd love to spend all of my time with you—"

"You can," he reminded her. "You're choosing not to."

She wagged a finger at him. "Have you been studying the dictionary? You finally used that word correctly."

Dean caught her finger and brought it to his lips. "I'll stay out of your way."

"You need to rest," Fawn countered, one brow arched. "Healer's orders."

He tugged her closer, lowering his voice. "You'd leave me here defenseless with Cali? What if her hands wander?"

Fawn's eyes slitted. "Then cut them off and find a new palace healer."

He'd already requested a healer from town to tend his wound, though Fawn didn't know it yet. A little irritated that jealousy didn't work, he tried to think of another way to either make her stay or convince her to let him go.

"You need to stay here and rest, and she needs to get new dresses," Cassandra chimed in. *"You can watch through me while you lay in bed. You'll be there without her knowing."*

Dean perked at his *familiar's* suggestion. "You're right," he replied out loud.

Cassandra whipped her head around to look at him. *"You agreed too quickly."*

"I'm glad you finally see reason." Fawn went up on her toes to kiss his cheek. "I promise to let Braddock and Cassandra murder anyone who looks at me for too long."

They won't need to. "You two protect her," Dean said with all the concerned authority he could muster.

Braddock narrowed his eyes and nodded slowly. After another goodbye, Monroe, Fawn, and Naomi climbed into one carriage.

Violet petted a massive tigon and motioned to her guards. "You don't have to go. I have Ares and Griff." The tigon shook his head and waited for her to tuck herself inside the carriage. He stood sentry by the door like it was his job. *Maybe it is.*

Tigons were fae jungle cats with white fur, black stripes, and a lion-style mane of quill sheaths that sharpened when aggravated. Dean had forgotten to tell Fawn the Tropical Prince sent War, his tigon *familiar,* to accompany Violet on her trip, and when Fawn stepped into the courtyard earlier, she nearly shattered glass with her screams.

Braddock vaulted gracefully onto his tall mount—fae strength making it effortless—and maneuvered to the far side of Fawn's carriage. Between a tigon on one side, and Braddock on the other, no one would be stupid enough to attack them.

To the crowd, Dean waved and walked inside.

Well, not everyone. The tigon and Cassandra tracked him as he strolled up to Ares and Griff. War and Cassandra could see through a royal's glamour because they were royal *familiars,* but to everyone else around them, Dean was just air.

He approached the two men and said quietly, "I'm going to need one of your horses today."

Griff nearly came out of his skin, and Ares startled slightly but chuckled, shaking his head. "You royals are all the same."

"For fuck's sake," Griff muttered. "You could have told us while still visible."

"One of you will need to stay here," Dean continued, "and no one else knows I'm going."

Both men groaned, stuck out their hands, and played a

quick gesture game to determine a winner. Ares won and pumped his arm in the air. "Have fun explaining to Roman why you're not on the trip."

Griff shoved him. "Shut up. He can't get pissed if the king orders me to stay."

Ares smirked. "Sure."

Griff looked in Dean's general direction. "If you could write to our darling prince and let him know I'm being forced to leave Violet, I would appreciate it."

Violet wasn't the prince's mate; she was his mate's sister. *Interesting.* "You have my word," Dean promised.

Griff grabbed a piece of leather from his pocket and tied back his hair. "Tell Violet I drank milk this morning if she asks where I am. She'll understand." The man gave a lazy salute and jogged back toward the palace, glamoured to appear like he took his horse with him.

Dean seized the reins and saddle horn, hauling himself into place. Royal fae strength made it simple, though his wound still throbbed with every motion.

Ares stared in his general direction. "Should you be riding in your condition?"

"No." Dean wiped the sweat from his brow and prayed he didn't rip his stitches.

Ares threw his head back and laughed. "Yeah, you royals are all the same."

❧

Watching Fawn smile and laugh with the others while shopping loosened something in Dean's chest. The quiet bond told him she'd not had much of that since her parents died. In the months leading up to their chance meeting he'd felt enough flickers from her to drive him to search for his mate, but nothing compared to how vivacious she was today.

Naomi stayed close to Fawn's side, a bouncy little thing with reservations of her own. Both women had their round ears covered, and Dean wanted to pull their hair back and dare anyone to treat them differently. Fae didn't see humans as lesser, just a weak liability in their eyes.

"*Incoming*," Cassandra warned him right before Cali walked into the shop.

His blood boiled. She'd been at the table when Fawn invited the others to shop with her, and Dean didn't doubt the woman showed up on purpose.

The others hadn't noticed them yet, but Cali rectified that within seconds. "Shouldn't you be tending to your mate?" she asked loudly. His mate whipped around, the smile dying on her lips. "Since you are the one who stabbed him."

A few gasps and whispers from the other customers followed her proclamation, and Fawn's cheeks burned red.

"It was an accident," she said defensively.

Naomi appeared at Fawn's side with an arm full of dresses. "I don't remember you being invited. Leave."

Cali turned to the modiste. "I'm here to pick up my dress for the ball," she said politely. Shit, Dean forgot about the ball tomorrow night. He'd speak with the modiste about rushing Fawn and Naomi's to be ready in time.

The shop owner smiled kindly, which pissed Dean off. "Yes, Miss Galla. I'll be right back."

Violet emerged from a dressing room and looked between the women. "Is everything alright?"

"I'm here to pick up my dress for the ball." She kept her voice sweet. "But according to the *future queen's* friend, I'm not welcome."

Dean drifted silently closer, ready to drop his glamour and

protect his mate, though he worried she'd be furious if he stole her chance to defend herself.

"Do not turn this around on me," Fawn shot back. "You insulted me the moment you walked in."

Cali laid a hand on her chest. "I only spoke the truth. You stabbed the king with witnesses present. I personally don't take kindly to someone hurting a person I love."

Fawn stiffened, and Dean bit back a curse. "What happens between *my mate* and I is none of your business." *Good girl.* "I understand you're upset he ended your engagement, but you need to take it up with the gods. They're the ones who passed you over and chose me as his mate."

Dean swore he'd have his feisty mate tonight. Watching her put this woman in her place made it impossible to keep his hands off her.

Violet's eyes softened with sadness as she swallowed hard. He felt for the girl. The gods fated Roman to her identical twin sister, but by sending his *familiar* to guard Violet, the prince's heart clearly chose her over his mate. It seemed Violet felt the same way, and as Dean knew, fate could be cruel.

He only hoped Violet understood the difference here and why Fawn had every right to defend herself.

"You will never love him the way I do," Cali said, her voice low and raw. "I know him better than anyone else, and it's only a matter of time before he realizes it."

Pain laced every word, and he felt a twinge of guilt. Her hurt did not excuse her treatment of Fawn, but a part of Dean understood why she lashed out. He'd speak with Lilith again. There had to be another way to keep Fawn safe without Cali staying in the palace.

Fawn laughed humorlessly. "You don't get it, do you? How you feel about him doesn't matter. It's how *he* feels that does. If he loved you, I would have never stayed, but he doesn't." She took a steely step forward. "And don't ever presume to know how I feel about him."

Dean only hoped he could wait until they were home to bury his cock inside her and show exactly how much her words meant. Her fire turned him on, and her insinuation that she might love him too gave him an unmatched high.

The shop owner reappeared with Cali's package and looked around nervously. "Here, Miss Galla. Your father already paid."

Cali accepted the package with a smile. "Thank you. I'll see you next week for the rest of my order."

She gave Fawn one last scathing look. "If he despises me and loves you so much, then why is he keeping me around?" Without waiting for an answer, she left, leaving Fawn to deal with the aftermath of curious stares and whispers.

Dean dropped his glamour, making the nearest customer scream. He walked to Fawn's side and addressed the others, "Cali Galla spewed lies and hate at my undeserving mate, and anyone who repeats her words as truth shall be punished severely." He cupped the back of Fawn's head and pulled her close. "You were magnificent, darling."

"What are you doing here?" she mumbled into his chest and tipped her head back to look at him. "You're supposed to be home resting."

He chuckled. "I am resting."

Monroe entered the shop holding two boxes and scanned the room, paling. "What happened?"

Naomi sounded ready to kill someone again. "Cali."

Monroe shook his head. "That woman needs to deal with her heartbreak like everyone else by getting drunk or laid or something." Fawn sputtered out a laugh, and Monroe looked at Dean. "Why are you here? You're supposed to be giving her space."

Dean scowled. "I did give her space. She didn't know I was here."

"We really need to get you a dictionary," Fawn muttered, but he felt her affection down the bond—affection and something else.

"Did they get all of your measurements?" he asked, changing the subject.

Fawn nodded. "We were finishing up when your ex-fiancé walked in."

He leaned his head back and stared at the ceiling. "I wish you'd stop calling her that."

"And I wish I didn't have to see her every day," she retorted.

Damn it. He knew Cali's barb about living in the palace would dig under Fawn's skin. How would he explain himself?

He chose not to answer her for now. "Monroe, take the ladies to the next stop on your list. I'll finish up here."

Fawn's eyes searched his, and he implored her to trust him, still he felt her hurt and confusion. "I'll catch up with you at the next shop," he promised.

After they left, Dean paid for everyone's things and spoke with the modiste about a few alterations to Fawn's things.

22

Fawn couldn't shake Cali's taunting about Dean allowing her to stay in the palace. Why hadn't he moved her out yet? Fawn couldn't think of a single good reason he'd let her stay.

Violet had left after the Cali debacle to meet her friends Lydia and Veronica, hugging Fawn tight before disappearing down the street with Ares. Dean had caught up with Fawn and the others, glamoured to look like a different man so as not to draw too much attention to their group. To her annoyance, the king was incapable of being unattractive. His current disguise had dark brown hair and a handsome face. Not as striking as his real one, but still unfairly handsome.

To Fawn's amazement, he stayed back with Braddock, allowing her room to breathe. She prayed he hadn't caught her inner turmoil before she shoved it down and tried to banish Cali's words until they were alone. By his inquiring expression aimed her way, she surmised he knew she hid something. She needed time to prepare herself for the dreaded conversation.

In her peripheral, Dean whispered something to Braddock, who responded with a nod. The king waved his friend off, returned his eyes to Fawn, and winked when he caught her looking.

He'd seen her naked, yet he still had the ability to make her blush from head to toe like a schoolgirl. Her mate had too much charm for his own good.

"Can we grab dinner in town?" Naomi asked Dean and Braddock. "I'm starving."

Monroe floated to Braddock's side and gave his husband the best doe eyes Fawn had ever seen. "I'm craving pasta from the tavern by the pleasure house."

He blinked his rounded eyes, and Braddock melted. "I'll take you."

"Pasta does sound good," Fawn agreed, as did Naomi. Their group stepped on to the cobblestone walkway and followed Braddock and Monroe toward the south end of the street.

Dean grabbed Fawn's hand and pulled her into a side alley. "I need to speak with you. We'll catch up with them later."

She distanced herself from him and flicked her hand toward him. "Speak."

He tilted his lips into a half-cocked smile. "Plotting a second murder attempt already?" Dean grinned wide at her slitted eyes. "If this is how you like to play, I'll need to wear a thin layer of armor to bed."

He wiggled his eyebrows, and she pursed her lips to keep from laughing. "What is this about?"

He prowled forward and backed her against the stone wall. "Tell me what's wrong."

Fawn placed her hand on his chest to keep him at arm's length. "We can speak about this when we're back in our rooms."

"No. Look at me, darling, and tell me what you're feeling." He tapped his chest. "You cut me off and it's driving me mad."

Fawn dreaded the conversation, but it had to happen. If he

couldn't wait until they were back, she'd settle for storming down a sidewalk instead of out of a room when things went sour. "Why is Cali still living at the palace, and when is she leaving?"

The muscle along his jaw fluttered and his grey eyes stared at her with an inner conflict she didn't understand. She concentrated on the faint tingle of emotions from her mate, horrified to discover guilt and remorse... *or sadness.* It was hard to tell. Had he lied to her about being in love with Cali? No. That couldn't be right, but why else would her question make him feel guilty and sad? Fawn thought she'd have felt his deception down the bond, but she was proof that emotions could be hidden.

Say something, she begged silently. *Tell me she's leaving soon instead of looking like I asked you to strangle a kitten.*

Silence.

Backing away wasn't an option, so she shoved him as hard as she could. His big body didn't move at her attempts to push him away, and she felt like a cornered animal. With more force, she tried to push him again, but he snagged both of her wrists in one of his large hands.

"Stop. Whatever you're thinking, you're wrong," he said and brought her hands to his mouth to kiss. His silence infuriated her, and she jabbed her bound fists forward, clipping his mouth. Instead of dropping her wrists like she'd intended, he held tighter. "There's my girl." His affectionate smile tempted her to hit him again.

Shoving down her true feelings, she slumped her shoulders, hoping to sway him into pitying her. "Please. I want to leave."

Wrong thing to say. Damn it.

Dean yanked her arms above her head and pinned them to the wall. The tip of his nose ran from her temple to her jaw and back until his lips were hovering at her ear. "What did I tell you about threatening to leave me?" She twisted against his hold, but his other hand bit into the soft flesh of her hip to hold her still. "You won't escape me, darling."

She'd meant leave the *alley*, not leave him. "That's not what I meant. Let me go."

How many times had she asked him to release her in some capacity since their initial meeting, and at what point would she be considered a hostage? *When you truly want to leave*, a pesky voice whispered in the back of her mind.

"Cali has to stay," Dean said, his tone maddeningly cryptic.

Fawn waited for the remainder of the explanation that never came. She stared at him, trying to discern if he truly thought that answer was enough to pacify her. "*Why?*" she demanded.

"I need her," he said after a beat.

Need her? Jealousy crawled over her skin like ivy, wrapping every nerve. The tight grip she had on her emotions shattered as she sneered, "If you want her around so much, then you have no need for me."

Maybe she would leave after all.

Dean felt an ugly pulse twist their bond, and realization struck. He grinned, unable to help the satisfaction coursing through his veins and straight to his cock. Fawn was *jealous*. He'd never antagonize her to this extent on purpose, but seeing his mate lose her carefully guarded composure was a heady aphrodisiac.

"Are you jealous?" he purred into her ear and jerked back when she tried to knock his skull with her own.

"I'm not jealous," she lied. "I'm fucking furious. You hid your fiancé from me after going on and on about marrying me.

Every time she crosses my path, she does her best to humiliate me. She lives in *our fucking home*, and you have the audacity to tell me the only reason she is around is because you *need* her? Fuck you."

Her admission stunned him. He would have captured her lips in a bruising kiss if he didn't think she'd try to rip a chunk out of his face with her teeth. His chest burned with his own emotion, the one he dared not voice, and he laughed, too happy to contain it. "*Our* home," he murmured.

Fawn stopped struggling, brows drawn. "What? Did you hear anything I said?"

"You called it *our* home." He smiled like a fool and gave in to the urge to kiss her.

She indeed bit him—*hard*. He hissed and pulled back with a bloody smile. "You admitted your home is with me."

Fawn's weary confused eyes scanned his face. "Are you insane?"

"Yes." He pecked her nose, and she tried to head butt him again, ripping another laugh from his chest. "Darling, I don't want her around. I can't kick her out for political reasons—not because I want her." He treaded thin ice saying as much as he did, but fuck, he couldn't let Fawn think he wanted anyone but her. "I *never* wanted Cali. The way she treated you killed whatever flimsy friendship we had."

Fawn huffed. "I'll not endure her treatment in my own home. She might have to stay, but she doesn't need a functioning nose to do so."

My own home. He needed to have her completely. *Now.* Her fierceness and willingness to trust him with little to go on touched him in ways he'd never felt before. "Do you still want me to fuck you?"

Everything quieted except her rapid breathing. His mate's eyes flicked to his lips, and she licked her own. She sniffed and lifted defiant eyes to his. "It's the least you can do to apologize."

"Oh, darling, I'll apologize as many times as you want. But I need to glamour you as someone else, unless you'd prefer us both invisible."

When he pictured their first time together, it hadn't been in an alleyway, but he couldn't wait, and by the looks of her, neither could she.

"Glamour me," she whispered. "I don't mind if people watch." He nearly came undone then and there.

Others would see someone else, but luckily for him, he could see through his own glamour. He'd never be able to create another woman as beautiful as her.

Dean released her wrists and backed away. Fawn rubbed them with annoyance, and his lips twitched to hold back another smile. "Take off your dress," he ordered and waited to see his mate's lush secrets.

She removed her dress in a sensual rhythm like it was second nature, her fingers following the fabric as it slipped down, skimming over her skin. With every inch she revealed, he vowed to forsake the gods and worship her until the day they died. Even then he'd kneel at her altar in the beyond.

Fawn freed herself of the last cloth barrier, standing in only her new sandals she'd purchased today, and Dean closed the distance between them in two strides. He dropped to his knees where he belonged in her presence and caressed her hips, one hand gliding around to cup her cheek, the other venturing to the warm paradise he'd dreamed about since tasting her for the first time.

The pad of his finger grazed across her clit and through her folds until it reached his personal heaven. Her soft gasp morphed into a moan as he slipped his digit inside. "Dean," she whispered, tilting her hips to urge him deeper.

Releasing her ass, he ran his hand over her thigh and lifted it over his shoulder. The sight of her glistening pussy taking his finger snapped the last of his resolve. He removed his hand and buried his head in her soaked cunt, running the tip of his tongue along her sensitive skin.

Her swollen clit begged to be sucked, but he needed to taste her more. His tongue thrust inside of her body, sliding easily into her dripping heat.

She cursed and pressed her hips against his face. "More. Fuck, please, more."

He grabbed her hips and tugged her against his face until breathing was a chore, fucking her relentlessly. His nose bumped against her clit with every stroke, and she moaned long and loud, grasping his hair with one hand.

"Gods, Dean." Her cries grew louder. Good. Let them hear. Let them see his queen fall apart.

He couldn't get enough of her, and his fingers pressed into her soft flesh hard enough to bruise. Silken walls quivered around his tongue, and he hummed against her. "Come for me, darling."

Her orgasm ricocheted through him as if it were his own and he moaned against her. He moved quickly to suck her clit, prolonging her pleasure until she shook her head and shuddered with a smaller orgasm. Dean switched back to her entrance to savor every drop of her cum until she melted against the wall.

Lowering her leg, he stood, never letting his hands leave her body. His fingers brushed over her hardened nipples, and she jolted. "Are you ready?"

Her glassy eyes met his. "Gods, yes."

Dean dipped his head to kiss her and reached between them to undo his pants. She broke the kiss and forced his hand away. "Let me."

He wanted to kiss her again, but she bent her head to focus on his buttons, and he had half a mind to rip them off. Needing to touch her, he tucked her hair behind her ear and kissed the rounded shell. "I wish you wouldn't hide these."

Fawn's fingers paused and he wanted to kick himself for bringing it up. "Okay," she said in a soft, raspy voice and continued unbuttoning.

She freed his cock with a triumphant smile men went to war for and wrapped her smooth hand around the shaft. He lurched forward and hoisted her into his arms, unable to wait a second longer.

A movement out of the corner of his eye caught both their attention and they turned to see two men watching them with interest. "Are you ready to give them a show, darling?"

Fawn smirked. "Fuck me like you mean it, *sweetheart*."

He quirked a brow. "That's eleven. If you keep this up, you won't sit for a week."

Confusion crossed her face, but he slammed into her before she could reply. She gasped and dug her nails into his shoulders. "Too big. I—it hurts."

"You were made to fit me, darling." Her pussy choked his dick like a vise, and his eyes rolled back. "Fuck, baby, you take me so well." He slid his cock out until only the tip remained inside her. "Look how perfect you are all swollen, and red, dripping for me."

Her head lifted from the wall and bent to watch as he buried himself again. "Shit," she breathed. Dean thrust harder, and she squeezed around him on a moan. "*Yes.*"

"You're going to look pretty leaking my cum down those beautiful thighs." His hips moved faster, and her heavy eyes locked in on his. He reached up, hips still thrusting, and tangled his fingers in her hair, licking and kissing along her throat. "I'm going to fill every bit of you until all you smell like is me."

Fawn moaned, moving her hips against his. Her walls fluttered, and he released her hair to strum her clit. "*Oh.*" She screamed his name and clawed at his shirt, her cum coating his cock. His balls tightened, cords straining in his neck, and he released, filling her cunt until it leaked down her thighs.

One of the men watching whistled and said something obscene. He worried she would regret their public display or hide from embarrassment, but his mate forever surprised him. She turned to the men and blew them a kiss.

If he hadn't already loved her, that would have pushed him over the edge.

23

The next afternoon, Fawn stared at the pile of boxes delivered from the modiste. "This isn't my order," she told the delivery men as they stacked more boxes.

"They told us to bring them to the king's rooms, Miss," one man explained.

Dean motioned for the men to leave. "Thank you, gentlemen. That'll be all." They bowed quickly and left, leaving Fawn and at least twenty boxes in the middle of the bedroom. "I had the modiste add a few more dresses in the styles you chose."

Fawn pointed at the mountain of boxes. "You clearly don't know what 'a few' means. Fire your schoolteachers. They did a terrible job." She toed one of the boxes nearest to her. "How did she make them this fast?"

Dean looked through the boxes until he found one with a blue ribbon and carried it to the bed. "She has an entire team of seamstresses."

"Thank you," she said, pecking him on the cheek. Having more dresses made for her was sweet, and the thoughtful gesture endeared him to her.

"A maid will be by later to put away the others, but I need you to try this on." He lifted an elegant, blue gown from the box, and Fawn's jaw dropped.

It was the draped style of her other dresses, but the rope attached around the bodice shined with an unfathomable amount of blue jewels. "Are those sapphires?"

She reached out to trail a finger over the beautiful detailing. A glint in the flowy fabric caught her eye and she leaned closer. "Did they thread gold into the skirt?"

Dean examined the skirt. "It appears they did. I told them to make you a ballgown fit for my bride."

Fawn straightened. "Ballgown?" She vaguely remembered Cali mentioning a ball yesterday, but she didn't think she'd go seeing as how it was the first she'd heard about it.

"I forgot about the ball tonight," he admitted. "It's to celebrate the new kings in the Mountain and Desert Kingdoms. I spoke with the modiste and had her make you a gown. I asked her to rush your order."

Rennick and Amos, the Desert King, were born on the same day and took their thrones at the same time. "Will they be here?" It'd be nice to see Amelia again.

"No." Dean laid the gown gently on the bed and twirled his finger for Fawn to turn around. "My mother never misses an excuse to throw a ball. She's been planning this one for months, though she'll hate missing it for the late Desert King's funeral."

Any mention of Dean's parents set Fawn on edge. After hearing how his father treated him growing up and his mother's compliance, meeting them was the last thing she wanted to do. "It's beautiful. Thank you."

"Stop thanking me." He loosened the rope at her waist and slid the sleeves from her arms until the dress pooled at her feet.

"You are my mate. I want nothing more than to take care of you."

"How will I take care of you?" she questioned, feeling guilty. "Maybe you can get sick so I can nurse you back to health?"

His finger traced down her spine, sending bumps across her skin. "I'll play healer and patient with you anytime you'd like."

She shivered and stepped out of her dress, bending to collect it from the floor. Dean tapped her arms, and she raised them so he could slip the dress over her head.

The smooth fabric fell over her skin and settled perfectly around her figure. She tightened the jewel-encrusted rope at her waist and held out her arms. "How do I look?" She twirled, feeling a light breeze on her legs. Inspecting the skirt, she discovered slits all around, but the way the fabric lay, you couldn't tell from looking at it. "I don't remember seeing dresses with these at the shop."

Dean stared hungrily at her body, eating up every inch of her appearance. "You're beautiful, darling." He reached out and moved his hand against her skirt until he found a slit and slipped his hand inside to brush her thigh. "I asked her to alter your skirts a little."

She stopped his hand, knowing if they got started, they'd never make it to the ball. Maybe that wouldn't be a bad thing. "Why did you have them add slits?"

He grinned wickedly and removed his hand. "Easy access."

She gaped at him. "You're ridiculous!"

Dean laughed, and Fawn marveled at the sight. He really was a beautiful man. "Now that I've had you, darling, I'll want you every second."

She understood the sentiment, but... "I want our relationship to be more than sex."

He sobered quickly, reaching for her to draw her close. "It already is. If you never touch me again, I'll fuck my hand until the day we die."

The organ in her chest tripped and fluttered at an alarming rate. She'd heard of love at first sight; people meeting and falling in love instantly. That wasn't what this was, but it was fast tracked.

She'd known him only a week and half. *A week and a half.* Yet the feeling in her chest confounded her. Surely not. Did the bond make them love one another or was she just a fool? For sanity's sake, she'd pretend the former. In truth, it was probably the latter.

"Don't be hasty," she teased. "I have needs too."

"And I will fulfill every one," he swore like an oath, conviction in every word.

Fawn went on her toes and beckoned him for a kiss. It was chaste but packed with meaning. "Does the bond make mates love each other?" *Why did I ask that out loud?*

The radiant smile he gave her melted away any lingering embarrassment. "No, darling, it doesn't. Do you fancy yourself in love with me?"

Mortification almost drowned her. She'd been caught up in the moment and made an idiot of herself. "No, it's just a question," she sputtered and rounded the bed to put space between them. "Your ego is too big for your own good."

Dean hummed in response and followed her to the other side of the room. She studiously ignored him in favor of studying the beautiful rope on her dress. "That's twelve for lying to me."

She glared at him. "Why do you keep counting?" Trying to feign nonchalance as she scooted around him, she scoffed. "I'm not lying, you pompous man."

Dean hooked his arm around her waist and hoisted her

into his arms then sat on the edge of the bed. She tried to wiggle free, but he only tsked. "Thirteen. Time to pay up, darling." He flipped her onto her stomach and moved her skirt to expose her bottom half.

"What are you doing?" she demanded. He ripped her silk underwear from her body, and she gasped with outrage. "That was silk! Do you know how expensive that is?"

"I can afford more." She kicked her feet and yelped when his hand came down on her bare bottom with a loud smack. "Count."

Did he just... "Are you spanking me?"

Dean caressed the spot he'd popped. "I told you I would. Count, or we start over."

She had two choices: fight like hell to get free or admit she was trapped and play his game. Going limp, she muttered, "One."

"Lovely," he praised and landed another slap.

"Two," she gritted out, already plotting her revenge.

Another. "Three."

Again. "Four."

He alternated cheeks, soothing each one with a gentle touch before striking again. Halfway through, he adjusted her slightly and licked her throbbing flesh, placing a kiss before landing another blow. The lick did things to her she'd rather not explore, and she resolved to ignore the heat building between her thighs.

"You're doing so well," he murmured. Another lick. For fuck's sake. "Almost done."

Another few rounds of alternating swats, licks, and kisses. She squirmed in his hold for friction.

Only two left, only instead of his tongue on her ass, his finger slipped through her folds, and she moaned. "Dripping for me already." A few more passes of his finger caressing her sensitive flesh and pressing lightly on her clit. He'd better fuck her after this, or she might just kill him.

His finger disappeared and she groaned, as did he. She twisted to glance at him to find his finger in his mouth and his eyes on her. Never breaking eye contact, he slapped her bottom again. She cried out, her flesh sore. "Twelve."

Still watching her, his finger slipped back to her pussy and her head fell forward. Fawn bit her lip to hold in a moan, but when his thick finger slipped inside, she couldn't help it.

She clenched around him, and pushed deeper, adding another finger on his outward stroke. "Your cunt loves to be fucked with anything, doesn't it?"

Her walls clenched, and she rocked against his hand. The pressure disappeared, and she growled, hoping the grasp she had on his leg hurt. She glared at him, and he caressed her face with his clean hand. "You're beautiful when you're unsatisfied."

The fucking nerve of this man. Before she could retort, his spanked her ass for the last time. "Thirteen," she gritted out, anxiously waiting for him to finish what he started.

Without warning, he plunged three fingers into her cunt, stealing her breath. He didn't just thrust in and out, he'd pull out all the way and run his fingers across her pussy to caress her clit before pushing back inside her. The sensation was too much but not enough. She grabbed his leg harder and tried to chase his fingers when they retreated each time.

She whined and whimpered, desperate. "Please," she begged.

Dean chuckled, the sound low and smooth. "This is a punishment, darling, and you'll take what I give you."

In and out, gliding, caressing. "I can't take it," she cried. "*Please.*"

He moved faster and put more pressure on her clit. Then

finally, her orgasm built, so close she could taste it. The anticipation might kill her, and with one final thrust, she exploded. Black dotted her vision as her muscles seized. Her cries were loud, and if she'd been in the right state of mind, she'd worry people in the hall could hear her.

Once her body slumped with satisfaction. Dean sucked his fingers clean, pulled Fawn upright, and cradled her in his lap to whisper the words that changed everything.

"I love you, Fawn. I always will."

Her eyes met his, and she saw and felt the love shining through. It was the same feeling she'd been too afraid to name "I love you too."

24

The nerves Fawn tried to hide showed in the slight tremble of her arm as she threaded it through Dean's. "Breathe, darling. Everyone will love you."

She nervously touched the hair covering her ears and blew out a shaky breath. Coming here had been a terrible idea. "Half of your staff thinks I'm your mistress."

"Not quite half," he corrected her. "They won't be saying your name with poison again."

She gave him a dubious look. "You cannot control what people think."

"No," he agreed, "but I can control what they say."

She huffed. *Men.* His word might be final, but he was not a god. "Did you implement a law? If not, I'm sorry to inform you that you can't control what people whisper behind closed doors."

A guard opened the door behind the dais and announced the king, effectively ending their conversation. Dean nodded to the guard and led Fawn past two thrones until they stood at the edge, looking down at the crowd.

"Is this the entire village?" Fawn muttered under her breath.

"These are the nobles, the upper echelons of our kingdom," he explained. "My mother insists on an exclusive guest list. When you throw events, you can invite whomever you wish, noble or not."

Fawn's heart seized. She'd be queen and expected to throw parties for people. Shit. She had one real friend and a small handful of people who she really liked. Never had there been a more ill-suited person to plan events.

Dean held his hand up, silencing the room, and everyone stared at them with rapt attention. "Good evening, friends. Thank you for coming."

Friends. The Dean she knew would sooner chew off his own arm than call these people friends. What a perfect politician he was. "Tonight we gather to honor the two new kings of Eden." Polite applause filled the air, but Dean held up his hand again. "However, we have bigger things to celebrate." He looked down at Fawn and smiled fondly. "I would like to introduce my mate and your future queen, Fawn Whitman."

A quiet fell over the crowd, followed by a loud buzzing of conversation. "Quiet," Dean snapped like a whip. "I know many of you have questions. It was well known my mate died when we were teenagers, but that turned out to be a lie." The whispers grew louder and the king held up his hand once more. "I will find out who betrayed me, and they will die for what they've done, but those close to me know that I always thought she was alive, but others told me I was imagining things."

Fawn looked up at him, blocking out the crowd, touched that he would reveal the secrets he kept hidden from his people. His people would have called him mad or too unstable to lead had they thought he admitted to feeling his mate's ghost.

He motioned to Fawn with his free hand. "My beautiful mate was safely tucked away in the Mountain Kingdom. I found her at King Rennick's coronation, and I am honored to present her to you today." He stepped away and swept a hand toward her. "Your queen."

Cheers and applause rang out, though some clapped reluctantly, eyes filled with suspicion. She couldn't blame them because even to her it sounded impossible the king would think his mate to be dead. Had she not been the mate in question, she would have been skeptical, too.

Dean's legs started to bend, but he stopped, looking around the room. Fawn felt his irritation grow, and she scanned the room for the source of his ire.

A lethal voice she barely recognized echoed off the walls of the beautiful ballroom, casting fear over the crowd. "Kneel before your queen or die where you stand."

Every person in the room hit their knees, including Dean, and Fawn gawked at him. "I'm not even queen yet," she whisper-yelled. "You cannot force them to kneel."

He lifted his head to look at her, genuinely bewildered. "I did not force them. I gave them a choice."

She bit the inside of her cheek to keep from laughing at his sincerity. He rose and kissed her gently. "Whether we are married or not, you are their queen, and they will treat you as such."

"You're insane," she breathed.

His wolfish grin did things to her she needn't think about in public. "We've already established that, darling."

He guided her to the two thrones on the dais and gestured for her to sit down in the throne to the left while he took the right. Reaching over, he took her hand in his and beckoned over a guard. "We will start receiving now."

Alarm bells rang in Fawn's head. "Receiving? As in, people come up to speak to us?"

Dean chuckled. "What did you think we would be doing?"

She flung her arm toward the dancing crowd. The music had started back up and couples twirled around the floor. "Dancing."

"We will, but people will want to meet you." He squeezed her hand. "I need to see if anyone carries a hostility toward you. It may lead us to whoever wants you dead."

The blood drained out of her face and pooled at her feet. "That's supposed to make me feel better?"

He frowned. "I would never let anyone hurt you."

"That's not the point," she argued. "No one wants to meet people who hate them."

"Darling, they wouldn't dare be rude to you, but I am good at reading people. If I sense something is off, I will have Braddock investigate them."

The confidence with which he spoke would have been inspiring if Fawn didn't feel like puking. *You need to get used to this*, she scolded herself. *You will be queen.* Until now, she hadn't really thought through what that meant. She should have.

The dancers looked beautiful twirling around the floor and staff moved silently along the perimeter of the room, offering people refreshments. "What about the staff?" she asked. "When will I meet them?"

His mouth tipped into a crooked smile. "Whenever you'd like. My mother never bothered, and I didn't think to set anything up."

She scowled at him. "Have you met them?"

He nodded. "Most. I cannot remember everyone's names, but I have done my best to introduce myself."

She felt like an ass for assuming he hadn't; she knew him better than that. "I'd like to meet them soon."

A woman appeared at Fawn's side and held out a glass of champagne. A sliver of cloth protruded from her mouth, and she carried a small chalkboard on a string. On it, she'd scrawled: "*Would you like a drink, Your Highness?*"

Fawn smiled kindly and accepted a glass. "Thank you. What is your name?"

The woman looked startled and glanced at Dean, who aimed a dark stare back. She scrambled to erase her board and retrieved a piece of chalk from her pocket to write, "*Beatrice.*"

"It's nice to meet you, Beatrice. I'm Fawn."

Beatrice blinked, then added: "*It's an honor, Your Highness*" to her board. She dipped a quick curtsey and scurried off the dais.

Fawn tapped her fingers on the arm of her throne. "I wonder what happened to her mouth."

Dean sipped the champagne another server handed him and hummed in response. Fawn fidgeted with her skirt when people lined up at the steps of the dais, waiting for the guard to let them through.

The first couple approached, introduced as Samuel and Catrina Galla. *Wasn't Galla* Cali's last name? Oh, fuck. This might be worse than meeting Dean's parents. The woman's eyes brightened when they landed on Dean. "Hello, Your Highness." The older woman looked delighted to see the king, and Fawn feared her eyes would dim when she turned them on her.

She braced herself for disdain, but instead Catrina made her way over to Fawn while Samuel greeted Dean. The woman curtsied and raised her head with a warm smile. "It is a pleasure to meet you, Your Highness." This couldn't be Cali's mother. In no world would that wretched girl come from this woman. She leaned closer to Fawn and lowered her voice. "I should be upset on my daughter's behalf, but I never wanted her to marry the king. He didn't love her, and I was afraid he never would." She patted Fawn's hand with a motherly air. "I finally understand why. He never looked at Cali the way he looks at you."

Fawn's throat tightened and she tried to swallow the lump in her throat before replying. "I appreciate that very much."

Catrina straightened and stepped to the side for her husband to take her place. The man smiled politely and bowed low. "We are glad our king has found his true mate," he said, smooth and articulate. "It is a relief that the Garden Kingdom heir will remain strong."

Odd thing to say but better than the hate she'd feared. "Thank you, sir." He bowed again, took his wife's arm, and allowed a guard to escort them down the stairs.

"Of all people to go first, it had to be Cali's parents?" she whispered. "Who's next? Yours?"

Dean laughed loud enough to draw attention. "Cali's parents are kind people. If I thought they'd disrespect you, they wouldn't have gotten within one hundred feet of this palace."

She sighed and sat back, ready to be thrown to the wolves again.

Dean watched Fawn mingle with Naomi and Monroe far enough away to give her "space," but close enough to keep her in sight. He'd tried to convince Cassandra to come and stay by Fawn's side, but the serpent refused. She hated crowds and had said, *"Stop treating her like fragile glass."*

He knew his behavior was over the top—he was a rational

man—but going through the loss of her wasn't something he'd survive again. It wasn't as if he were leashed to her. Again.

"Stop staring at her," Braddock remarked. "She's close enough that either of us could get to her before someone hurt her."

"They could if I'm not watching. What if someone pulls a dagger on her?" The thought alone lit violence in Dean's soul. "You won't let me watch her, and I can't move to stop them if I'm not watching."

Braddock pointed two fingers at his eyes then pointed them toward Fawn. "I have her in my line of sight and I'm faster than you."

Dean held back a scoff. A non-royal fae, no matter how fast, was exponentially slower than a royal, and they both knew it. "The faster we find whoever was behind the assassination attempt, the faster I can be at peace when we're apart." Braddock raised his brows. "More at peace than I am now," Dean amended, glancing over his shoulder at his mate.

A man approached the girls and motioned to Fawn with a smile Dean didn't like. Dean started forward, but Braddock snatched his arm to hold him in place. "If she is to be queen, she needs to handle herself. Do not make her look weak in this sea of sharks."

Dean recognized the young nobleman. *Howard.* His father died mysteriously a few years back and Howard took over the estate. The man's self-importance knew no bounds.

A few people around Fawn's group had stopped their conversations to listen with wide eyes.

Howard raked his eyes down Fawn's body again, and Dean fought the urge to pull her close. He didn't mind people looking as long as it remained just that: looking. Something in Howard's eye unsettled Dean. He decided he'd kill him later, just to be safe.

"You looked pretty on that stage last time I saw you," Howard said. Her nostrils flared, and Dean tried to decipher the man's words. *Did he mean the dais?* "I must say, I was surprised to learn you are the king's mate."

Fawn smiled tightly and clasped her hands in front of her. "As was I. Are you from the Mountain Kingdom, then?"

"I was visiting on business." Howard crossed his arms and licked his thin lips. "Will you dance in the local pleasure house?"

The pleasure house? He stared at Fawn for her reaction, but she kept her face blank. "That is none of your business," she replied curtly, her irritation growing. "I assure you, there are plenty of beautiful dancers who work there already."

The side of Howard's mouth lifted in a nasty smile. "I've seen your *assets*, Your Highness," he drawled lecherously. "It'd be a crime to deprive us of them."

Dean cursed when Cali pushed her way to the front of the growing crowd with Emi at her side. *What the fuck is her sister doing here?* Dean had banned Emi from the palace after that first disastrous dinner. The two women whispered to each other and, Cali giggled, catching Fawn's attention. Her irritation slipped into embarrassment, and Dean's spine went rigid.

His mind raced putting the pieces together. Either Fawn worked at a pleasure house at some point, or this man was insinuating his queen was a whore, neither of which deserved the condescension this man used.

Fawn feigned indifference; her cool mask sliding into place. "Do you speak to everyone this way? Because I must say," she looked Howard up and down, "I am not a fan of unwarranted arrogance."

Naomi smirked, and Howard's ruddy cheeks darkened. "I treat a whore like a whore," he sneered, dropping the flimsy jovial mask.

"I'm afraid you don't," Fawn snapped. "Pleasure house workers and whores are desired enough to be paid for their time. You, on the other hand—" her lip curled with disgust "—were turned down by dancers and thrown out of our establishment." His face looked almost purple now. "That's right. I remember you. You couldn't even *pay* to touch someone."

"You can play at queen all you'd like, but everyone knows you're a fraud," the man raged. "The king will tire of you sooner or later and go back to the woman who deserves him." He flung his hand toward Cali. To Cali's credit, she looked horrified at the exchange, her smug smile long gone.

Fawn's breathing picked up, and her hands fisted at her side. "Would you like to know the best part of being queen?" she asked him. He opened his mouth to answer but she cut him off. "Deciding the fate of men like you. Dean, *sweetheart*." She reached for his invisible arm, and he grinned. The little minx had known he was there all along.

Dean appeared instantly, and Howard stumbled back, but Braddock stopped his retreat. "Yes, darling?"

"I don't want him stepping foot in any pleasure house in our kingdom." Howard's face contorted with rage as she added, "or our palace."

Dean leaned in and kissed her forehead. "As you wish. Would you please move back a few steps?"

She gave him a quizzical look but did as he asked. "Thank you." Dean turned back to Howard and retrieved his dagger from his belt. "I don't want you to get blood on your new dress."

In one motion, he slit Howard's throat. Screams and cries filled the air, and people tried to scramble for the exit. "*Lock the doors*," Dean bellowed.

Braddock dropped Howard and looked down at his bloody arms with annoyance. "This is my favorite shirt."

"*Dean,*" Fawn shrieked. "What have you done?"

He wiped his dagger on his pants and sheathed it. "He'll never set foot in a pleasure house or our palace again."

Fawn's gaze jumped from him to Howard and back again. She sighed loudly and rubbed her temples. "In the future, please ask me before killing someone."

"I will," he lied, and she narrowed her eyes knowingly. He winked and led her back to the dais.

Sobs and chatter infiltrated Fawn's senses as some of the attendees cowered in groups. Others stood around chatting like watching your king slaughter a man for insulting his wife was normal happenstance. Dean raised his hand and the room fell quiet save for sniffles and hiccups.

"Anyone who disrespects their queen will meet the gods," he announced, his voice brokering no room for argument.

Fawn poked him in the side. "I will not allow you to kill people for being assholes," she whispered.

We'll see. He turned back to the crowd. "Anyone who disrespects their queen will suffer whatever consequences she decides."

Braddock directed two guards to clear Howard's body and a few maids to clean up the blood. One passed out, and Cali rushed over to help her with Emi at her side. Dean called over a maid and told her to have the musicians play something sensual.

They both sat on their thrones and watched their people. Some were still crying, and he'd let them go before too long, but first they would admire his bride to erase Howard's poison.

"There's another person with a chalkboard," Fawn observed, a line forming between her brows as she scanned the crowd. "And another. I don't understand."

Dean prayed she'd have a better reaction to this than she had to Howard's penance. "I had everyone who called you anything but my mate rounded up and their tongues cut out."

"*What?*" She jumped out of her throne, horrified. "Gods, Dean, what the fuck is wrong with you?"

He leaned forward and tugged her in front of him. From his seated position, they were almost eye-to-eye, and he pulled her even closer. "I am not a man who can sit idly by while someone hurts you. My mother remained silent while my father abused me, and her betrayal cut deeper than his ever could. If you hurt, I destroy. It will always be this way, darling."

Dean held his breath. Would she try to leave him? He'd need to get new locks that only he had the key to for their rooms if she tried. That would be a hassle.

"You couldn't have revealed this part of yourself before I fell in love with you?" she tried to joke.

"The first time we met, I threw a server across the room for making you smile," he reminded her. "You've always known."

A sensual number floated from the musician's box and Dean slipped his arm around his mate's waist. "We need to address what Howard accused you of."

Fawn went rigid in his arms, and something flashed in her eyes. "Accused? As if dancing in a pleasure house is a crime?" Oh, she was mad.

Dean released her, allowing her to back away, and ran the pad of this thumb over his bottom lip. "You like showing others what's mine?"

She lifted her chin defiantly. "Yes."

He lounged back on his throne, his eyes tracing her body. "So do I. Dance for me, darling."

It took her a moment to recover from her shock, and he fought with a smile. "This is hardly the place, Dean," she spoke softly. "Not everyone is comfortable with public nudity."

"Leave on your clothes, if that makes you more comfortable." He'd have her give him the full show later. "But do not let that piece of shit insult your art. Show them how beautiful it is."

Fawn's eyes softened, and she sauntered forward, swaying her hips to the beat. Leaning over his lap, she kissed him sweetly. "Thank you."

Dean watched his mate dance, giving life to the music around them. The sexual nature of her moves charged the air like a well-placed lightning strike and everyone (who wasn't still crying) watched, entranced by her.

A deep satisfaction took root as every eye followed her around the stage.

25

A few days later, Fawn leaned over to smell a gorgeous pink flower in the palace gardens. The sweet scent intrigued her, unlike the florals of the Human Kingdom. Flowers weren't prevalent in the Mountain Kingdom, and the beautiful foliage of the Garden fae lands took her breath away.

Dean trailed behind her and Naomi, speaking with Monroe. He laughed, the sound shooting straight to her core. Would she ever tire of her mate? Would there come a day when his smile didn't make her heart beat faster? She didn't think so.

"The first time I came to the Garden Kingdom, I walked through their forests for hours gathering flowers to set around our cottage," Naomi remarked, lost in a memory.

Fawn understood. She'd never been much for flowers, but these were something else. "Do you think they would let us cut flowers from here?" she mused.

Naomi slid her eyes to her. "The king would let you burn the gardens to the ground if you wanted."

Fawn couldn't argue, but she didn't want to cut flowers here if it wasn't normally allowed. She might be a future queen, and he might be unhinged, but she still needed to live by the rules if she wanted respect. "Can you ask the staff if it's allowed?"

Naomi nodded, entranced by another bush. "I think Violet took some with her before she left, so I bet it's fine." Violet and her friends had left the day before to continue on to the other kingdoms on their tour.

A sudden movement in the nearest tree caught her eye, and she edged closer for a better look. Several dark eyes on a fuzzy tan head peeked over a branch. Long legs held its body in place, and she froze. The biggest spider she'd ever seen stared back at her and inched over the wide branch toward her.

Tarantula. A boy in her class in the Human Kingdom once snuck his pet tarantula into school. Fawn had thought the fuzzy creature was cute, but their teacher did not and demanded he take his little friend home.

She inched closer, using the same voice she reserved for children. "Hello, little one." The spider watched her, unblinking, and crept forward. "What are you doing hiding out here?"

She doubted large spiders would be welcome wandering around a public place and feared someone would try to hurt it. "Someone might hurt you here," she explained. "I'll take you to the forest." The tarantula had a larger body than the small one she'd seen as a child. Was it a large one or a fae one, and if the latter, could it understand her?

As far as she knew they couldn't, but she spoke to it anyway. "I won't hurt you." Fawn pressed her hands together, placed them at the edge of the branch, and the spider scurried into her waiting palms. Its legs prickled against her skin, sending a shiver down her spine. The creature froze. "It just tickles," she assured it, absurdly afraid she'd hurt its feelings. "Dean, look!" she said excitedly.

Dean hurried to her side, and she turned, holding up her prize with a wide grin. "Isn't it cute?"

The king let out a sharp scream and scrambled back. "What in the fuck?"

Fawn's jaw dropped at the deathly pallor of her mate's face. She looked from him to the spider and back again. He moved behind Monroe, and the shorter man gasped with outrage. *He's scared.* She burst out laughing until tears trickled down her face. Dean scowled at her from behind Monroe. "It's not funny. Put it down."

"Are you scared of a harmless tarantula?" she taunted and walked toward him.

The fearless king who killed men without blinking now held out a hand and backed away. "Fawn, do not come any closer."

Naomi covered her mouth to smother a laugh, and Monroe darted to her side. "Dean's right," he agreed. "You should put it back. Or kill it."

Fawn whirled around and pulled her new friend to her chest. "I'll do no such thing. I'm taking it to the forest to set it free."

Dean shook his head. "You're not bringing that thing anywhere. Put. It. Back."

The tarantula climbed from Fawn's hands to her chest, clinging to her dress. Dean's face paled further, and he pointed at her. "It's going to rip out your throat."

She smirked. "If you're that worried, then come and get it."

"Guards!" Dean hollered, and Fawn threw her head back laughing. "Some protector you are." She smoothed her hand down the creature's rounded body.

Dean puffed out his chest and marched toward her, hands trembling. He started to reach for the spider, and Fawn nipped at his hand with her fingers. "Boo!"

He yelped and jumped back. Fawn doubled over, holding the tarantula to her body to keep it from falling off. Naomi laughed loudly and Monroe scolded them, "It's not funny."

"It really is," Naomi replied. "Did you hear him scream?"

"Fine," Dean growled. "We're dumping it in the forest on our way to the stables."

Fawn gulped. She'd agreed to start horse riding lessons today. Oh, gods.

Dean glared at the creature clinging to Fawn's shoulder. How could she let it crawl across her bare skin? The thought made him gag, and she only snickered. They'd gone to the forest to release the wild beast, but it refused to leave Fawn's side. "You have to set that thing aside to get on the horse."

Fawn rolled her lips together and reached up to pet the creature. "I will. I wouldn't want to spook the horse." *Or me,* he added to her sentence silently.

"Is this to pay me back for killing Howard?" he asked, still not understanding why it upset her. *You kill one man and cut out a few tongues and suddenly you're "unstable."*

"Get over yourself," she admonished and glanced at the spider. "I happen to think it's cute, and it likes me." If she kissed the spider, he'd wash her mouth out with soap.

Fawn handed the thing to Naomi, and the woman giggled as it scrambled up her arm. "I think it's cute too. I wonder if it's male or female?" She moved her hair aside so the tarantula could perch on her shoulder. "I bet there's a book in the library about them that will explain how to tell."

"You're not bringing that into the palace," Dean informed the women. "If you insist on keeping it, it has to live in the gardens."

Fawn's eyes rounded. "What if someone hurts Tickles? I'll never forgive you."

"Tickles?" Monroe squeaked. "You actually named it Tickles?"

"You named it?" Dean asked, incredulous. She couldn't be serious about keeping it. He thought she'd let it go in the gardens and be done with it. "I'll put out a decree that all tarantulas are under the protection of the crown."

"You should have named it Creepy Pasta," Monroe muttered. "Look at its legs." He stepped farther away from Naomi.

Jeremiah returned with a small tan gelding, its dark mane glossy, and set a tall mounting block by its side. The horse was small by fae shire standards, but still larger than a human shire. He thought a smaller horse would ease his mate's discomfort.

On its broad back sat the long saddle he'd commissioned their first day at the stables. It was almost double the size of a normal saddle, and had the shire not been so large, it would have been too big.

"What is this?" Fawn asked, stepping closer to graze her finger along the leather.

"I had a two-person saddle made for us." Dean positioned the mounting block at the horse's side. "It'll be more comfortable for you."

Fawn's mouth turned down and she dropped her arm. "It takes longer than a week to make a regular saddle. A custom saddle takes longer. How is this possible?"

Jeremiah snorted. "You'd be surprised what our men can do when given a royal order." Dean had paid them handsomely to finish the saddle quickly.

His mate glanced at Monroe and Naomi for help. "You'll do great," Naomi encouraged. "You already know how to mount."

"Knowing how and doing it are two different things," Fawn said. "I tried once, and I cried."

"I don't blame you," Monroe chimed in. "I like to look at horses, but I'd prefer to do so at a safe distance." He had moved a good way behind Naomi when Jeremiah brought out the horse.

"I like horses," Fawn replied, "but heights are a different story."

"Time to ride," Dean said, beckoning Jeremiah over. "You're going to mount first."

Fawn scooted away from the mounting block and clutched her skirt. "What if I fall off the other side?"

"I'll be there to ensure you don't," Jeremiah assured her.

Dean moved closer to her. He won't catch her like some hero or Dean might kill him. "I won't let you fall," Dean promised. "If you start to tip, I'll grab your waist."

Fawn's hands trembled, and he almost called the whole thing off. He wanted her to overcome her fear so they could share this together, but feeling her trepidation was torture.

She squared her shoulders and stepped onto the block. "I'm ready."

Dean placed his hand on her lower back and kissed the top of her head. "There's my brave girl."

"You make me sound like a child," she grumbled.

"Darling, I assure you, you are anything but."

A pretty blush colored her cheeks and his hand drifted to her bottom and squeezed. She swatted at his hand. "Behave."

With much coaxing, Fawn mounted, clutching the saddle horn for dear life. Dean climbed on behind her and wrapped one arm tightly around her waist.

Jeremiah helped position her foot into the right stirrup and patted her leg. "You did great." Dean glared at where he touched her calf.

"We're only going to take a small turn around the stables," he told her. "That's all we'll do for today, and each day we'll go a little farther."

"Okay." Her voice was tight, and he bet her eyes were closed.

The horse started forward, and Dean loosened his arm to let her feel the movements. She yelped a few times as her rigid body slipped side to side, and he tapped her middle. "You need to loosen your hips. Use your core to keep your upper body straight but let your lower half sway with the horse."

She panicked when the horse bit at a fly on his leg, the motion bouncing them a little. "What does that mean?"

Dean lifted his hand from her waist to move her hair behind her ear and bent his head down. "It means hold your shoulders like a queen and move your hips like a whore."

She sucked in a sharp breath and the bond sparked with arousal. Snaking his arm around her middle, he held her upper body still. "I've seen the way your hips move when you dance. Do what you do best, darling."

He felt her relax slightly as her desire rose. *Interesting.* Maybe rubbing her clit while they rode would make her forget her fear. Unfortunately, they were almost finished with their turnabout, so he'd have to try that theory another day.

They returned to their friends, and Fawn's tremble had lessened to a light shake. *Progress.* After helping his mate down, he pulled Jeremiah aside.

"I need you to make a few alterations to a saddle."

"Another long one?" Jeremiah asked. "We only made one. It will take another week."

Dean shook his head. "Use a regular saddle you have already made. I'll need this by tomorrow."

"What alterations are you needing?"

Dean grinned.

26

The next morning, Fawn and Dean sat in the royals' private dining room enjoying their breakfast alone. "I have a surprise for you tonight," Dean told her with a salacious smile.

"If it's another leash, I will stab you on purpose this time."

He barked out a laugh and stabbed a piece of ham to pop into his mouth. "What's funny?"

A woman who looked to be in her fifties asked as she glided into the room. Her greying blonde hair twisted into an elegant updo, and her pale beige skin was flawless. Dean stiffened beside Fawn and a man with a permanent scowl, salt and pepper hair, and a slim but muscular build followed her in the room behind Cali. Fawn's knuckles turned white around her fork.

"Mother," Dean greeted with a fake smile. His eyes flicked to the man. "Father."

Gods, if you're listening, please open the ground beneath me.

"Dean," his father answered curtly.

"Good morning, Dean," Cali beamed and ignored Fawn. This bitch.

"Who is your friend?" his mother asked, but the look in her eye said she already knew.

"Mother, Father, this is my mate, Fawn." Dean settled a lethal gaze on his father. "We need to speak about the death certificate you supposedly found."

The former king's expression hardened. "What are you suggesting?"

"I'm not *suggesting* anything," Dean replied coolly. "I'm saying you lied about my mate's death. I don't know why, but you will answer for what you've done."

His mother's hand flew to her chest, and Cali looked scared. "Are you threatening me?"

Dean rose and rounded the table. "Yes. Beg for your life if you want, but it will be up to Fawn if you keep it."

The older man's lip curled. "I heard about your display at the ball. You are tarnishing our family's reputation and our people's faith in our ability to rule."

Dean threw his head back and laughed. "Unlike you, I ensure my family receives the respect they deserve."

"Everyone needs to take a breath," the former queen tried. She made her way to Fawn's side and held out her hand. "I'm Anne, Dean's mother."

Dean left his father and stood at Fawn's side. She stood and took his mother's hand. "I'm Fawn. It's nice to meet you."

Much to Fawn's dismay, Cali stayed at Anne's side. Were they good friends? Did his mother wish her son was marrying Cali instead?

Dean's father approached Fawn, and her mate took a defensive stance, ready to strike. "Fawn," his father said, tipping his head respectfully. "I'm Henry. Despite what my son claims, I was given your death certificate, as well as those of your parents."

Fawn smiled politely even though she wanted to tell her abusive father-in-law to go to hell. "My parents passed away in a rebel attack in the Mountain Kingdom when I was fourteen," she explained. "I survived."

Henry's eyes flared slightly before he blanked his expression. A seed of doubt at the man's guilt planted in Fawn's gut. He'd looked genuinely surprised at her admission. If he'd knowingly given Dean false information, wouldn't he know the truth?

"I am sorry to hear that," Henry responded, and Fawn believed him. She hated him for what he did to his son, but in this, she believed him to be innocent.

"Shall we enjoy our breakfast?" Cali interjected. "I'm starved."

"What are you doing here?" Fawn asked her before she could think better of it.

Anne gasped, Henry ignored the barb and took a seat, and Cali sat to Dean's left with a smile. "Anne and I were catching up last night and she invited me to breakfast. We became very close while planning mine and Dean's wedding."

If Dean could kill someone in front of everyone, Fawn could too. Sensing her train of thought, Dean wrapped his arm around her shoulders and guided her to her seat. He sat down and leaned down to kiss her. Nothing deep, but enough to send a message.

Servers hurried in, setting plates before the newcomers and filling their glasses. "Fawn," Anne began, "tell me about yourself."

She'd rather not but had no reason to refuse. "What would you like to know?"

"Your birth record in the Human Kingdom said you're half-human, but since the other records they provided were false..."

"That's correct," Fawn confirmed and tucked her hair behind her ear to point at it. "My father was from the Mountain Kingdom, and my mother was from the Human Kingdom. I grew up in the Human Kingdom until I was fourteen and moved to the Mountain Kingdom."

Henry listened attentively. She expected him to make smart remarks, but he seemed genuinely interested.

"You've been in the Mountain Kingdom this entire time?" Anne asked and picked up a blueberry.

"Fawn worked at the pleasure house there," Cali offered with a saccharine smile. Henry choked on his food, and Anne took a hasty drink of water.

"Cali," Dean snapped. She looked at him with innocent eyes, and Fawn wanted to scratch them out. She wasn't embarrassed about her hobby, and she'd be damned if anyone insinuated she should be ashamed. Before she could tell Cali to fuck off, her mate continued. "Have you forgotten what happened to the last person who disrespected my mate?"

The color drained from Cali's face. "You wouldn't hurt me."

Fawn remained quiet, curious to hear his response. If he needed her for political reasons, did she have a certain immunity?

The look he gave her would have terrified the toughest of men. "Don't test me."

That's it? Fawn frowned. Couldn't he at least cut out her tongue?

Anne cleared her throat and tried to smile. "Did you enjoy growing up in the Mountain Kingdom?"

Fawn took a drink of water to give herself time to calm down. Fuck Cali for making this more awkward than it already was. "I did. I lived with my grandparents on their horse ranch until my early twenties. Then I got a job as a palace maid and lived in the staff quarters."

Anne's face lit up. "Dean loves horses."

"We went riding yesterday," Dean added. "She's a natural."

She reached under the table and pinched his leg. "Did you grow up in the Garden Kingdom?" she asked his mother.

"I grew up in the Tropical Kingdom," Anne replied. "This kingdom is more beautiful, but the Tropical Kingdom was better on my skin."

Cali and Anne both laughed, and Fawn and Dean exchanged a look. Fawn didn't know what she meant by that, but it irked her that the other two women acted like old friends. Fawn would never be close with Anne, not after she stood by and did nothing while her husband abused her son, but that didn't mean she wanted Cali close with his family.

Anne peppered Fawn with innocuous questions, she and Cali laughing at private little jokes. Henry didn't say much, and Dean fielded any questions that made Fawn uncomfortable.

The torture ended, and Dean ushered Fawn out of the room with hasty goodbyes. "You didn't tell me they were back," Fawn hissed.

He stabbed a hand through his styled hair. "I would have if I'd known."

"Dean," a vaguely familiar voice called out.

Dean and Fawn spun around and came face to face with Lilith. How old was this woman? She looked at least one hundred. Fae weren't immortal, and the woman's youthful walk and sound mind only solidified Fawn's belief in witches.

The king bowed his head. "Lilith. Terrorizing the palace today?" he teased fondly.

The old woman's lips twitched. "I need to speak with you."

Dean pinched the bridge of his nose. "Now? I can't leave her alone with my parents in the palace."

"Who says I can't go?" Fawn demanded.

Lilith's pale eyes danced with amusement watching the two. "You can't." Fawn glared at her. A little womanly solidarity would have been nice. "Nothing will harm her while you're gone." Dean opened his mouth to reply but she held up a hand. "You may call Cassandra to stay with her but not Braddock."

"No," he snapped. "I'm not leaving her without someone who can carry her to safety if needed."

"I can walk," Fawn interjected, earning a scowl from her mate.

"You must," Lilith told him, never taking her unsettling eyes from his.

After giving Lilith a scathing look, he turned to Fawn. "I have to go with her, but I'll be back as soon as we're done."

Fawn looked curiously at the old woman. Who was she that Dean bent to her will with little resistance. Turning back to her mate, she nodded. "I don't mind, but I'm not staying in our rooms again."

He clenched his jaw. "Why not? We were going there anyway."

"*We* being the operative word. I'm not sitting there alone when I can find one of my friends."

"Cassandra will be there," he reminded her.

She turned to Lilith for help, but the old woman offered her nothing. "Cassandra can't speak to me. I'm not staying in the rooms, and I'm only telling you as a courtesy."

"Fine," he gritted out. "I'll call Cassandra."

Fawn and Cassandra meandered through the gardens, looking for Tickles. Dean kept his word and issued a protective order on all tarantulas, and after the incidents in the palace regarding tongues, Fawn felt safe enough to let the spider free in the gardens. Naomi had found a book on spiders in the palace library and declared Tickles a male. Whether she read his molt correctly or not is up for debate.

"Tickles," Fawn called out, hoping to lure the little bugger into the open. She'd have to ask Naomi if tarantulas had ears. Part of her had wanted to keep him with her, but he needed to catch his food and eat, and while she liked him, she drew the line at catching things to feed him.

Tickles scurried out from a bush and toward Fawn. "There you are."

Cassandra started forward but Fawn grabbed her with both hands. The serpent jerked around, and Fawn screamed, falling to the ground. Tickles ran as fast as his noodle legs would carry him until he sat protectively on Fawn's shoulder.

Cassandra hissed and Fawn scrambled backward across the stone walkway. "He's my friend," she told the *familiar*, cursing when she remembered the serpent couldn't hear. Trying again, Fawn pointed to Tickles then pointed to her face and smiled.

Cassandra's tongue slithered out and Fawn backed up more. She was certain Dean's *familiar* wouldn't hurt her, but she didn't trust the beast around the spider.

"Do you need assistance?" a deep, commanding voice asked.

Fawn tilted her head back, meeting the eyes of a large man much older than her. He wore fighting leathers and had a long sword strapped at his hip. "No, she won't hurt me."

The man held out his hand to help Fawn stand, but Cassandra darted forward and knocked it away with a terrifying hiss.

"I'm not going to hurt her," the man snapped at the *familiar*. "You're the one who made her scream."

Fawn pushed to her feet and dusted herself off. "She can't hear you. She doesn't have ears." She held out her hand. "I'm Fawn. Thank you for trying to help me."

"General Craven," the man said, withdrawing his hand quickly when Cassandra hissed again.

"Don't mind her," Fawn replied, hitching a thumb in Cassandra's direction. "The king told her to protect me, and she takes her job seriously. She almost killed my tarantula." She pointed at Tickles.

The general's eyes moved to the spider on her shoulder and he laughed. "You're giving the boy a hard time, aren't you?"

Fawn tilted her head. "The boy?"

"Dean," he clarified. "I've known him since he was a child."

Fawn bobbed her head. "Yes, well, he deserves it."

The general laughed again. "I wanted to meet you at the ball, but I had to meet the king and queen at the border and escort them to the capital."

"This must be anticlimactic for you, then." She swept a hand over herself. "Just a plain woman who consorts with animals."

The general studied her until she fidgeted under his gaze. "I think you'll make an excellent queen." He turned to leave but thought better of it and looked at her one last time. "Do not walk around alone."

With that, he left Fawn staring after him, wondering if he'd threatened her or helped her.

❧

General Craven couldn't do it, not now that he'd seen the girl. He thought he'd choose power over loyalty to the crown, but one look at her protecting a little creature from a great serpent, and he knew the kingdom needed her.

He wasn't stupid enough to get in Samuel's way, but he couldn't carry out the assassination. The general had been a good man once, back before the former king had sunk his claws into him and made him into a fucking monster. That good man was long gone, but the loyalty to his kingdom was not.

He marched through the gardens and made plans to get his family out of the kingdom as quickly as possible. No one told Samuel no and lived.

27

Dean stared at Lilith and drummed his fingers against the arm of his chair. "What is this about?"

Lilith poured herself a cup of tea and took a seat across from him. "I needed you to leave Fawn's side."

Dean shot to his feet, his panic and anger crashing against him like a tidal wave. "If you pulled me away to allow someone to hurt her, I will fucking gut you and keep your head in a box."

"Sit down," Lilith clipped. "This must happen for her to live."

"Do you know who is trying to hurt her?" He closed the distance between them and loomed over Lilith's small form. "If you're hellbent on saving her, then tell me and save me the time."

"I cannot do that," she replied, her face unreadable. "Believe it or not, I'm bound by the rules of the aether."

Dean's brows lowered. "What the fuck is the aether?"

"Also known as heaven, the heavens, Elysium, and a plethora of other things. As a Fallen Fate, my ability to see all possible futures is limited."

"You have got to be fucking kidding me." He backed away and fell into his chair. "So you *don't* know it all."

She shook her head. "Not anymore, but I know enough to guide you—if you'll listen."

Dean closed his eyes to connect with Cassandra and froze. General Craven spoke to Fawn, laughing. He'd never cursed having a serpent as a *familiar* until that moment. Who bonds a royal to a *familiar* without ears?

Dean shot to his feet. "She's with General Craven. I have to go."

Lilith nodded once. "It has been long enough. Go to her."

He sprinted for the door and to the gardens with a sinking feeling in his gut.

Dean found Fawn sitting in the gardens, petting Tickles with Cassandra coiled at her feet. His rib cage rattled with the exertion of running. He'd never pushed himself that hard, and he had to put his hands on his knees. What should have taken twenty minutes took less than ten. "Are you okay?"

Fawn jumped up and advanced toward him. "Oh my gods, what's wrong?"

Sweat clung to Dean's hair and dripped down his face. He swiped at it and straightened. "What did General Craven say to you?"

She bent her brows together. "General Craven? He wanted to say hello. He was very nice."

He laughed humorlessly. "The general is anything but nice."

Fawn glanced at Cassandra. "She didn't like him either. What am I missing?"

Dean hung his hands on his hips, his breathing finally

returning to normal. "When my father had me punished by combat, the general was my opponent."

Fawn gasped loud enough to frighten Tickles, and emotions fought for dominance in Dean's chest. Anger won out. "I would have let Cassandra kill him," she spat. "How dare he?"

Moving to pull her close, Dean froze when Tickles looked at him from her shoulder with beady black eyes. He paused, the need to hold his mate warring with his need to flee. "Can you put the monster down so I can hold you? I need to hold you."

Seeing General Craven alone with his mate ripped at something inside him. No matter what Lilith said, he didn't trust the general not to hurt her. Lilith didn't know everything anyway. Did his father know that? What a mind fuck.

Fawn deposited Tickles on the ground and walked into Dean's embrace.

It took Fawn a ridiculous amount of time to convince Dean that General Craven didn't upset her. Knowing he was the man who put scars all over her mate's body infuriated her, and had she known, she would have signaled for Cassandra to kill him.

They were safely back in their rooms, and Dean had a shit-eating grin on his face. "Are you ready for your surprise?"

A sheet covered a waist-high object at Dean's side. "I don't know. The last surprise you gave me was a leash."

Dean waved her off. "You have to get over that."

"I will bring it up at least once a week for the rest of our lives." She walked closer and fingered the sheet. "Show me and get this over with."

He frowned at her but removed the sheet and gave her space to look. She blinked. Surely she wasn't seeing what she thought she was. "Is that a cock attached to a saddle on a rocker?"

Dean prowled forward and ran his fingers across the smooth leather of the saddle. "It will help you learn to ride."

"I already know how to ride a cock. What is this?" Fawn bent over and touched the stitching at the base of the cock where it attached to the saddle. The shaft and head were made of the smoothest leather she'd ever felt. "Where do they sell these?"

"I had Jeremiah make it with help."

Fawn started and snapped her wide gaze to his. "You what?" Her face flamed and she considered hitting him. "How am I supposed to face them again?" *Oh my gods.*

Dean covered her hand with his and guided it to the leather shaft. "You don't mind people watching you fuck but them knowing you'll fuck a saddle is too far?"

She gawked at him and waved her hands in the air. "Do you hear yourself? In what world is *fucking a saddle* a normal occurrence?"

Dean moved her hand over the smooth leather. "Ours." Her traitorous nipples tightened at his sultry tone. He skimmed his other hand up her waist to her breasts to caress her soft mound. "You like the idea."

Gods damn her, she did. This was her mate, her forever, and if she couldn't be honest with him, who could she be honest with? "Yeah," she replied, her voice husky, "I do."

"I'll get you ready to take your new toy." He went to his knees and parted the overlapping strips of her skirt. A low groan rumbled from his chest. "You wore them today and didn't tell me?"

His hooded eyes met hers, and she bit her lip. "I knew you'd find out at some point."

"Fuck, Fawn." He brought a finger to the strip of damp red

silk between her legs. "You're going to kill me." Leaning forward, he snaked his tongue between her legs and licked the soft material.

Dean hooked his fingers under the sides of her underwear, slid them down her legs, and stuffed them in his pocket. "I want those back."

His half-cocked grin heated her skin. "These are mine. I'll buy you more."

Rough hands ghosted over her thighs, leaving tingles in their wake. "Touch me."

"With pleasure." He hooked her leg over his shoulder and tugged her hips to his face. He lapped at her folds, devouring every drop of her arousal to create more. "One day I'll lay you out on the table and eat you for dessert."

Silken strands of his hair slipped through her fingers as she held on to steady herself. "More," she pleaded in a whispered breath.

If she thought he'd devoured her before, she'd been wrong. He sucked and licked like a man who'd starved himself for weeks. His magic tongue slipped in and out, driving her to the brink faster than what should have been possible.

Her walls fluttered and her muscles tightened. "That's it," he murmured against her. "Let go, darling."

Pleasure flooded every inch of Fawn's body, and Dean clutched her tight to keep her afloat. He continued his assault until she draped her body over his in a panting mess.

He lowered her leg and stood, reaching between her legs to gather any lingering cum. "I think you're ready." Licking his fingers clean, he hummed.

Holding the rocker still, he looked at her pointedly. "Mount, darling."

The leather cock taunted her, tall and proud. "It's too big."

Dean positioned himself near the head of the saddle to give her room. "It looks average to me."

Cocky bastard. Reluctantly grabbing the saddle horn, she stuck her foot in the stirrup and threw her leg over. Her dress tucked under legs, and Dean released the saddle. Fawn sucked in a sharp breath and white-knuckled the horn when it rocked violently. Dean plucked her skirt loose and parted it down the middle, twisting the pieces to the side. "Sink down, baby. Let me see you take it."

Never in a million years did she think she would be fucking a saddle. She gingerly notched the head of the leather cock in her entrance and lowered herself. The buttery leather slid smoothly, splitting her open. She moaned and dropped her head back. "Gods."

"Fuck," Dean groaned. "Never thought I'd be jealous of an inanimate object." He positioned himself at her side and slid his fingers to her clit. "Ride, darling."

The cock's pliant shaft moved with her as she rocked her hips. The saddle rocked with her, nearly throwing her off balance. "*Oh.*"

"Keep your shoulders straight," Dean murmured, "and move your hips with the saddle."

Concentrating on her task felt impossible with the sensations shooting through her. "I..."

"Focus. You'll need to pay attention to your posture no matter the distractions." He circled her clit harder. "Roll your hips for me."

Delirium took over and paying attention was a faraway dream. Her hips moved faster, seeking the promise of a high. Dean's other hand slipped the sleeves of her dress off her shoulders and cupped her heavy breasts. She gasped and moved faster as he caressed her sensitive peaks, alternating pinches with soothing touches.

She shuddered with her oncoming orgasm, and Dean released her breasts to bring her face to his. Her hips momentarily slowed down, and it was difficult to move with her lips held hostage by his own. He stopped rubbing her clit, and she protested with a whine. "Move, or you don't get to come."

Fawn focused on rolling her hips while keeping her upper body still. The movement came easier now, and he slid his fingers back to where she needed them most. "Good girl. Keep fucking it like the pretty little whore you are."

Words deserted her, and she opened her mouth on a silent cry. "That's it," he murmured against her lips, dragging them to her neck. "You're almost there."

She moved faster, rolling and bouncing her hips until everything exploded around her. "You're perfect," he praised against her sensitive skin. "Beautiful. I wish you could see yourself."

Nothing in Fawn's body worked; every muscle melted like gelatin. "I think I'm going to like riding horses."

Dean barked out a laugh, slowly lifted her from the saddle, and carried her to the bed. "We're not done, pet."

"Don't call me that," she mumbled half-heartedly as he laid her out on the soft mattress.

Warmth laved at her nipple, and she twitched, still sensitive from her riding lesson. "Every part of you tastes sweet." He sucked her other breast, whispering sweetness against her skin. "I'll never get enough of you, wife."

Wife. She liked the sound of that. "We're not married."

Dean lifted his head and pushed her farther back on the bed. His long body stretched over her, and his cock prodded her entrance. "We're getting married the second you agree." He slammed into her, and her back arched off the bed. "We'll go wherever you want to go afterward to celebrate our wedding, just the two of us."

She felt every part of him as he thrust into her. "I'll marry you," she breathed. She'd give him anything he wanted.

A guttural moan vibrated through him as he emptied himself into her. His movements slowed, and he buried his head in her neck, careful to stay toward the front. "You always know what to say."

Fawn ran her fingers through his hair. "I meant it. I'll marry you whenever you want."

He lifted himself onto his elbow and tucked her hair behind her ear, grazing the top. "Do you want to plan a big wedding?"

Absolutely not. "No. I'd rather it be small with our family and friends, but I'd like my grandparents to come."

He kissed her softly and pulled back. "We'll send word tomorrow."

"Is it true that I'll be as strong as a royal when we marry?"

Dean's free hand idly smoothed down to her breast and toyed with her pebbled skin. "Marrying a royal strengthens your magic to match ours. You won't get a *familiar*, but your glamour will extend farther and work on non-royal fae."

Fawn worried her bottom lip. "If it amplifies my magic, what if my magic is still too weak to reach that of a royal?"

His hand stilled for a moment before moving south to grasp her hip. "It will still be stronger than any non-royal."

"Will we have children right away?"

Dean's cock hardened inside of her, and he rolled his hips. "Darling, I've been trying to put a baby in you since the first night."

"I take tincture to prevent pregnancy," she said with a tinge of regret. He thrust harder and she clawed at his back. "*Dean.*"

"Then stop. I want you swollen with our child." He moved faster, and her eyes rolled back in her head. "I would keep you pregnant if I could."

They moved together, bodies slick with sweat. Wet, slapping sounds mingled with moans of pleasure, filling the air around them. "I love you," she chanted over and over.

He echoed her words like a prayer, until they were both sated and spent. Dean pulled out of her, went up to his knees, and tapped the inside of her thigh. "Open, darling."

Fawn's knees fell open, and he reached between them, pushing his leaking cum back into her cunt. "Every drop counts."

28

The piece of fabric in Fawn's hand scraped against her palm, and she almost puked. "Not this one."

She tossed the offending fabric into the "no" pile and picked up the scrapbook of pressed flowers. Flipping through a few pages, she stopped on a page filled with bright yellow petals. "These are pretty."

Monroe leaned over. "They're yellow." His look implied she should understand his meaning.

She looked back at the lemon-yellow flower pressed in Monroe's book. "What does that matter?"

Monroe tutted and flipped to another section of flowers. "Yellow will make you look like a corpse. Here." He pointed to a light blue flower. "These suit you better."

"I'm not going to wear them," Fawn grumbled, tracing the crisp edges of the petals "But I do like this one."

Naomi peeked over her shoulder. "Ooh that one's pretty."

Fawn had made the mistake of mentioning her and Dean's upcoming wedding to her friends. Naomi could have been reined in; Monroe, however, was an uncontrollable tornado.

He'd kept every wedding planning book he'd made from when he and Braddock married, and he waited all of three hours before showing up in Fawn and Dean's rooms with Naomi in tow.

Dean had agreed to allow Fawn, Monroe, and Naomi to use his study to plan, staring begrudgingly at the materials and books Monroe scattered across the floor. He and Braddock lounged in chairs in the corner, talking while Monroe jotted notes in a sketchpad.

Monroe set down his notebook and held up two swatches side by side. "How long will it take your grandparents to arrive?" He held them up to Fawn's face and threw one to the side.

"When I traveled to the Mountain Kingdom at a normal pace—" Naomi glared at Dean. "—it took a week."

Monroe fanned himself dramatically. "I cannot believe I am having to plan an entire wedding in a week."

"It's a small wedding," Fawn stressed and motioned to everyone in the room. "It will just be us and a few others."

"Even small weddings take time," Monroe insisted. "We must see the modiste today to have a dress designed and made. The gardeners will need to be contacted about floral arrangements. Have you even looked at which room in the palace you want to have it in?"

Fawn glanced at Dean for help, but he just shrugged with a wink. The asshole. "Isn't there a designated wedding room?"

"*Oh my gods,*" Monroe wailed. "This is more dire than I thought. Clear your schedules. Do you have any idea how many different banquet rooms there are?"

Naomi and Fawn stifled their laughter at their friend's obvious distress. "I don't care where I get married," Fawn tried to placate him. "We could get married here in the study and I wouldn't care."

"I wouldn't either, darling," Dean concurred.

Monroe's face was a picture of horror. "You are so lucky you met me."

At that, Fawn and Naomi collapsed into giggles, but Monroe went silent, his eyes fixed on the open study door. Cali stood in the hallway with Cassandra at her side, staring at the scattered materials on the floor.

Was it a coincidence they were together, or had Cali befriended the serpent before Fawn arrived? Evidence suggested everyone had liked Cali very much. Did any of them wish she was marrying Dean instead?

Even from across the large room, Fawn saw the woman's eyes shimmer. She looked frozen in time, as if the sight had turned her to stone. "Are those the wedding books we used?" Her voice cracked as her eyes lifted to Monroe.

Everyone stayed silent as Cali's heart broke in front of them. Monroe stood elegantly and crossed to the door. "They are the same books I used for my wedding." He gentled his voice. "You are not the first person I lent them to, and Fawn won't be the last."

Cali turned hurt eyes to Fawn. "You don't deserve to use them. You don't know anything about him, do you? Did you even know he loves radishes?" Her lower lip trembled. "I haven't seen any on his dinner plate since you arrived, but I always made sure he had them. Now you're using the same books I used to plan the start of our lives together." Tears salted her cheeks, leaving track marks on their way down. "You don't deserve *him*." She ran off and Cassandra slithered after her.

"I need to check on her," Monroe fretted. "I've never seen her that upset. Not even the day she met Fawn."

It was a chore for Fawn to keep her face neutral when she felt like she'd broken up a happy home of friendship. Damn it.

She refused to feel bad for the woman who had tried to humiliate her at every turn.

Refused.

And yet...

"Naomi and I will clean up here." She shooed Monroe toward the door. "We can plan another day."

Monroe apologized again, gathered Braddock, and swept after Cali in a whirlwind of skirts and guilt.

Dean approached and crouched beside Fawn. "I hate radishes." He helped gather swatches of fabric and placed them into Monroe's oversized book. "Do not feel guilty."

"I don't feel guilty," she said slowly, shutting her mouth at his pointed look.

"Do not feel guilty," he repeated. "Any hurt Cali feels is fate's doing, and any notions she has of love are misguided."

"And she's been a bitch to you," Naomi added. "I'm glad she cried."

Fawn's head snapped up to look at her best friend. "That's a terrible thing to say."

She shrugged. "And trying to make you feel bad for being half human is worse."

Her logic was sound, but it still felt cruel to bask in Cali's misery. Seeing her shamed for being awful? Fawn would love that. But seeing her cry because the man she loved was planning his wedding to someone else with the same books she'd once used? No, Fawn didn't like that at all.

"We'll clean this up and go to the stables early," Dean said, gathering papers haphazardly and trying to put them in some semblance of order. "You can put your new skills to use."

The wicked grin spreading across his face made her entire body go up in flames.

The next afternoon, Dean held Fawn loosely at the waist with one hand and the reins with the other. Fawn still radiated tension in the saddle, but at least she no longer screamed at every misstep.

Today he took them on a longer ride through a more secluded stretch of the palace grounds. The Garden Kingdom was by far the most beautiful of the five, with its full trees, riot of colorful flowers, and rolling hills of pink grass hills. Their trail wound through the woods and over stone bridges spanning bubbling brooks.

Picturesque didn't begin to cover it. "Is the entire kingdom like this?" Fawn tilted her head back to look at him.

"Some areas have lakes that stretch for miles," he told her. "In some places the pink grassy knolls are endless; in others it's nothing but dense forest. Here, it's a mix of everything."

"I'd like to see the big lakes," she said as their horse picked its way over a narrow bridge. "I've seen lakes, but none as big as that."

"It will be our first stop on our wedding celebration trip," he promised. "Have you ever seen an oasis in the Desert Kingdom?"

Fawn shook her head. "I've never been."

"I haven't either, but I've heard they're beautiful." He squeezed her close. "My first trip out of my kingdom was to Rennick's coronation."

She beamed at him. "I like the idea of us seeing it together for the first time."

"I like the idea of having you to myself for a few months." He brushed his lips over hers, the fullness in his chest nearly overwhelming him.

She tried to twist to see him better. "A few months?"

Dean hiked a shoulder. "Depending on how many places you want to see. Half the time will be travel."

Fawn turned forward and drummed her fingers against the saddle horn. "I'll have to bring Tickles with us." The teasing lilt in her tone was the only thing keeping Dean from fainting on the spot. Days on end in a carriage with that monster?

While he didn't think she'd subject him to that knowing how he felt, he wasn't taking chances. "I already made arrangements."

The drumming stopped, and she peered up at him through narrowed eyes. "I'm not setting him free. He's domesticated."

He decided not to point out that she'd not known Tickles long enough to make that assessment. "There is a local woman who used to run an animal sanctuary."

Her eyes narrowed more. "You're not asking for help adopting another tarantula, are you?"

His hand twitched at her sardonic tone, needing to redden her ass. "I had Braddock speak with her about Tickles. She's very knowledgeable about most animals, including tarantulas."

She grabbed Dean's rein hand and tugged gently until Art, the small fae shire paint they rode, halted. "We're not giving him away."

"I wouldn't do that to you," he said, affronted. "I hired her to oversee the construction of his own section of the garden to make sure it has everything he'll need. She will tend to him if we're ever gone."

Fawn's eyes sparkled and affection hit Dean in the chest. "Thank you. I'm sorry I thought you'd give him away. I should have known better."

Dean picked up the reins with one hand, his other still firmly around Fawn's middle, and spurred Art into motion. "You're forgiven. Have you changed your mind about fucking me while we ride?"

She sputtered out a laugh. "I'm doing everything in my

power to not think about falling off, and you want me to concentrate on riding your cock too?"

He slipped the hand on her stomach down to cup her pussy, and she jolted with a sharp breath. "You concentrate on staying upright," he murmured against her ear. "I'll worry about making you come."

Dean tugged at the strips of her skirt until he slid beneath the fabric, groaning when his fingers met still more fabric. She threw her head back and laughed. "Did you think I'd sit in a saddle with nothing but bare skin and silk?" Moving her skirt aside, she pointed at the footless, cotton tights adorning her legs. "I'd rather not have to eat heaps of yogurt and bathe in garlic for days just to combat my stupidity."

Dean's face twisted. "What do those have to do with anything?"

"Don't worry about it."

And he would do nothing but worry about it.

Samuel hurled his brandy against the wall, shards of glass flying in every direction. The king was set to marry the Whitman girl in one week.

General Craven hadn't checked in last night or this morning, and when Samuel sent a guard to retrieve him, the man reported no one was home. It wasn't like the general to vanish without notice, and Samuel suspected he'd have to use his backup plan.

Cali *would* be queen. His family deserved the royal designation, and he would do whatever he must to secure it. Even bloody his own daughter's hands if he had to.

29

Fawn waited for the barmaid at the local tavern to take her drink order. She, Naomi, and Monroe were celebrating one of her last nights as a single woman. Not that she considered herself single, but the other two insisted. She could do with a night out with her friends anyway.

And Braddock stood sentry, ready to maul anyone who stared at Monroe too long.

A man sidled up to Fawn and smiled. "Are you new in town?" He had dark, curly hair, pale, beige skin, and nice teeth. Most fae men were tall, and he was no exception.

Realizing she'd been staring, she chuckled. "Am I that obvious?" She glanced at her friends over her shoulder, and they gave her a thumbs up. They'd told her if a man offered to buy her a drink, she had to accept. It was a tradition, according to Monroe.

Braddock hadn't been too happy to learn his husband participated in the ritual at his own pre-wedding celebration, but Monroe had waved him off. "*It's flattering —and a free night out.*"

"I earn enough money to buy the entire tavern," Braddock had grumbled.

"Let us have our fun." Monroe had then shooed her toward the bar.

"No, but I haven't seen you here before, and I would've noticed," the man said. Fawn almost rolled her eyes. She didn't think dealing with his ridiculous lines was worth a free drink. "I'm Sadler."

She took his outstretched hand. "Fawn."

"Fawn," he echoed, with a half-smile. "I like it. Can I buy you a drink?"

"Yes, thank you." She wanted to get this over with and return to her friends.

"Invite him to a corner table," an all-too-familiar voice whispered in her ear.

She nearly jumped out of her skin and spun around, bumping into something solid but seeing nothing. Either she lost her mind, or her mate was playing invisible man again. "You couldn't give me one night?" she whispered, without heat.

"Did you say something?" Sadler held out her drink.

"Nope," she squeaked and cleared her throat.

Dean's breath ghosted against her cheek. "The corner table, Fawn."

"Would you like to sit at a table?" She searched the room and spotted one against a far wall. "I see one over there."

"I'd love to." Sadler swept out his arm. "After you."

She hurried to the table, set her drink down, and pulled out a chair. Dean's large hands grabbed her waist and stopped her from sitting. Her skirts ruffled and her underwear ripped away.

Fawn gasped, and Sadler's concerned eyes traced over her face. "Are you okay?"

"He can't see your skirts move," Dean whispered so low she almost didn't hear.

Sadler took a seat, and Dean slowly pulled her down into his lap. She jerked when his warm fingers circled her clit and ran through her folds. Fawn bit her lip and tried to concentrate on the man across from her. "Are you from here?" she asked, fighting to steady her voice.

Dean picked up his movements, dipping his finger into her heat. Part of her loved the thrill; the other part wanted to kill him. How in the fuck was she supposed to speak to this man with her fiancé teasing her?

"I am." Sadler drank his ale. "Where are you from?"

Fawn had never liked mundane conversation, and she liked it even less with Dean's fingers gliding across her slick lips. "The Mountain Kingdom. I moved here about two weeks ago."

Sadler took another drink. "What brought you here?"

Dean roughly pushed his fingers inside up to the knuckles. The bastard curled them just right, and she squirmed, holding in a moan. Trying to think of a lie through her lust-addled brain proved more difficult than she thought. "I moved here with my friend. She's from here."

"Who is she?" Sadler leaned his elbows on the table with interest. "I might know her."

Dean moved his fingers faster, and when her muscles started to pulse, he removed them. Both relief and frustration coursed through her. "Naomi. She's right there." She pointed at her friends, who were already watching.

Monroe waved with a goofy grin, and Braddock scowled in their direction.

Dean lifted Fawn slightly, aligned his cock with her entrance, and slid her down until her cheeks met his thighs. She clamped a hand over her mouth to stifle the sounds trying to escape. Sadler was going to think she was crazy, hovering in the air and emitting weird noises.

"To everyone else, you haven't moved," Dean murmured. "But they can see your face and hear you."

Fucking hell.

Sadler turned back to her and nodded. "You know Monroe?"

She adjusted herself on Dean's cock for more friction, but his hands held her firmly in place to keep her from moving. It felt more torturous than when he fucked her with his fingers. "Yes. I met him at the palace when I moved here."

"He's a nice guy," Sadler agreed. "His husband is terrifying though." He glanced back over to where Braddock glared at anyone who walked too close to Monroe. "Do you work at the palace?"

Dean flexed his cock inside her, the slight jump enough to set her on fire. She tried to move her hips again, but his fingers dug into the cushion of her flesh. "Be still. You'll warm my cock until I allow you to move."

Fawn rolled her lips together. "I do." Not a complete lie—being the king's mate was a full-time job. "Tell him you're a maid," Dean instructed, the crowd's chatter smothering his voice from carrying across the table.

Pretending to look around the room, she whispered, "You have to stop. He'll recognize me when I'm announced as queen."

"I glamoured your face when you walked in," he said, far too amused.

She jabbed her elbow back into his gut, delighting in his surprised grunt. Who changed someone's face and didn't tell them? "I'm a maid. What do you do?"

Sadler's face lit up. "I'm a cartographer for the crown."

"You make maps?" she asked, not entirely sure.

"I do. I'm working on a new one that's giving me a hard time." Honest to the gods, the man reached into the satchel she hadn't realized he carried and retrieved a rolled-up piece of parchment and a pair of round, gold spectacles. He slid them into place, pushed their drinks aside, and unrolled the map. "It's the capital."

Trying not to be rude, she leaned over the table to look. Arcadia, the name of the Garden Kingdom capital, was written in perfect scroll across the top. Beyond downtown streets and a few landmarks, the page was sparse.

Dean rocked her hips to steal her attention, and she sucked in a sharp breath. "How do you know the distances between everything?" He rocked her again and she gripped the edge of the table. Fortunately, Sadler didn't notice as he launched into an explanation about measurements and chains.

Fawn tried to pay attention to the poor man, she really did, but if not for Dean idly rocking her back and forth, she'd have dozed off within minutes. Who knew drawing maps was so boring?

"—and it takes a lot of arithmetic," Sadler droned on. "I graduated top of my class, so it wasn't an issue for me."

Dean chuckled, brought two fingers to her mouth, and eased them inside. She twirled her tongue around them, and he slid them out and under her skirt to massage her clit.

"*Gods,*" she breathed.

Sadler laughed. "I know. It really is amazing. Wait until I tell you about using the constellations."

Dean's fingers picked up speed, and right as her body started to tingle, he stopped and pinched her clit. She hit her fist on the table and clenched her teeth to keep from cursing.

Sadler stopped talking, his hands mid-air, and frowned. "Are you okay?"

She nodded too enthusiastically and tried to laugh, but it came out strangled. "I banged my knee."

Dean tugged her flush with his chest and whispered, "Ride my cock, darling, and look him in the eye while I fuck you."

Needing something to cool her down, Fawn grabbed her drink, downed the clear liquor, and almost spit the disgusting drink out.

"Are you sure you're alright?" Sadler had dropped his hands, his face pinched with worry.

She tried to smile back. "Just numbing the pain. It really hurt."

Her chest, heaving and flushed, drew Sadler's attention. The dress she wore tonight dipped in a deep V, and his gaze landed on her cleavage. His eyes darkened, as if remembering why he'd bought her a drink to begin with, and he smiled suggestively. "Want me to massage it?" *What a creep.*

Dean lifted her until only the tip of his cock remained inside and slammed her down, not giving her the chance to adjust before doing it again. "Oh *gods*," she choked out.

"Eyes on him," Dean said, anger threading his voice. She knew him well enough to know he wanted to rip Sadler's arm off for offering to touch her.

Realizing she could get payback of her own for this unfair little game, she gave Sadler her best sultry smile. "You could come to my place after." Dean's growl made her laugh, and she tried to pass it off as a flirtatious giggle.

Sadler shifted in his seat and licked his lips. "I'd like that."

The warmth of Dean's hand returning to her clit made her eyes roll back in her head. She rocked her hips with his movements and her breathing picked up, unable to mask anymore.

"Fawn? Are you..." Sadler made a choking sound, and she met his dark eyes.

"Now everyone sees you rocking that needy little cunt on the chair," Dean chuckled. "Give them a show, darling."

"We can leave now." Sadler reached beneath the table to adjust himself. "This is the hottest shit I've ever seen."

"He's right, but you're all mine," Dean whispered, his voice rough and gravelly.

Shit, she forgot about her friends standing to the side watching them. No one could see her real face, but they knew who she was. She would never be able to look them in the eye again.

Dean slipped a long finger alongside his cock and pressed the spot she needed. She quivered and released a string of expletives.

Sadler jumped up. "Babe, we can go in the back if you're desperate."

Fawn cried out and jerked around Dean's cock, coming harder than she'd thought possible. Her cum coated his cock and dripped down the sides, sticking to their thighs. Dean moved her body faster until his loud moan filled the air. Sadler stepped back, confused. Strings of hot cum released from her mate's throbbing cock until it mixed with hers and covered them both.

"Oh my gods," she rasped. People stared, turning her on even more.

Fawn *saw* Dean's long arm reach past her and take Sadler's ale. The man's face paled and he stumbled back. "Where did..." He looked around. "You appeared out of thin air!"

Others around them gasped and whispered, and Fawn twisted around to look at her mate, sporting his usual disguise.

"I've been here the whole time; you were too busy talking maps and staring at her tits to notice." Dean chugged Sadler's ale and slammed down the mug.

"You didn't have to insult his maps," she muttered, feeling a little sorry for the guy.

Dean grabbed her neck, yanked her back, and kissed her—a possessive claim, as if fucking her in front of the entire room wasn't enough.

Lifting Fawn off his cock, he set her on the ground, stood to tuck himself back in, and nodded to Sadler. "We'd love to stay and chat, but I need to fuck her again, and that little chair won't cut it."

He smacked Fawn's ass and led her out of the tavern, leaving a roomful of gawkers wondering what the hell just happened.

The next day, Fawn tried to hide her discomfort as she waddled down the hall with Cassandra at her side. The night before, Dean had fucked her all night, in all positions, to *"remind her who she belonged to,"* he'd said. She'd reminded him that it was he who demanded she sit with Sadler alone. He wasn't upset with her, but seeing another man go after her had snapped something inside him. His words.

She'd had fun with him at the tavern, and they'd probably do it again at some point. The time ticked by with each step, and she wondered how much longer Dean would be. He'd wanted her to join him in a meeting with his father, but she'd told him she'd rather walk on nails barefoot. He'd reluctantly left her to her own devices but insisted on Cassandra or Braddock accompanying her.

She'd opted for Cassandra and a walk through the gardens to visit Tickles. At the bottom of the stairs to the main floor, she rounded the corner and ran smack into Emi.

"I'm sorry," the girl apologized profusely. When she realized it was Fawn, her eyes widened, and she curtsied. "Your Highness."

"Emi, right? We've never been officially introduced."

Emi curtsied again. "I'm just here to find my sister, then I'll be gone, I promise. My father asked me to retrieve her."

Fawn's brows knit. "You don't have to apologize for being here." The girl had been nothing but polite, and Fawn didn't understand her fear.

Emi looked just as confused. "Oh, thank you."

She started to skirt around Fawn but spun around. "Wait." Moving closer, she lowered her voice to a whisper. "Stay away from my sister."

Fawn's scalp tingled, and her spine steeled. "Are you threatening me?" This family had pissed her off enough. If she had to order Cali out of the palace herself, she would.

Emi shook her head and looked around frantically. "No. You don't understand. I'm trying to help you." The girl sounded scared, and Fawn's confusion grew. "Please, just stay away from her. If you see her coming and you're alone, get away as fast as you can."

"Emi, do you know something?"

"I must go. I'm sorry." The girl ran off and disappeared around the nearest corner.

Cassandra coiled into a small pyramid, staring at Emi's retreating form.

"Is that why you're always with Cali?" Fawn asked the serpent. "Do you sense she's a threat?" Cassandra looked at her like she was stupid, and Fawn sighed. "We need to teach you to read lips."

30

Fawn tried not to worry about Emi's warning. Maybe Emi only meant her sister was a bitch, not that she'd plotted something nefarious. Then again, Fawn hadn't known Warren wanted to kill her. Her judgment of people couldn't be trusted.

An hour wandering the gardens' hedge maze left Fawn hungry and bored. Her stomach growled, and she set Tickles down. "I'm going to get food, little guy. I'll see you tomorrow." She still wasn't sure if he understood, but she talked to him anyway, just as she did with Cassandra.

She wound her way through the maze and glanced at Cassandra's massive form. "Will they allow you in the kitchens?" The *familiar* ignored her and she shrugged. "Guess we'll find out."

Cali's voice penetrated the air from the other side of the hedge wall. "I know you need her to have your heir, but why do you have to marry her?"

Fawn ground to a halt, unable to move or blink. A deep male murmur responded too low to make out.

"But what if you actually fall in love with her?" Sniffling. "Promise me you won't." More soft murmurs.

Did nobles call their children heirs too since they were ranked higher than others? If Cali had found another man to latch on to, that would make Fawn's entire year. Then they could move out and have a happily ever after somewhere else.

Fawn's ribs felt like they cracked under the force of her heartbeat as she ran quietly on her tiptoes to the edge of the hedge wall to see who stood on the other side. She poked her head around the corner to get a glimpse of Cali's secret lover.

She spotted two figures, and the ground seemed to vanish beneath her. *No.* She shook her head to force the image to reform into something else, but nothing worked.

Dean, *her* Dean, cupped Cali's face in his hands, whispering to her with so much love and adoration on his face that Fawn had to look away. Her eyes burned, nearly blinding her, yet she forced herself to keep watching. Maybe she was wrong. Maybe it wasn't what it looked like. *He loves me. He wouldn't do this.*

"I miss you," Cali admitted softly, almost too quiet for Fawn to hear. "You're always with *her*." He said something in reply, but only low rumbles reached Fawn. Then the cracks in her ribs extended through her entire body as she watched her mate lower his mouth to Cali's. The passionate kiss stole Fawn's breath, and a sob escaped before she could muffle it.

Dean and Cali turned quickly, and his face turned ashen. He scraped his hands through his hair, his grey eyes darting between the two girls. "*Fuck.*" Fawn focused on his emotions, praying for anything to explain this away since he wouldn't.

Nothing. The bond had gone silent.

He started toward her. *Yes,* she silently begged. *Please explain why you had your lips on someone else.*

Cali grabbed his arm and tugged him back, her voice pleading. "Stay with me."

Cassandra had moved toward them, leaving Fawn behind. *Is that why she's been following Cali around?* The hurt was unbearable. Dean turned to Cali fully, ignoring Fawn, like she wasn't worth his time now that the charade was up.

She turned and ran back through the hedge maze until her legs burned and a stitch in her side forced her to slow down. Images of Cali and Dean played on a loop, breaking her heart until there was nothing left.

None of it made sense. She'd felt his love for her. Could he love her that much and also love Cali? Fawn squared her shoulders and marched toward the palace. *He might love her, but he loves me too, and I'm going to fight for what's mine.*

"Your Highness?" Fawn whirled around at the sound of Emi's voice and the girl gasped. "Oh my gods, are you okay?"

The worst thing to do when someone is upset is ask them if they're okay. Her fragile hold on her emotions snapped, and the hurt poured out of her like salty rain. She tried her old tricks to shove it all down, but nothing worked.

Emi ran over and wrapped her arm around Fawn's shoulders. "I'm so sorry you found out that way."

Fawn raised her blurry eyes. "You knew?"

"I didn't know for sure, but I suspected they were still seeing each other." Emi led her toward the palace courtyard. "I never found proof, but Cali mentioned taking matters into her own hands so they wouldn't have to sneak around."

"That's why you told me to stay away from her."

Emi nodded. "I love my sister, but since getting engaged to the king, she's slipped farther into her delusions. My parents don't see it. They never did," she added bitterly.

Emi pushed through a side garden gate into the palace courtyard and released Fawn's shoulders. "I'll take you to my house and you can hide out there until you decide what to do."

"I'm going to fight for him," she declared. "He loves me,

and we're mates. I'm not giving him up, but I need time to think of what to do next."

Emi's brows hit her hairline. "Good for you. My sister would make a terrible queen." Unhooking the lightweight hooded cloak around her shoulders, she held it out to Fawn. "Put this on so people don't recognize you. The guards will report back to the king."

Fawn fastened the cloak at her throat and pulled the over-sized hood low to shield her face. She'd accept the sanctuary Emi offered and figure out her next course of action.

&

Fawn stood in the receiving room of the Galla's home, waiting for Emi to return with tea. The family lived lavishly on a grand estate just outside the palace walls.

Fabric rustled and Fawn turned around to Emi standing in the doorway sans tea. "Do you need help? I don't mind," Fawn offered. "I was a maid at the Mountain Kingdom palace for years."

"I thought you were a whore," Emi deadpanned.

Fawn recoiled at the girl's lifeless tone and even more life-less eyes. "I worked at the pleasure house for fun, but my primary job was a maid."

Emi's lip curled into an ugly sneer. "Why would the gods mate someone like you to a royal?"

"Did I do something to upset you?" *Or do you have an evil twin?* The girl she'd run away with and this one couldn't be more different. The light glinted off a metal blade in Emi's hand, and Fawn swore.

"You're a weak slut who doesn't deserve the royal title," she said, her voice too calm for the situation.

Fawn gauged the distance from herself to the door. Emi

stood halfway, and she didn't know how fast the girl was. "Did your sister try to have me killed before I came here?"

Emi rolled her eyes, the action making her look like a normal eighteen-year-old, and not the psychopath she was. "Cali told Daddy that Dean claimed to still feel the mate bond even though you were dead. Daddy spoke with Henry about it, but everyone wrote Dean off as delusional. But Daddy didn't want to chance it. He'd fixated on Cali being queen and our family being elevated to royal status. He dug around and discovered you were alive and well, living in the Mountain Kingdom."

Fawn's mind spun. "He tried to have me killed because he wanted to be related to a royal?" She waved her hand at the grandeur around her. "Don't you have enough?"

"It's not about money; it's about prestige," Emi stated and held up her dagger. "If you'll give in, I'll make it quick."

Fawn didn't believe that for a second. Emi ran forward, and Fawn darted to the side and rounded the closest settee. The other girl anticipated her move and went the other way. Fawn screamed, knocked over a side table, and bolted into the hall.

Looking side to side, she ran left and hoped it led to the entrance. "Fawn," Emi sang. "You'll never find your way out of here."

Why is this house so fucking big? Her sandals slapped the marble floors like a beacon, but she couldn't afford to stop and take them off. *They must not have rugs in their halls so they can hear their victims running away.*

Fawn careened around another corner and cried out with relief when she entered the foyer. Almost there. A hand reached out and snatched her hair from behind, yanking her back. Her scalp screamed, but it was nothing compared to the excruciating pain of Emi's dagger sliding between her ribs.

Fawn's knees gave out and she sank to the floor as Cali

strolled through the front entrance looking smug. "Where are the servants?" Her eyes hit Fawn with confusion and then dread when they trailed to her chest. "Emi, what did you do?"

Cali ran forward and dropped to her knees beside Fawn. "Get my bag."

"No," Emi said flatly. "If she dies, Dean is yours."

Cali glanced back down at Fawn and sat back on her haunches. "Please tell me you didn't do this for me."

Emi's slow grin held a promise of evil. "Why? Would that make you feel guilty? You signed her death warrant when you ran to Daddy, crying about Dean thinking he still felt her emotions." Cali paled. "Daddy hired General Craven to kill the half-human bitch, but the general disappeared. He didn't have time to find another to do his bidding before Dean married her and knew *I* was the only person he could trust to do it." Her face fell into girlish fear, lip tremble, and all. "Who would think a sweet young girl barely out of school could do something this horrible?" She cackled. "Let her die, or we'll all die in her place. The king won't let us live when she tells him what happened. Leave now, and we'll all get the life we deserve."

Cali stood and stepped away. "Does Mother know?"

Emi rolled her eyes. "She never would have agreed. She's too soft like you." She made a shooing motion. "Leave. You don't need to watch this."

Fawn tried to talk, to beg Cali for help, but she couldn't draw in a deep enough breath. She tried to cough and cried out from the pain. Her last hope at survival walked out of the room without looking back.

Emi hovered over her, smiling. "I've never watched a *person* die before. With animals it's hard to tell their emotions, but with you, they're written all over your face. It's fascinating to watch you accept your fate."

A sickening feeling twisted in Fawn's gut, and the world around her faded away.

§

Cali disappeared into the hallway, took off her shoes, and sprinted toward her old room for her healer bag she kept here for emergencies.

Bile crept up her throat at the thought of her family doing this for status. Their father had always been ambitious, but this was horrifying. To think Cali was the catalyst... she'd never forgive herself if Fawn died. She should have bowed out when Dean picked his mate over her, but she loved him and hadn't wanted to give him up without a fight.

She'd be lying if she said Emi's offer hadn't tempted her. It would be so easy to say Fawn ran away after seeing the glamour of Dean and Cali in the gardens, and if Fawn had run, Cali wouldn't have cared.

But Cali couldn't watch an innocent person die. That went against everything she believed in. She swiped her bag and ran back to the foyer. Leaving Fawn with Emi had been a risk, but she banked on the fact that Emi would find Fawn's suffering interesting and would leave her be until she died on her own.

She paused before walking into the foyer. Going in without a plan was foolish. Emi wouldn't hurt her, but she would kill Fawn before Cali could get to her.

"I found her like this," Emi cried. "I don't know what happened."

A dangerous hiss and more fake cries from Emi. She wouldn't know a real emotion if it stabbed her in the heart, but she was an excellent actress.

Cali ran into the room and Cassandra rose up protectively over Fawn's unconscious form and bared her red fangs. Cali held up her bag and opened it to show her healer supplies. "I'm going to help her."

Only fate could have sent Cassandra to Fawn's side when she did. The serpent had been accompanying Cali more and more lately, and she sent a silent prayer to the gods for the *familiar's* newfound interest.

Emi's mask fell into one of annoyance behind Cassandra, but Cali ignored her. Slowly, Cali dropped down beside Fawn and assessed the damage. Bubbled up blood leaked form the sides of her mouth, and one side of her chest caved with each labored breath. *Fuck.* Cali had only vented a punctured lung once in her life, and it was with a mentor at her side.

"It's going to be okay," she lied to herself. Fawn blacking out was for the best because this was going to be excruciating.

Emi started pacing behind Cassandra as her composure slipped. The calculating glint in her eye told Cali all she needed to know: her sister wasn't done.

An aggravated Emi who didn't get her way was dangerous. Cali didn't know what her sister was capable of. At best, she'd run and exact her revenge later—and there *would* be a later. Emi didn't let things go.

Emi's scheming kept her occupied, allowing Cali to stare Cassandra in the eye and mime stabbing Fawn then point at her sister. Hot tears tracked down her face as she did it again, imploring the serpent to understand. Emi was her sister, she loved her, but she was sick, and that sickness wouldn't ever go away.

Cassandra nodded once, flipped, and extended her red fangs. Emi started fake crying again. "I'm so scared. When will Daddy be home?" she asked Cali. "He'll know what to do." Her sister's ability to deceive and manipulate terrified her.

Cassandra looked back, and Cali nodded once, sealing her

sister's fate. Cali squeezed her eyes shut and clapped her hands over her ears to muffle her sister's screams.

Collecting herself, she opened her eyes, avoiding her sister's body, and assessed Fawn again. "I'm sorry," she whispered and unloaded her bag for the procedure. "I'm going to save you."

31

Dean sat behind his large oak desk and waited for his father to speak. For the first time in his life, the former king looked defeated.

"I didn't lie about the death certificate," he said finally.

Dean laughed humorlessly. "You're accusing the Human Queen and King of sabotaging my relationship with my mate?" It was a bold accusation that could start the first-ever war between kingdoms.

"No." His father sat back in his chair and scrubbed a hand over his face. "When we went to the Human Kingdom, your mother insisted I catch up with the king while Charlotte took her to the archives." Dean stayed silent, and Henry shook his head. "I didn't question her when she told me about your mate's death. Why would I?"

"Question who?" Dean couldn't believe what his father implied.

Henry looked weary and aged beyond his years, not in body, but in spirit. His proud shoulders slumped, and his eyes dulled. "Your mother. She came to our room crying and blubbering about your mate's death. She had the records in her hands."

"And you think she lied?" Dean clarified. Why would his mother do that?

"I do. Queen Charlotte had no reason to lie about one of her subjects. Hell, she gave the Mountain King permission to retrieve his mate from the human lands."

"What reason would Mother have?" Dean's ears rang. He'd been prepared to kill his father, but his mother? His quiet, meek mother, who followed her husband's every order and turned the other way instead of defending her son?

"I don't know, but her deception could have ruined us all." His father's familiar anger appeared, contorting his face. "She knows the importance of a mate bond. Without it, there was no guarantee your children would have been powerful enough to protect our lands."

Dean had been prepared to call his father a liar, but he knew the man too well. He'd learned to read him at an early age for self-preservation, and the man's anger and confusion were genuine.

"I know you hate me," his father interrupted his thoughts. "I know I was harsh on you, as my father was on me, but it had to be that way. You couldn't grow up to be weak."

Dean barked out a sardonic laugh. "Harsh? You had the general beat the shit out of me." He stood and ripped his shirt off, the buttons flying across the room. "Look at what he did to me."

His father's eyes traced over his scars without a hint of regret. "And you are now better than any warrior in all of Eden. We are not only the protectors of our kingdom; we are the protectors of our world. We cannot risk the slightest crack in our strength."

The chair groaned under Dean when he dropped down and

leaned back. What kind of parent looks at the damage they've done and feels nothing? "You have until Fawn and I conceive to find another place to live."

"What?" his father sputtered. "You cannot kick us out of the palace."

Dean clasped his hands on his desk to keep from snapping his father's neck. "I would never let a monster like you around my children. You're lucky I've decided to let you live." Standing, he walked to the door and opened it for his father to leave. "I cannot say the same about your wife."

His father stared at him as if he were the monster, and Dean held back the urge to laugh in the man's face. "You have no idea what kind of monster I can be to those who hurt the ones I love."

"You said children," Henry said slowly. "Royals only have one heir. Is your mate pregnant with someone else's child?"

"We plan to adopt more children," Dean replied, unsure why he told his father anything.

"Your mother will be heartbroken if you do not let her see them," his father admonished. "She always talks about when you have an heir."

An heir. That was all his father saw him as, but he would never make his daughter feel like she was a means to an end. "She should have thought about that before she lied about my mate's death."

With a last, long look, his father left. Dean shut the door and sat back down, staring at the wall, a numbness spreading through him. His mother watched him become a broken shell of himself when he thought Fawn had died. He'd always known she was a coward, but he never thought she was blatantly cruel.

The question was why?

Dean closed his eyes to connect with Cassandra to find out where Fawn was. *"We're in the maze in the middle of the gardens,"* Cassandra greeted him.

"I'll be there shortly. Let me know if you exit the maze before I'm there."

"Hurry," the *familiar* ordered. *"I can't hear what she's saying, but I think she misses you."* Dean cut the connection and jogged to go find his girl, grinning like an idiot. He missed her too.

Minutes later, pain struck him in the chest, and his knees nearly buckled. Am I having a heart attack? He focused on his breathing and realized it wasn't a physical pain. *Fawn.*

He snapped his eyes shut. *"What's happening? Where's Fawn? Is she hurt?"*

"She's safe, but she's upset. I don't understand why," Cassandra admitted. *"We saw these three, and she started crying."*

Cali and a man Dean had never seen before stood in an embrace, and his mother stood beside them. They were speaking, but Cassandra couldn't hear them. *"I really wish you had ears."*

"Me too."

Cali and the man turned toward Fawn and Cassandra. They looked upset. Dean's mother spotted Cassandra and her eyes widened. She said something quickly and stepped out of sight. Cali grabbed the man's arm and pulled him away from Fawn.

"Get closer," Dean urged.

Cassandra slithered along the walkway until she circled the couple, and the man tried to jump away. Cali smiled at Cassandra and said something.

"Why is your mother hiding?" his *familiar* mused.

"I don't know." What about seeing those three would upset his mate?

Cassandra turned, but Fawn had vanished. *"She must have run."*

Dean cut the connection and sprinted toward the maze.

Dean ran through the gardens with no sign of Fawn. Whatever they said to her in the maze upset her, and he had a sinking feeling it had to do with him. The heartbreak he felt from her scared him shitless. There was no place she could run that he wouldn't find her, but he hoped she'd talk to him before leaving the palace. Still, he needed to find her as soon as possible to fix whatever the three of them had broken.

He started toward Tickles' new enclosure but fear almost doubled him over. What the fuck was happening? A burning pain lanced his chest, and he stumbled. *Fawn.* He started to run and scream her name but skidded to a stop as the bond faded, much like all those years ago.

Panic cut off his breath, and his vision spotted. *Not again.* Cassandra interrupted his spiraling thoughts. *"You need to get to the Galla estate and bring a healer."*

No, no, no, no. *"What the fuck is going on?"* Cassandra blocked out her surroundings, and he knew his worst nightmare was coming to fruition. She cut their connection, and he sprinted toward the courtyard.

Dean paused at the gates to instruct a guard to sound the alarm in the palace. Any member of the Galla family was to be imprisoned until further questioning, and every healer in the palace was to report to the Galla estate.

If Fawn died, not even the gods could save the kingdom from his destruction. If she didn't get to live, no one did.

Dean burst through the Galla's front entrance, wild and feral with fear. He took in the foyer: Emi's dead body covered in bright red veins, Cassandra hovering over a body with Cali on the other side, working diligently. The serpent moved her massive body out of the way, and his entire world stopped. His beautiful mate lay on the floor, her skin the color of death, with blood spilling out of her mouth and chest.

Dean hit his knees and reached for her, but Cali elbowed his arm away. "Don't touch her."

She didn't even look up from her work to warn him; she just knocked his hand out of the way and kept working. He'd never felt as helpless as he did watching Fawn's shallow breaths shudder out of her blood-tinged mouth.

Cali did something, and Fawn's body jerked. "What's happening?" he demanded, his words cracking. Dean gently pushed a piece of hair out of Fawn's face. "You can't leave me here."

"Stop speaking about her as if she's dying," Cali snapped.

He nodded and swallowed around the knot in his throat. "I love you," he murmured, hoping Fawn could hear him. "When you're better, we'll find Tickles a friend. We'll find him ten, but first you have to wake up."

If she didn't live, neither would he. The gods could give the throne back to his father or bless a new heir, for all he cared, because there wasn't a day in this life he could survive without her.

32

Dean kept vigil at Fawn's bedside, watching her chest rise and fall. Other healers arrived and helped Cali finish her work. They praised her for keeping a level head and saving Fawn's life.

Dean owed her everything, and whatever she wanted—other than him—he would give in abundance. They'd given his mate a tincture to keep her unconscious so the patch over her wound wouldn't be disturbed. A temporary valve, they'd called it. Dean didn't care what it was called, as long as it saved her.

He dipped a clean cloth in a nearby water basin and continued to clean the blood from Fawn's face. A heavy presence entered the room, and he knew without looking that Lilith stood behind him.

Once they told him Fawn would be okay, he'd started piecing together Lilith's riddle. If Cali had moved out of the palace, she might not have been there to save his mate's life. And all those years ago, he'd wondered who Lilith wanted Cassandra to stay with. *Cali.* Had she not followed her, she couldn't have kept Emi from stopping Cali from saving Fawn.

There were other pieces to her cryptic messages he didn't understand, and only one person had the answers.

"Why couldn't I tell Fawn that Cali had to stay to save her life?" Dean dropped the bloody cloth in the basin and twisted around.

Lilith approached Fawn's bedside with measured steps and peered down at her sleeping form. "She would have reacted differently to seeing you and Cali in the gardens." Lilith's brows squished together. "I don't know how. That part isn't clear, but she wouldn't have gone with Emi."

"Going with Emi is what almost got her killed," Dean ground out. "How is that bad?"

"If Emi hadn't been the one to attempt to kill her, someone more skilled would have. No matter what course of action you took, she would have been killed. This was the only scenario where she lived."

Dean scoffed. "If you don't want her dead, why was death her possible fate?"

"Death is everyone's possible fate. Some I see, some I don't. In the aether, I have no power to stop it, but here, I can make a difference."

Lilith's chin lifted, the pride and defiance in the stance so utterly mortal that it took Dean by surprise. "Is a Fate supposed to care if people live or die?"

"No," she responded softly, "but living among mortals makes it hard not to." Her slender lips pressed together. "Fuck the gods and the rules of the aether."

Dean sputtered a laugh. He'd never heard her speak with such emotion, let alone curse. "For what it's worth, Eden is better with you in it, and I'm not just saying that because you saved my mate. You saved me years ago, and you do what you can to protect our world."

Dean detected a slight sheen in the Fate's eyes. "Dean Hawthorne, are you trying to get your picture on my wall?"

He grinned wide. "You were going to put me up there anyway."

"May I come in?" His mother poked her head into the room, and Dean's blood simmered in his veins.

Lilith's eyes thinned. "I'll give you two some privacy." At the door, she ignored Anne and told Dean, "Fawn will wake up tomorrow."

He tipped his head in thanks, and his mother entered the room, the picture of concern. The urge to kill her overcame him. "Why are you here?"

She recoiled and stumbled back a step. "I've come to check on my daughter-in-law. What has gotten into you?"

Dean had asked Cali about what happened in the gardens to upset Fawn and send her into Emi's arms. She'd admitted to his mother approaching her with a plan to send Fawn running. Emi was supposed to help Fawn leave, not take her to their estate to kill her.

"Why did you lie about Fawn's death?" Anne blanched, and he lifted a hand. "Do not attempt to lie."

The queen's chin trembled, and she searched the room for another chair. Falling into one in the far corner, she met his furious stare. "Your father and I would visit the other kingdoms periodically to discuss political matters. After you were born, on each trip, I collected the birth records of every child born on the same day as you." She settled her gaze on Fawn, a wash of regret encompassing her. "When you heard Fawn's name, I knew who she was—a half-human girl in the garden region of the Human Kingdom."

"What do you have against humans?" he demanded. "There is nothing wrong with her heritage."

His mother's hand shot to her chest. "Nothing!"

"Then why?" Dean fought down the emotion clogging his throat. "Why did you steal her from me? And once you saw how much she meant to me, why did you try to take her again with your bullshit glamour act?"

"I knew a half-human girl was too weak to be a fae queen," she replied, all traces of remorse gone. "You need a queen who matches you in strength and knows the ins and outs of our politics. You think a weak maid with no training has what it takes to rule at your side?"

"You will die for what you've done," he vowed, and she stood quickly to run but he beat her to the door and wrapped his hand around her throat. "You took her from me. Fate brought her back, and you tried to take her again." He squeezed tighter until she turned blue. "Don't worry, Mother. I'll not sully her room with the piss and shit you'll release when you take your last breath." Dean dragged her to the door and handed her to the man guarding the hall. "Take her to the dungeons."

"*Dean*," she screamed and ripped out of the guard's hold. Her strength outmatched theirs, a fact Dean had overlooked.

He snatched her around the neck again and spoke to the guard. "Get a healer."

His mother tried to fight him, but thanks to her lack of interference growing up, he was stronger than even his father. She couldn't match him. One of the palace healers, an older man who'd treated many of Dean's childhood wounds, jogged down the hall with the guard on his heels.

Dean jerked his chin toward Fawn's room. "Get a sedative for my mother."

Anne fought harder against his hold. "You can't do this! I am your *mother*!"

He laughed bitterly. "You're nothing but the bitch who stole my mate and stood by while your husband abused me for years." The healer appeared with a damp cloth and placed it over Anne's nose. Her body sagged and Dean tipped his chin to the guard. "Take her. Remember, she is a royal and can make you see whatever she wants you to. Once her cell is locked, do not under any circumstances unlock it until I tell you to."

≀●

Did someone pour sand down my throat? Fawn thought groggily as she blinked open her eyes. Pain radiated through her chest and abdomen, and her head throbbed like crazy.

"Fawn?"

Dean? A warm hand caressed her cheek. "Wake up, darling."

Her eyes roved until they landed on his face. "What's going on?" Why did her mouth taste of copper?

"Get a healer," Dean ordered someone Fawn couldn't see. He turned his handsome face back to hers. "What do you remember?"

Her brows bent as she searched her memory. Everything came flooding back. The hedge maze. Emi led her away to kill her. Cali walked away. "You were kissing Cali in the gardens." She laid her head back and forced the burning in her eyes to subside.

"That wasn't me." He grabbed her hand, but she snatched it away. "My mother glamoured Cali and another man to look like me. Did you hear him say anything?"

The queen used her royal glamour to make Fawn think Dean was unfaithful? "No. Well, you—*he* said fuck, but it came out like a growl. You do growl from time to time."

He reached for her hand again, and this time she let him. "The fact that you doubted me means I don't show you I love you enough." She tried to sit up and hissed as a sharp pain shot through her torso. "Don't try to move," Dean said, panic edging his voice.

Fawn rolled her head to look at him. "You show me you love me more than enough." Her eyes filled with tears. "You really do, but I had no way to explain what I saw. I saw you, and it looked as real as you do now. Why would I ever think your own mother would glamour me just to sabotage us?"

Dean's lips brushed against her cheeks, kissing her tears away. "I understand. I don't blame you."

"I wasn't leaving," she whispered.

He pulled back. "What do you mean?"

"I wasn't running away," she clarified. "I told Emi I planned on fighting for you. I knew you loved me, and even if you loved her too, I was going to fight."

A blinding smile spread across his face and love pulsed down the bond. "I love you and only you."

She swiped her nose with the sheet—gross, but better than snot running down her face. "I love you too." Fawn looked around the infirmary room. "How am I alive?"

Dean smoothed her hair out of her face. "Cali saved you."

That couldn't be right. "Emi told Cali to let me die so she could be queen, and Cali left me on the floor."

"She came back and told Cassandra to kill Emi," he said softly. "Were it not for her, you'd be dead."

"Why would she do that?"

"I'm not as evil as I pretend to be," Cali teased as she walked into the room. Fawn swallowed a gasp. The woman looked haunted. The look in her eyes didn't match her playful tone. "I need to examine you."

Fawn couldn't figure her out. "You walked away."

"To get my healer bag," Cali replied without looking up. "I wouldn't have let you die without trying to save you first."

Words escaped Fawn as she stared at the woman listening to her chest. "Thank you."

Cali nodded slightly and glanced at Dean. "Do you mind if I speak with Fawn alone?"

Fawn didn't bother protesting; she knew Dean wouldn't let her out of his sight.

"I'll be right outside," the traitor said to Cali and Fawn. She gawked after him, too stunned to yell and too sore to throw anything.

Cali checked Fawn's wound, and when everything checked out, she set her supplies aside and folded her arms across her chest. "I need to apologize for how I've treated you."

Great, now I feel guilty for not wanting to be alone with her. "You're forgiven. I was going to fight you for him too when I thought you were having a secret affair." Cali had the good graces to look ashamed. "That was a terrible thing to do, by the way."

Cali bit her lip and dropped her gaze to the floor. "Look," she started. "I am sorry for how I acted. I thought you were the villain in my story."

Fawn huffed out a laugh and groaned with the movement. "I guess in a way I was."

"No." Cali dashed at a tear. "Fate is the only true villain in our lives."

The infirmary door burst open, and Naomi and Monroe ran in. "You're awake," Monroe cried and hurried to her bedside. Cali and Fawn exchanged a loaded look, both conveying their regrets. With a tip of her chin, Cali slipped from the room, leaving Fawn to wonder if there would ever be a day they could be friends. Probably not; there was a lot of hurt on both their ends, but anything is possible.

Naomi dropped into Dean's chair with a small box in her

hands. "Did you hear that Cassandra ate that little bitch that tried to kill you?"

Fawn's eyes bugged out of her head. "She *ate* her?"

"She *bit* her," Dean chuckled, sauntering through the door. He frowned at Naomi now occupying his chair and stood by Fawn's feet. "Cassandra's venom kills instantly."

"I brought you a surprise," Naomi said and handed her the box.

"I'll open it for her," Dean offered and intercepted the box. "She can't sit up."

Monroe shook his head quickly. "I don't think you want—"

Dean's scream startled everyone, and his face turned a shade no living person should sport. Tickles had jumped from the box onto Dean's chest and hung on for dear life. Braddock ran into the room looking around. Dean's eyes rolled back in his head and his body dropped like a rock. Braddock dove forward and saved the king's head from smashing against the ground.

Everyone stared at Dean's limp form and burst out laughing.

33

Dean watched his wife laugh with her grandparents across one of the palace drawing rooms. They'd postponed the wedding until she completely healed.

He'd offered to marry her in the infirmary, but she'd insisted on waiting. Today, as they walked down the aisle, she confessed why. *"I want to fuck my new husband any way I want,"* she'd said, causing him to go impossibly hard in front of everyone. Then he'd had to sit through their wedding dinner, and now their reception.

It was a small group of their family and friends gathered in an overly extravagant room, drinking and laughing the night away.

Fawn looked across the room, and when her grandmother turned to speak to her grandfather, she poked her tongue into the side of her cheek in rapid succession.

"That's it," Dean announced, jumping off the settee. "Thank you all for a lovely evening, but I would like to take my wife to our rooms."

Fawn's cheeks burned, and she refused to look at her

giggling grandmother. They said their goodbyes, and Dean scooped her into his arms.

"I'm going to make you pay for that," she threatened.

"Darling, I promise your grandmother knows we've had sex."

She whacked his chest. "That's not the point."

"If you hadn't been a little tease, I would have minded my manners."

They approached their rooms, and he cradled her with one arm, opened the door with the other, and carried her across the threshold. "Are you ready to bless every surface, wife?"

"Fuck me, sweetheart," she taunted with a wicked grin. Dean stalked into their bedroom and gently tossed her onto the bed. She sank into the soft mattress with a giggle and went up on her elbows.

He backed away, never taking his eyes off her, and pulled his desk chair to the middle of the room. He sat and crooked a finger. "Strip for me until there's nothing left but the silk between your thighs."

Fawn sat up slowly and stood, that salacious smile spreading. "You like to watch as much as you like to be watched."

"Only you, darling."

After kicking off her sandals, her slim fingers reached behind her and unfastened the golden rope at her waist. With slow, practiced movements, she pushed the sleeves off of her shoulders until they fell away, the material pooling at her feet.

"You didn't wear a breast band," he said, roughly.

"I'd hoped you'd touch me, but you didn't," she pouted, twisting the gold wedding band on her finger. "I had to slip away to the bathroom and touch myself."

Dean's breaths came out ragged, and his cock surged against his trousers. "Come here."

His mate obeyed, sauntering with a deliberate sway of her hips. "What will you do with me?"

He reached and tugged her the rest of the way and sucked one of her dark pink nipples into his mouth. Nails dug into his shoulders, and her body leaned into him for more. Switching to the other breast, he grazed a bite over the taut peak, and she moaned. "More."

Dean released her and sat back. "Dance."

Her lust-filled gaze held his. "You're a tease," she complained and spun around. He thought she'd walk off and demand he finish what he started, but her upper body disappeared behind her legs as she bent forward. He couldn't resist running his hands over her silk-covered ass.

She slapped his hand away. "No touching."

Chuckling, he raised his hands and leaned back again. Her spine unfurled as she straightened; her hips rolled. Fuck, his wife was sexy. She lowered to hover above his lap with her back to his chest and moved in a way he'd never seen before. Her ass grazed his stomach, his cock, his thighs, threatening to snap his resolve to keep his hands to himself.

After the sweetest torture, she turned herself around and straddled his lap, looping her hands over his shoulders as she continued to move. Her hips swayed to a music only she could hear, and her head fell back as she lost herself in the rhythm.

His knuckles whitened against the side of the chair, the need to touch her overwhelming him. One of her hands drifted down until she slipped it in her underwear, the red silk hiding her cunt from view. *Why did I tell her to keep them on?*

Her hand moved in rhythm with her hips, and he cursed when she ground herself against his cock to press her fingers deeper. "Dean," she breathed, her sultry moans snapping the last of his restraint.

He slid a hand down the back of her underwear and

skimmed across her flesh until he met her hand. "Hands off," she rasped.

"If you think I'll let you fuck yourself and not join, then you don't know me very well."

Dean pushed a finger into her wet pussy and pumped in counter-time to her rhythm. She bucked against them and leaned forward. "Gods."

The roll of her hips ceased in favor of bouncing, her tits jiggling in his face. He buried his face in her flesh and ravished them as they fucked her with their fingers. Short cries burst from her in rapid succession, and her walls throbbed around them until she screamed and fell forward to bury her face in his neck. Fawn's orgasm spread through him, and he gritted his teeth to keep from coming in his pants. He'd never seen anything more erotic.

They pulled out, and he caught her hand, lifting it to his mouth. He slipped both of their fingers between his lips and sucked them clean. "Fuck, baby."

He cradled her in his arms, rose to his feet, and laid her out on the bed to feast on her body. Fawn lifted to a sitting position. "Wait."

"I don't think I can," he answered truthfully.

Placing her hand on his chest, she guided him back and dropped to her knees in front of him. "Hungry for my cock, darling?"

His mate hummed and stripped him bare, running her hands up his thighs until one wrapped around his thick cock. It jumped in her hand, and she licked her lips. "I've wanted to taste you all day."

Dean plucked the pins out of her hair and threaded his fingers through the loose strands. "Then let me hear you gag."

Warmth wet the underside of his cock and licked the precum from the tip of his head. He sucked in a sharp breath and squeezed her hair tight. "Open up, wife."

Her pretty dusky rose lips parted and ensconced his cock. A shudder racked his body, and he flexed his hips on instinct. "I can't hold back," he groaned. "I'm going to fuck that smart mouth of yours, and you're going to swallow me like a good little whore."

Fawn hollowed out her cheeks in answer, and he surged forward until she gagged. "Relax your throat."

Her defiant eyes lifted, and he knew she would end him with pleasure. Grasping his hips, she yanked him forward, swallowing as his head hit her throat. "Oh, fuck."

His breaths came in quick pants, and his vision blurred as his wife worked him like she was born to suck cock. Her hot mouth possessed a magic of its own, working him to the fastest release of his life. The tingle fired at the base of his spine, and he tipped his head back, thrusting his hips faster. He couldn't speak or think as his orgasm ripped through him.

He moaned her name, and her lips trembled around him. Fawn's eyes rolled back in her head, and her body twitched with her own release. She swallowed every drop he emptied into her mouth and released his cock with strings of drool still connecting them.

"The bond," she panted. "Holy shit."

Dean crouched in front of her. "Now you know how I feel all the time." Marrying Fawn had strengthened her magic to that of a royal, letting her feel the bond in full—his orgasms included.

"We should have married sooner," she declared, ripping a laugh from him.

"I would have married you at Rennick's coronation," he murmured. His cock thickened, and he kissed her lightly. "On the bed so we can consummate this marriage properly."

Fawn scrambled onto the bed and spread her legs, showing him her perfect, dripping cunt. Dean crawled over her and rubbed his cock through her slick folds until she squirmed under him. "I need you inside me," she begged.

He hooked one of her knees over his shoulder and drove into her. The blankets slid with her body across the bed, his hold on her thigh and hip the only things keeping them connected. Together they moved, their bodies coated with sweat and the smell of sex thick in the air.

Dean removed her leg from his shoulder and leaned over her so they were face to face. "I'll love you for eternity. Not even death will stop me." He slowed and ground his hips so every stroke dragged across her clit.

Fawn cried out and matched his movements. "For eternity," she breathed.

Their mouths collided with desperation, hungry to fuse themselves together until they didn't know where one of them stopped and the other began. The climax built between them —his, hers, *both*. A fiery pleasure burned through him, and he yelled her name, thrusting into her to empty himself into her cunt.

They lay there panting, looking at each other with enough love to satiate them for every lifetime.

For eternity.

Briar hauled her little brother, Bellamy, by the middle, his feet kicking behind her. Fawn pinched the bridge of her nose, wondering what he'd done now. Briar turned twelve tomorrow, and her nine-year-old little brother said he had promised a present. Fawn had foolishly expected something sweet, but the angry look on Briar's face proved otherwise.

Dean wrapped his arms around Fawn's shoulders and chuckled. "What's he done now?" Their two oldest trudged closer, and Fawn slapped a hand over her mouth. Briar's light beige skin and golden-brown hair were speckled with something resembling mud and Bellamy had it coating his deep amber face.

"What is all over you two?" Dean asked, wrinkling his nose when they came closer. "Is that sh—poop?"

"His gift was a mini catapult he used to launch balls of horse crap at me," Briar fumed.

"She smashed one in my face," Bellamy growled back, sounding too much like his father. "It got in my mouth!"

Briar picked a piece of shit off of her sleeve and smashed it in his curly dark brown hair. "You deserved it."

"Where did you get a catapult?" Fawn demanded.

Bellamy puffed out his chest. "I made it."

Dean nodded, impressed and Fawn popped him in the stomach. "Do not encourage him."

He rubbed his abs. "It's impressive, but we do not use our projects to throw poop at people." Pausing, he added, "Or anything."

"Daddy!" their six-year-old daughter, Brooke, cried out.

Dean and Fawn turned around to see their youngest daughter, Brooke, bawling in Monroe's arms. "She said she doesn't feel well," he said frantically. "She's not warm, and I don't know what to do."

Lilith—these days disguised as a middle-aged woman—followed behind him. "I told him she'd be fine."

"Hello, witch," Fawn greeted her, earning a small smile in return.

Dean had convinced Lilith to spend more time with them instead of hiding in her cavern. It took a while, but eventually, she came out of hiding a few times a week for dinners and visits. She'd really taken to the children.

"Come here, little monster," Dean cooed and scooped his daughter into his arms.

Lilith moved closer to Fawn and murmured, "I'm not sure why, but you should step back." Fawn frowned but obeyed. Thank the gods she did.

Brooke laid her blond curly head on her father's shoulder and cried. "My tummy hurts." She punctuated her statement by vomiting down the front of Dean's shirt.

Oh no. Dean would change as many diapers as you wanted, but he could not handle vomit. Everyone froze, staring wide-eyed at the king. It took a second for him to register what had happened, and he started dry heaving violently. Fawn grabbed Brooke and handed her to Briar, who already had her arms outstretched. She knew the drill when Dad came in contact with vomit.

Dean leaned over with his hands on his knees, gagging loud enough for the entire kingdom to hear. Monroe clamped his mouth shut to keep from laughing, and Lilith shrugged at Fawn.

Bellamy started dry heaving too, and Fawn cursed the gods for giving her two males with the weakest stomachs in the world.

Rushing to her husband's side to remove his soiled shirt before he puked, she called over her shoulder, "Monroe, will you take Bellamy inside please? Briar, find Great Grandma and have her clean Brooke."

Fawn's grandparents had retired when they adopted Brooke to help with the kids. They had Monroe, Braddock, and Naomi to help, but Fawn suspected she just wanted to be near them. Her grandfather insisted on working in the stables with Naomi's husband, Jeremiah.

Briar, Bellamy, Lilith, and Monroe hurried back to the palace with Brooke. Monroe pinched his nose. "What is all over you two?"

"Horse poop," the prince and princess responded at the same time.

Monroe stepped a few steps away and scolded them the entire way back.

"Stand straight so I can get your shirt off," Fawn ordered her husband. His skin turned a greenish-yellow color, and she prayed she could get the vomit off him before he lost his lunch.

She ran behind him, grabbed his collar, and ripped his shirt down the middle. "Arms straight." He stuck out his arms and puffed out his cheeks to hold his breath. Fawn slid his shirt down his arms and threw it behind her. No puke made it onto his skin, and she breathed a sigh of relief. "You're clear."

Dean closed his eyes and spun around to put as much distance as possible between himself and the shirt, gagging every few steps. She chased after him and rubbed his back as they walked. "You're okay. It's gone."

Her husband dragged in a deep breath and blew it out. "I fucking hate when they do that."

"I know," she soothed. "By the time we get back, Grandma will have given her anti-nausea medicine."

"Thank you, darling." Dean pressed a kiss to her head. "I hope I didn't scare her."

"She's seen this enough times to know you'll be fine. We'll check on her after we get you a fresh shirt."

He bent over and stole a kiss as they walked. "I love you."

She leaned her head on his shoulder and murmured, "For eternity.

CURRENT AND UPCOMING WORKS

FAE KINGS OF EDEN (INTERCONNECTED STANDALONES)

Viciously Yours (Rennick & Amelia)

Obsessively Yours (Roman & Violet)

Tragically Yours (Dean & Fawn)

Brutally Yours (Amos & Clover)

VINCULA REALM (DUOLOGY)

The Umbra King (Rory & Caius part 1)

Aeternum (Rory & Caius part 2)

ABOUT THE AUTHOR

"Anything is a toy if you play with it."

-Andy Dwyer

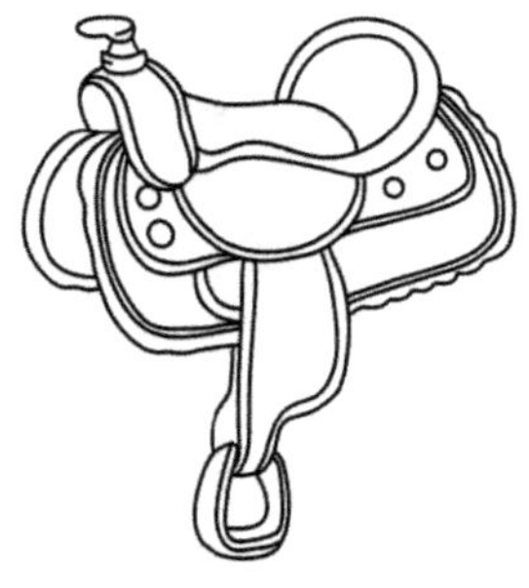

LET'S CONNECT!

Scan the QR code below for links to my website, newsletter signup, social media, and more! Or visit beacons.ai/jamieapplegatehunter

ACKNOWLEDGMENTS

I want to thank everyone except the eight people on my nemesis list. You all can fuck off.

CONTENT WARNINGS

Graphic violence and death, morally black actions by a main character, exhibitionism, explicit scenes and language, emotional child abuse, physical child abuse by combat, traumatic death of parent(s), depression